THE G[_____]
POCKE[___]

CU00704228

THE GREAT POCKES

R. B. TAYLOR

Also by **R.B.Taylor**

St Barlaam's Day

Robert Taylor's original feature screenplay *Muggers* premiered at Cannes in 1999 and was nominated for the Australian Writers' Guild Best Original Screenplay award.

A second original feature screenplay, *Cliffy* premiered on ABC TV (Australia) in 2013 to critical and popular acclaim and outstanding ratings. He has optioned or been assigned a further twelve feature film scripts in the US, the UK and Australia, to Oscar-nominated and Palme d'Or, Golden Lion and Golden Globe-winning producers.

He has taught screenwriting at universities in the US, the UK and Australia. He lives in Bath, Somerset with his wife, Juliet.

The Great Pockes is his second novel.

Copyright © 2021 R.B.Taylor

All rights reserved. No part of this book may be reproduced in any form or by any electronic or mechanical means, including information storage and retrieval systems, without permission in writing from the publisher, except by reviewers, who may quote brief passages in a review.

ISBN: 9798735478553

Crossed Quills Publishing

16-17 Newton St Loe, BA 2, 9BT, UK

This is for Lise-Lore and Graham

The origins of the Great Pockes remain shrouded in controversy and conjecture.

Whatever its origins, much of the following is actually true ...

Table of Contents

1. These Piping Times of Peace...1

2. After the Manner of Egypt..67

3. That which hath been is now ... .169

4. ... and that which is to be, hath already been 232

1. These Piping Times of Peace

*R*obin *Hoode, Robin Hoode, with his band of men/Robin Hoode, Robin Hoode went riding through the glen.*

The guests at the rear of the Great Hall clapped their hands and stomped their feet. The high and mighty, the wealthy and titled who were seated at the front rattled their jewellery.

'Christ and his holy crown of thorns,' muttered Henry. 'Are they listening to the lyrics?'

'Clearly not, dear.'

He took from the rich/He gave to the poor/

Robin Hoode! Robin Hoode!!

'One more time!' the singer shouted. 'Let's hear you!'

'Do they have to play so loud?' Henry grumbled.

What was it with these young minstrels? Glorifying outlaws and rebelling against authority. It was all down to Arthur and Harry. They were keen on this modern stuff. They had "discovered" the minstrels busking outside the Palace and had implored their father to "give them a slot". Call that music?

The Great Hall at Westminster Palace was brimming with society's finest; its rich and its rulers, its talented, its entitled,

1

and its just plain beautiful. The conversation sparkled. No, it *glittered* as brilliantly as the jewels in the ladies' tiaras, as brightly as the satins and silks of the men's doublets and breeches. The brightest talent in the realm entertained: strolling minstrels sang ballades, jugglers juggled, fire-eaters ate fire. The gala was held in honour of "our European friends" – which is how Westminster referred to England's former rivals and enemies these days. It was a tribute to the friendship and profitable relations which Henry had forged between England and her major trading partners. It was a dazzling display of wealth and power, a night that would be the talk of London society for weeks to come.

And Henry was the star in this firmament of his own making. Yet he brooded. Conversation, witty or intellectual, bored him and he wasn't mad on music, especially this rubbish. Give him his Domesday Book to pore over or a few accounts to balance and he was a happy man.

'This is a new ballade of our own composing,' the lute-strumming singer announced.

> *O, the King was in the counting-house, counting out his money/the Queen was in her parlour, eating bread and honey*

'Fuck!'

'Henry!'

'Listen to them! Are they mocking us?'

'I rather think they are, dear,' said his Queen.

Henry's glass of burgundy remained untouched. No one could accuse Henry of gluttony. Cheffie had put together a menu comprising oyster soup, a blancmange of haddock, blood-rare roast pigeon and whole spitfired boar in a mustard sauce, yet Henry barely picked at his kitchen's finest. Nor sloth – he was as hard a working monarch as had ever sat on the throne. Nor lust: he had been happily married to Elizabeth for seventeen years. In that time he had taken no mistresses, a first in English history, surely.

The minstrels finished their song. All eyes turned to their monarch. Henry's lips twisted in a smile and he slapped his hands on the table. He would show he was a sport but that was the last time they'd play Westminster; they'd be back on the streets busking for farthings and Arthur and Young Harry would be confined to the Palace for a month for having invited them.

Household staff served the next course: grilled whale tongue. Excellent! Whale, sturgeon and porpoise are Royal fish and it is the duty of the Receiver of Wreck to deliver any of these species caught or found in English waters. Henry always looked forward to this course. Whale tongue, whether grilled, braised or fried, is an acquired taste and Henry had acquired it. He hoed in, knowing his subjects must surely follow. He watched his guests poke the dish, take a tentative sample, and then discreetly tuck the offensive morsel up their sleeves or down their décolletage. It was his only amusement in an otherwise tedious night.

Where was he? Greed? No! Absolutely not. He had a country to run, three million – three million (!) subjects – to rule. The Exchequer coffers were bulging. Taxation was running a little high, perhaps, but Henry was the first king in centuries to balance the budget. That wasn't greed, that was prudence, that was. Sound fiscal management.

Pride? Possibly. He was proud of his achievements even if he didn't receive the plaudits he believed were his due. And it wasn't as if he was a vain man. Henry hated spending money on his wardrobe. He happily loafed about in any old breeches and a blouse. It was his Special Advisor, Foxe the Chronicler's, grand idea to order a new suit of clothes for every banquet. It kept the Clerk of the Wardrobe and his team very busy men – no unemployment, no idle hands in Henry's reign! More importantly, it was a political ploy, aimed to dispel Henry's miserly reputation. Moreover, garbed in such finery, Henry dazzled his subjects with His Majesty and splendour. That was the theory anyway.

Which left Envy. Henry stabbed at the last of the whale tongue. It was true; he obsessed over the reputations of his predecessors, Alfred the Great and William the Conqueror, Richard the Lionheart and all the other warrior kings. But what had they bequeathed him? What was there to show for all those battles – Crecy, Poitiers and Agincourt? All those years, those *centuries* of bloodshed and warfare? Nothing. All the overseas conquests were gone, replaced with a mountain of debt. Which he, Henry VII, had eradicated.

Henry took a swig of his wine. A footman leapt to top his glass.

'Can't I finish the bloody thing first?'

'Henry!'

Henry growled and took another swig.

People just didn't understand that warfare was expensive. Might may be right but money is where the real power lay. If Henry had been around at the time there would have been no Crusades. Why anyone wanted the Holy Lands was beyond him anyway; all mudbricks and sand dunes. And camels and mosques. Henry would not have waged war with the Saracens; he would have *traded* with them. Obtained concessions, opened markets into Jerusalem and Galilee and all the rest. The Muslims would have welcomed the Christians with open arms. Everybody happy.

But how would history judge Henry VII by the Grace of God, King of England for all his trade deals, for all his financial acumen? Henry the Sensible? Henry the Prudent? Counting House Henry?

Henry scowled. They've never had it so good. But try telling them that.

'Do cheer up, Henry. It's all going rather well,' said Elizabeth.

Yes, well, it would want to be, the cost of the thing for starters. Henry knew his miserly reputation was well-founded and he was loath to raid the Exchequer to fund pageants and fabulous banquets like tonight's. It was another of Foxe's grand ideas. Spectacular events such as these gilded the Crown's majesty, revealing yet also shrouding the mystique mantling Henry's divine, God-given right to rule. All who attended found the fine food and wine, the entertainment, the *glamour* in this grandest of settings irresistible. Everyone wanted to be a part of the H-VII show and the banquets and pageants gave them that opportunity. It would take a brave noble to rebel against Henry's rule when all the said noble's wife wanted in life was a seat at His Majesty's high table.

The seating was meticulously arranged. Elizabeth sat at his side with their three children, Arthur, Margaret and young Harry, artfully arranged around their parents and paraded for all to see. The happy united Royal Family. It painted a picture of stability, a line of succession, an assured future. Arthur was a precociously handsome and confident young prince. Already the hopes of an everlasting Tudor dynasty seemed in safe hands. He'd get over this minstrel-rebel thing, it was only a phase. Henry and his queen were trying for a fourth; a king could never have enough sons to protect their father's throne. Even daughters were sometimes useful. They could be married off to friendly royals, thus creating more powerful dynasties, or to old enemies, thus forging new alliances. Bit hard on the girls, being little more than bargaining chips but that was the system, that was how ... God planned it?

Servants cleared the plates. Assorted European dignitaries were honoured with places at high-table: the Spanish, Portuguese, Flemish and various Italian ambassadors and their wives. God knows, there were enough Italians. Why didn't they just unite? The French ambassador had rather inconveniently cried off at the last minute with a case of the grippe which necessitated a seating rearrangement, bumping guests up one table in rank from the farthest at the back to high-table itself. Interspersed amongst the Europeans sat the Chief Minister, Sir Reginald Bray and his wife, the Lord Chancellor, Sir John Morton, who also doubled as Archbishop of Canterbury, and the ever-observant Foxe the Chronicler. Henry kept his three officials separated at public events. There was great rivalry amongst them for Henry's favour and King's Council meeting always amused Henry as they fought to be the last man to leave the chamber. Last man in had the final word – that was their theory.

Beyond this *sanctum sanctorum* tables radiated in status or according to whom Henry was trying to impress. Nobles friendly to him sat to one side. Those who weren't –

Cumbria, Suffolk, Devon and Somerset foremost – Christ, that many? – were sat in Henry's eye line, reminding them that their king was symbolically as well as literally, keeping an eye on them.

The Palace was the centre of political and economic power but Henry, Elizabeth and their inner circle were also influencers, avatars of taste and decorum. Invitations to official palace events were sought after and highly prized. By an unwritten royal decree, no mistresses were allowed at such events. Wives only. Wives were drawn to the royal court like bees to the hive and dragged their husbands along. Thus the Palace maintained its position at the apogee of all things social and cultural. Elizabeth played her role by inviting the wives of any potential dissidents into her inner circle. She shared gossip and intimacies, her hairdresser and dressmaker. The Lady Cumbria, for example, was looking radiant in her new gown: yards of silk and satin. Inlaid pearls, were they? And spun gold thread? Henry smiled. It must have cost Cumbria a fucking fortune. There was a time the young Henry would have exercised his kingly droit de seigneur with the likes of Lady Cumbria. Aaah, but such jaunts were a long time gone. Lady Cumbria, who was young enough to be Cumbria's daughter had outfitted her husband. He was looking decidedly uncomfortable in the mulberry satin breeches and waistcoat and royal blue jacket which would have suited a man half his age. That must have cost him a fortune too.

Cumbria was chief among the noble dissidents but his wife, drawn irresistibly to the glamour at court had demanded Cumbria buy a London address. As Foxe had pointed out, this meant Cumbria had less time up north hatching plots and less money to spend on raising a rebellion. Cumbria had defiantly tucked into the whale's tongue and stared with barely-concealed hostility at the European guests. Bloody foreigners were only good for one thing in Cumbria's book – target practice. He didn't mind guzzling their Burgundy or Rioja, though.

The next arc of tables hosted the mercers and traders. Parvenus such as these were banished to the outer reaches of the Great Hall in previous courts but times had changed and now wealth as much as land and title reflected a man's status. Men sat by each other according to *merit*. This social mobility inspired loyalty in the wealthy elite – Foxey was right on that one – and as their wealth and social standing rose so did their loyalty to Henry. And their tax bill.

Lord and Lady Cumbria were seated with Sir Andrew Farrer who was Chairman of the Merchant Adventurers and his wife, Lady Martha. The Merchant Adventurers had made fortunes exporting wool to Europe and the Farrers were the wealthiest of all. It was a sign of the times that the noble Lady Cumbria was fawning over the merchant's wife's jewellery. Wager London to a brick the Lady Cumbria would be down Clerkenwell first thing tomorrow, thought Henry, ferreting out the latest in cut sapphires and rubies.

Cumbria was looking more animated now. He was moving wine glasses and salt cellars around the table, almost certainly reenacting the Battle of Tewkesbury or Bosworth Fields. This was another reason why Henry paired the old nobles with the merchants. Cumbria sublimated his warrior's urges reliving his glory days whilst impressing merchants like Farrer who had never held a halberd in anger.

The next row of tables comprised the Wardens, Masters and Office Bearers (and their spouses) of the Worshipful Companies of London: the Goldsmiths, the Brewers, the Merchant Taylors, the Lorimers etc. Fifty-eight of these Liveried Companies had been granted Royal Charters. Collectively they were known as the populares or mediocres. The Middle Classes. Social mobility had risen exponentially under Henry's rule. He had to admit he had not foreseen this but he rewarded the mediocres with minor honours and invited them to his grand reception to see that all to which they aspired lay but one table away. And aspire they did.

An alarum sounded in Henry's ear.

'Fuck me!'

'Henry!'

Oh yes, wrath. Well, he did have a temper. He would have to own up to wrath.

Henry had appointed John Blanke, a black man from somewhere in Africa as Court Trumpeter. The jaunty alarum heralded a procession of scullions who bore aloft a pie the size of a stool-ball field.

Oh, no.

They laid the pie in the centre of the high table. Cheffie – the Royal chef de cuisine – followed with a footman who bore a salver with carving knife and fork.

This was the entremet.

'You'd better not fuck it up, Cheffie,' Henry muttered under his breath.

Cheffie bowed to Henry, flourished his carving implements theatrically, then deftly sliced the pastry top at which point a dozen thrushes were supposed to fly out. It had been a bit of a show-stopper in its day but it was little more than a party trick now. The first thrush emerged, fluttered its wings and promptly collapsed in a butter dish. The others managed to get airborne and flew in distraught circles, shedding feathers and shit in equal proportions.

It was a conversation stopper all right. Between ducking the faltering thrushes and evading their excrement the guests were uncertain how to react. Surely one didn't drink thrush-fouled Burgundy, even in the royal presence? Or did one ...?

Cheffie bowed to the guests and beat a dignified, if hurried exit. While footmen vainly tried to recapture the terrified birds, the scullions cleaned up the mess. Somehow, Henry contained his wrath, though Cheffie would feel it in the morrow.

Henry saw Cumbria chuckling. The smug bastard. Their eyes met. Henry felt his heart pump. Anxiety. Based on unfounded fears. That's what Foxe called it. But Cumbria *was* plotting against him; there was nothing unfounded about it.

A footman swiped at the last of the thrushes which fell in the Spanish ambassador's finger bowl where it gasped plaintively and drowned.

The night couldn't get any worse, could it?

B

acon hurried south along Chancery Lane and thence past Lincoln Square. The bells had long rung. Technically, he was a Nightwalker. He was a regular Nightwalker, in fact, though he had so far escaped prosecution. But tonight he was afoot on legitimate business.

'Hear ye!' The inevitable Watchman's challenge.

'My name is Robert Bacon and I have business with Sir Andrew Farrer.'

'Ye do, do ye?'

Bacon could smell the peppery stingo from yards away. Now, was the man a belligerent drunk or a lazy drunk?

'His son lies ill, near death perhaps, and nearer still thanks to dallying here with you.'

'Physic, are ye?'

'Yes.'

Well, no. Bacon had studied medicine at Bologna, the finest medical school in Europe. He was a surgeon, but the arcane laws which determined social standing in London placed the surgeon many levels below physician; roughly on par with butchers.

'I am making a note of this, Robert Bacon. Will you return this way?'

Neither lazy nor belligerent. A dedicated Watchman. All too rare in London.

'I shall.'

The Watchman nodded sourly and Bacon continued south-west toward The Strand. The air was relatively fresh and clean around here. The houses were bigger and were surrounded by gardens. They had sanitation and the streets were regularly swept. The Strand had once been an enclave of the nobility who made their London addresses here, but Bacon had noticed an influx of arrivistes, wealthy merchants in the main. Sir Andrew Farrer, Chairman of the Merchant Adventurers was one of the wealthiest. Farrer – and England – had ridden to prosperity on the sheep's back and the Merchant Adventurers controlled three-quarters of

England's foreign trade. Farrer sat on the King's Council and was one of Henry's most trusted financial advisors.

Geffrey was the Farrers' only son. Upon his son's marriage, Sir Andrew had bought the adjacent property, demolished the grand old house and built a grander one for Geffrey, his wife and two young sons.

A footman opened the door and Bacon was shown in. Beatrice was at her embroidery in a sitting room. Their two young children were presumably in bed.

'Good evening, Beatrice. Are you well?'

'Exceedingly. Thank you.'

Her tone was civil enough but she reserved a special disdain for certain of Geffrey's friends. Her needlework became careless, almost angry.

'Geffrey called for me.'

'Is your call professional? Or "social"?'

She winced as she pricked a finger.

'Are you all right? Let me get you something. I have lavender and aloe with me.'

'I have no need of your services, Mr Bacon. Geffrey is in his room.'

The stench hit him immediately. The air was dank, weighed down with foul vapours.

'My dear fellow. Come in, come in.'

'How are you feeling, Geffrey?'

'Wonderful. Couldn't be haler or heartier. A cup of wine?'

Bacon shook his head.

'Not like you to refuse a man's hospitality, Robert. Do you know the good friar? Sir Andrew called him in.'

Sir Andrew, not 'my father'. It was a strained relationship.

'Good evening, friar.'

He was an Augustinian, one of the mendicant order that looked after the poor and sick. Farrer was sick but hardly poor. He lay in his bed, burning with fever. The wine heightened his face's flush. The bedclothes were damp with sweat and encrusted with bodily fluids. He had recently returned from a tour of the Italian states and had fallen ill on his return.

'Do have a drink, Robert. Pour Mr Bacon a drink, Tepper. I've got some of that lovely new French stuff. Brandy. Delicious. And packs a wallop too. No, I insist. Have you heard about Montacute?'

Bacon listened to tales of Montacute's tangled love life and sipped his brandy. Fiery stuff, but smooth. He could see that Geffrey might develop a taste for it.

'What seems to be the problem? Let's have a look at you.'

'I hope you've got some magic tricks in that bag of yours. Truth is, I'm feeling rather rotten.'

The breathing was laboured. Bacon checked his pulse. Fast.

'Who's your physician?'

'Metcalfe.'

The Court Physician. Of course.

The antipathy between physicians and surgeons ran deep, as entrenched as, in fact, a product of, the English class system. Physicians went to Oxford and read Greek and Latin. Surgeons were apprenticed to barbers and were members of the Worshipful Company of Barber-Surgeons. Bacon's father was a small landowner in Shropshire and the young Bacon was apprenticed to a barber-surgeon. When his father died he invested his small legacy in a degree at Bologna where surgery was a more esteemed profession. The cutting of hair was not studied.

The English medical system was rigid: physicians diagnosed and prescribed drugs; apothecaries dispensed them. Surgeons did the dirty work – tending to wounds, broken limbs, amputations. Physicians would never stoop to touching a body let alone delving inside one. Surgeons also attended the poor – those who couldn't afford physicians.

If Sir Thomas Metcalfe learnt that a surgeon had attended his patient – especially one of Farrer's social standing – without his say-so there'd be hell to pay. An official complaint to the Worshipful Master of the Barber-Surgeons at the very least.

Geffrey's face contorted.

'What is it?'

'Headaches. Blinders. Worse than any hangover and god knows we've had some beauties, haven't we, Robert?'

'Any other pain?'

'Gut. And the damndest thing, the pain only comes on at night. All set for a night out in the grand metropolis. And – '

He clenched his teeth and grasped Bacon's hand, almost crushing it.

Bacon lifted Geffrey's nightshirt. One final symptom to check. If the armpits were swollen and sweaty it could be confirmed as the sweating disease.

They were.

'Not good?'

'Not good. But we haven't lost you yet, Geffrey.'

It was touch and go if he would survive. Not everyone died of the sweats, though its mortality rate was high. Bacon saw a dozen or more puncture marks on Geffrey's arms and torso. Leeches.

'Who bled him, friar?'

'One of your lot, presumably,' said the friar. The Augustinians had been skilled bleeders and were at the forefront of surgical practice until Pope Honorarius issued a papal bull (1131) forbidding men and women of holy orders to spill blood. Metcalfe had presumably ordered a surgeon or barber-surgeon to supervise the bleeding.

'Quite a lot by the looks of it,' said Bacon. He was not a fan of bleeding, fashionable though it was.

'Three pints.'

Three pints! And still the pulse was rapid. Bacon detected the faint scent of vinegar and wormwood.

'Sir Thomas ordered the concoction?'

'Yes,' said the friar. 'I made it up myself.'

No one knew what caused the sweats, so no one knew how to treat it, but the Augustinians were experienced herbalists and a cider vinegar and wormwood poultice was as good as any.

'How else have you treated him? Snake?'

The friar nodded. The snake, symbol of Satan, was cut up and applied to specific parts of the body. It was supposed to draw out the poison. Or the devil. Or both.

12

'And emeralds. Sir Thomas insisted.'

Crushed emeralds. Very expensive and useless as far as Bacon could tell. Aristotle was said to have found emeralds soothing for the eyes. Physicians had prescribed eating the crushed gemstones for the Black Death a century previous and residents of The Strand, perhaps to flaunt their wealth and social standing demanded it for any old ague. Sir Thomas Metcalfe should have known better.

'We are all praying,' said the prior, and, as if to prove the point, clasped his beads.

'By "we" do you mean all your brethren?'

'Yes, my son.'

'In all your priories?'

'Yes, my son.'

The friars were paid by the prayer, so all the Augustinians in all the priories in London meant one very expensive intercession.

'Hello, what's this?'

A patch of ulcers was clustered around Geffrey's groin.

'Oh, those.' The pain was reducing Geffrey's voice to a hoarse whisper. 'Just some ulcers, right?'

'Yes, but what caused them?'

'No idea.'

Bacon gently probed them.

'Any pain?'

'No. None at all.'

'How long have you had them?'

'Oh, a few weeks.'

The ulcers were clustered randomly and not in the "ring o' roses" which was the classic symptom of the Black Death. Was this a new form of plague? Or a new form of sweating disease?

'They're not buboes. So, it's not the plague.'

'That's a relief.' Geffrey's head swayed and he fell into unconsciousness.

'Has he been slipping in and out?'

'All day,' said the friar.

Not good.

Bacon considered his options. The ulcers were red and ugly though one or two had receded to little more than pock marks. A nasty rash was emerging on his torso.

'What about this rash? How long has he had that?'

A dwarf in full fool's fig sauntered into the Great Hall to a mighty cheer.

'Barabbas!' The cry went around the Great Hall. 'Barabbas!'

The jester lifted his arms, milking the applause. He raised a forefinger. The hall fell silent. The audience was as blancmange in the palms of his tiny hands.

'Fie! Fie! Fie!!' cried Barabbas. 'Any priests here tonight? Hello, archbishop! How do you make holy water? You don't know??? You boil the hell out of it!'

He shook his marotte. Its bells jangled merrily.

'I'm a single man, ladies. Ooh, you are a saucy one, madam. I'm single by choice. My ex-wife's choice.'

Nicholas Hardwick laughed along with the rest. His mentor, Sir Reginald Bray had asked him down from Oxford to discuss his future and he was invited courtesy of a last-minute cancellation. He was allocated a table in the farthest corner of the Hall. Merton College was renowned for its kitchen and cellar but the food and wine at Westminster were on another level. Taste was not the only sense that feasted lavishly. The music, the Venetian glassware, the Dutch tableware titillated eyes and ears. The smell of the food, combined with the scent that both men and women were wearing, intoxicated. The fashion was gorgeous and none more colourful than Henry and Elizabeth's. Bray had told him that Henry's suiting had cost 200 sovereigns. Twelve pounds a year was a reasonable wage, so Henry was wearing more than most men would earn in half a lifetime. Hardwick marvelled at the grandeur which served to exalt Henry, give substance to his charisma for all to see. And yet there he was, a few tables away. So near. And so far. It was a clever trick.

'I won't say my ex-wife was a bad cook. We hosted a dinner party the other night. We served the food. We cleared the plates. We buried the dead.'

Jingle jingle went the marotte.

The grandest men of the realm were gathered here in one space. Royalty, nobility, Merchant Adventurers, politicians, the Archbishop of Canterbury, Ambassadors, Guild Masters, the Mayor of London. Unfortunately, Hardwick was stuck next to a colourless court official who reluctantly introduced himself as Mr Dunne.

'What is it you do, Mr Dunne?'

Dunne grunted.

'Mr Dunne is the Master of Household Accounts,' sniffed Mrs Dunne, equally drab in her fawn and grey outfit.

'I see,' said Hardwick. 'Is it true that Henry's suiting cost 200 sovereigns?'

Hardwick was embarrassed that his question fell to such a level but gossip seemed to be the favoured currency of conversation.

Dunne grunted.

'More?'

He grunted again. Much more? The man's grunts could articulate a sizeable vocabulary.

'What is it you do, Mr Hardwick?' said Mrs Dunne.

'A humble fellow at Oxford, Mrs Dunne. Like myself, Sir Reginald is an old Merton boy.'

'I suppose he's offered you a job, has he? Palace is full of you Oxford types. Advisors,' Mr Dunne spat. 'Place is crawling with advisors nowadays. Advisors. And advisors' advisors. And advisors' advisors' advisors.'

'That's a lot of advisors.'

'All got to be paid, don't they?'

'The money's not coming from your pocket, surely, Mr Dunne.'

'Six hundred people in the household. All have to be paid and fed three times daily.'

John Blanke sounded an alarum. Hardwick had heard trumpets in Oxford but this man's command of tone and melody was exquisite. And so *modern*. Another street

15

musician. Another of Arthur's bright ideas, according to Mrs Dunne. Arthur had seen him play outside the Abbey and insisted he join the court. Henry could never say no to Arthur and had reluctantly agreed. There was no doubting Blanke's talent. He could blow alarums other musicians could only dream of. Sombre, romantic, joyful. And rhythmic.

'Six shillings a week we pay him to blow that thing a few times a day,' Dunne muttered.

Barabbas bowed and motioned for silence. Dunne cracked a smile. Mrs Dunne clapped her hands in anticipation.

'Here's we go, Mr Dunne,' said Mrs Dunne.

Barabbas took a deep breath and focused his vision. He clasped a hand to his breast.

> *My fair cousins/If we are about to die, we are now/To do our country loss; and if to live/The fewer men, the better share of honour*

Hardwick saw the Dunnes frown.

'No farting, Mr Dunne?' said Mrs Dunne.

'Bloody hope so. Only reason I came,' said her husband.

> *God's will! I 'treat thee, wish not one man more./By Jove, I am not covetous for gold.*

'Not fucking Agincourt again,' Henry muttered under his breath. Why Agincourt, now of all times? And what was it with Barabbas of late? He was a jester, a fool, and he thought he was a *poet*. He wanted to be taken *seriously*.

First the thrushes, now Barabbas. The atmosphere was sinking like Cheffie's entremet and Henry's anxiety was going through the roof. He had brought peace and prosperity to his realm. But yet again he pondered his legacy. Alfred the Great. William the Conqueror. The Black Prince. Even Edward the Confessor had a nice ring to it.

Henry the Stable? Henry the Peaceful? Oh, god. Henry the Loser?

'Does Barabbas write all this?' Hardwick said, oblivious to the table's disappointment.,

'He can't read or write," said Mrs Dunne. 'He makes it all up.

The conversation faltered. The couple on Hardwick's other side were engaged in gossip about people Hardwick did not know.

Tomorrow is St Crispian/Then he will tear his sleeve and show his scars/And say these wounds I had on Crispian's day.

Barabbas bowed. The applause was muted, hopeful.

'I say, I say, I say,' Barabbas chirped. 'The more I take, the more I leave behind. Who am I? And no, the answer is not our glorious king? Well?'

The finest minds in the country laughed at the sally then scratched their heads.

Watch it, Barabbas, you're getting very cheeky, thought Henry.

'Footsteps!'

The hall groaned indulgently.

'Come on, Barabbas,' muttered Henry. 'Stick to farting.'

'Perhaps, it's the size of the hall,' said Queen Elizabeth.

'On a good day and given a tailwind they'll hear him in Hammersmith.'

'I'd like to introduce you to Mr Blanke,' said Barabbas.

Blanke bowed, held his trumpet to his lips and blew a short melody.

Barabbas put his hand to his ear, listened intently and responded with an arpeggio of farts. The audience howled with laughter. Good old Barabbas! The maestro with his pitch-perfect arse!

He galloped off to tumultuous applause.

That was better. Henry sighed in relief. The conversation picked up. Laughter pealed around the Hall. Henry saw a worried-looking palace official enter. At least Henry assumed he was a palace official; there were so damn many of them scurrying around these days with worried looks on their faces. He approached Sir Reginald Bray and whispered in his ear, his hands gesturing his concern. Henry's stomach lurched. He saw Sir John Morton discreetly trying to eavesdrop. Bray nodded impassively, rose and moved toward Henry and Henry knew that the night was about to get worse.

'Naples has fallen without a fight, Your Majesty.'

Fuck, oh fuck. The fucking French had attacked Naples. That was why the French ambassador had cancelled. A grippe be damned. The bastard.

Henry was desperate to leave and consult with his advisors. He could see the news spreading through the Hall. He signalled to Blanke to play an alarum.

Henry rose.

'No, I shan't be repeating Barabbas' virtuoso, er, musicianship.'

The guests tittered politely.

'Thank you all for coming. I hope you enjoyed yourselves. Please stay. Enjoy the revels.'

He took his Queen by the hand. All stood as their monarch departed. Hardwick watched Bray and Morton leave, quickly followed by Foxe, Cumbria and the other nobles.

Dunne's arse had barely hit the seat before he leapt to his feet again.

'Sir Andrew. Sir Thomas.'

The pair nodded curtly before exiting with their wives.

'Who were they?' said Hardwick.

Dunne grunted.

'Sir Thomas is the Court Physician,' said Mrs Dunne. 'Sir Andrew is the Chairman of the Merchant Adventurers.'

'You're very well connected, Mr Dunne,' said Hardwick.

Dunne grunted.

B acon dozed in an armchair. He frequently stayed the night with a patient. He felt it part of his duty though few surgeons and even fewer physicians provided this level of dedication. Gruff voices awoke him.

'Who is this?'

'I have no idea, Metcalfe. Some friend of Geffrey's, I assume.'

'My name is Bacon. I am a surgeon and, yes, I am a friend of Geffrey's.'

'I did not call for you.' Metcalfe didn't bother hiding his contempt.

'Geffrey called for me.'

'Your lad needs a haircut, Farrer. Perhaps he called the right man after all.'

'My apologies, Metcalfe. If I'd known he'd call a surgeon,' Sir Andrew began.

'How do you plan to proceed, Mr Bacon? Lop off a leg?'

'That won't be necessary, Sir Thomas. But, for the record, I've administered a draught of opium and henbane for the pain and to help him sleep. Valerian for the rapid pulse. And lavender and aloe – '

'What on god's flat earth? This is a sick room, not a kitchen garden. The boy has a fever. He's been bled. In forty-eight hours, he'll be up and about.'

'Lavender and aloe,' Bacon repeated. 'For the ulcers – '

'Ulcers? What ulcers?'

Bacon decided to show due deference. Metcalfe was a powerful man in London's medical circles; he was the Court Physician after all.

'These ulcers and this rash.'

Metcalfe was momentarily confused – as Bacon knew he would.

'The snake and the emerald. They're drawing out the infection in the form of ulcers and a rash,' he said finally.

'So this is how you expected it?' said Farrer anxiously.

'Exactly as I expected it,' said the physician.

Not bloody likely, thought Bacon.

'Of course, if you'd prefer a *surgeon*'s opinion I shall withdraw my services.'

'Of course not,' said Farrer. 'If you'd kindly leave, Mr Bacon.'

'No,' said Geffrey. 'Robert knows what he's doing. I feel better for his treatment.'

'Recovery is almost certainly short term,' said Metcalfe. 'Amputation is a sure cure for a painful leg, but is it the wisest treatment?'

Sir Andrew was torn. He desperately hoped his son was recovering but Metcalfe was a *physician*. The *Court* Physician.

'Don't be ridiculous, Geffrey. You're in the best hands money can buy.'

If quality of care was equated with expense, that was true, thought Bacon. A guinea a call? Or more. Bacon's fee was a shilling.

'Best I go, Geffrey.'

His friend gripped Bacon's hand.

'You'll be back?'

Bacon hesitated. 'Of course.'

'You will listen to Sir Thomas, Geffrey. His counsel is sought by the king himself.'

Bacon gathered his instruments and concoctions. The sitting room was in darkness. Beatrice had retired to bed – not that she would have wanted to talk with him anyway.

Bacon reflected on his old friend as he retraced his steps along The Strand. They were from different ends of the social spectrum but ran into each other in establishments where social class was not so much an issue. They were similar in age – late twenties, but the similarities ended there. Farrer was beautiful; there was no other word for him, a man who drew members of both sexes to him. Bacon had the type of face which jesters joked about. Bacon was largely solitary and devoted to the study and practice of his surgery. Farrer was charming, gregarious, and enormous fun. But he was a wastrel; a degenerate some would say. The death of his father would make Geffrey one of the wealthiest men in the realm, but he showed little of his father's aptitude for commerce or hard work.

The Watchman was waiting for him by Aldwych.

'I'm going home now,' said Bacon.

'And where might that be, sir?'

Bacon gave his Aldgate address. It was not the most salubrious area of London. No surgeon lived in a smart part of the City. But he lived a short distance from Chaucer's home of a century ago and Bacon was very fond of Chaucer.

'W
here is he?' Henry demanded.

'Scotland, apparently,' said Sir Reginald Bray.

'Scotland?'

'Edinburgh.'

Sir Reginald had dispatched a court official to the French ambassador's residence, demanding a meeting, grippe or no grippe. He'd been looking forward to tearing strips off the French swine. But M. l'Ambassadeur had fled.

'Deep breath, Your Majesty,' said Foxe.

Henry took a deep breath and tried to calm himself.

'France invades Naples and the ambassador hotlegs it to Scotland? Why?'

'The Auld Alliance,' said Sir Reginald. France and Scotland. One of the oldest treaties in Europe. It was first signed in 1295 and renewed several times since.

It was nearly 2 am but Henry had called an emergency meeting of his closest advisors: Bray, Morton and Foxe.

'What does Alexander say about Naples?' said Henry.

Alexander. Pope Alexander VI, Rodrigo Borgia as was, Bishop of Rome, Vicar of Jesus Christ, Successor of the Prince of the Apostles, Supreme Pontiff of the Universal Church, Servant of the Servants of God.

'I have yet to hear, sir,' said Morton who, as Archbishop of Canterbury, was Alexander's highest-ranking representative in England, 'But, technically, Rome and France are allies.'

'And technically, Naples refused to hand over a decent lump of his duchy to the Papal States, so Alexander thought he'd teach Naples a lesson,' said Sir Reginald.

'It's complicated,' said Morton.

'Complicated?' said Henry. 'Sounds pretty bloody simple to me.'

'Nuancée.'

'What is nuancé-ed about it?' snapped Henry. 'France has attacked Naples and the fucking Italians – typically – have surrendered without lifting a sword.'

Advisors.

The French invasion placed Henry in an awkward situation. He could condemn France and rattle sabres and tell Alexander to go to hell but Henry had struck a deal with Alexander's predecessor, Innocent VIII who had issued a papal bull threatening to excommunicate any challengers to Henry's Divine Right to Rule. It was a tribute to Henry's negotiating skills, for, although it bought the Church Henry's loyalty, it legitimised Henry's claim to the throne.

However, Henry owed the pope and though Innocent was long gone, the agreement did not follow him to the papal grave; Alexander had made no secret that the debt was still in a kind of unwritten escrow. Bloody Florentines! Worse still, bloody Borgias. Alexander may be pope but he was a Borgia and they were all lunatics: murder, rape, incest – nothing was beyond that family. (Henry chose to forget that his own wife was Richard III's niece and had been in an incestuous relationship – allegedly – with the fallen monarch.) Hadn't Cesar Borgia been made cardinal at age 18? Henry was not averse to a little nepotism – royal succession depended upon it. But in the Church?

Henry felt suddenly tired. He was nearing 40 but felt much older.

'We really must do – or at least say – something in response, Your Majesty,' said Sir Reginald.

'The nobles are waiting outside, Your Majesty,' said Morton.

'No need for haste,' said Foxe. 'Sleep on it, Your Majesty. Approach the problem with a clear mind.'

Yes, sod the nobles, thought Henry. Let them wait till morning.

But sleep would not come. 3 am and not a wink. Henry's claim to the throne was shaky at best. His forebears were illegitimate on *both* sides. The Earl of Warwick had a stronger claim to the crown. Fortunately, Warwick would never see the light of day, rotting as he was in The Tower. Christ, even the Duke of Burgundy had some claim to the throne and wouldn't he love to press it. Who was Foxe to say his fears were unfounded? Sir Thomas Metcalfe claimed Henry's anxieties heated his blood which elevated his black bile. He prescribed leeches, concoctions and crushed emeralds endlessly. And not a scrape of difference.

Foxe sat with him, told him to think good thoughts. "Henry by Grace of God, King of England." Years of repeating the mantra and years of Foxe constantly reinforcing it had almost convinced him. He had won the crown on the battlefield at Bosworth, but many of his subjects argued that a battle-won crown did not equate with the God-given divine right to rule. But he wouldn't have won the battle without God's grace, surely? Or so Foxe kept telling him. Henry concentrated on the positives; England was not at war nor had she suffered from any recent famine. English pastures were abundant with grain and stock. Henry felt his wrist. His pulse was racing with hot blood. Henry could feel the black bile pouring from wherever black bile came from. How could Foxe say his fears were "all in the mind"? There had been the Stafford and Lovell rebellion, the Yorkshire rebellion, the Lambert Simnel rebellion. And now there was this Perkin Warbeck who claimed he was Prince Edward, Duke of York, alive and not murdered by Richard III's henchmen in The Tower. Hard to believe RIII would botch a simple murder. Hard to believe anyone would believe such an outlandish claim, but Warbeck had his supporters, Cumbria being a prominent one, and Warbeck was up in Scotland that very minute gathering forces. With the French ambassador. Oh, Christ. France, Scotland, Warbeck. Were they plotting to overthrow him? And would Cumbria and the other dissidents join them? Henry was surrounded by conspiracy.

'Enough, Foxe. Send for Barabbas.'

Barabbas had been drinking sack – for a little fellow he could really put it away – and prone to melancholy in his cups.

> *O, I have pass'd a miserable night, So full of ugly sights, of ghastly dreams,*

'No, no. Something funny, Barabbas.'
'How about this, Your Maj.'

> *When I a fat and bean-fed horse beguile ...*

The wisest aunt, telling the saddest tale
Sometime for three-foot stool mistaketh me
Henry chuckled. Three foot stool? That's more like it!

Then slip I from her bum, down topples she

Henry laughed. Slip from her bum!
Oh, that Barabbas!

'Impure thoughts, father.'
    'How many times a day?'
    'Many.'
  'Impure deeds?'
  'None. None at all.'
'Thought begats deed, my son. In the eyes of God the one sin is not greater than the other.'
Did God have eyes, Bacon wondered. Yet another doubt to add to the many that fogged his mind and chipped away at his faith. Yet, he suffered his penance; an hour on his knees – agony on the cold flagstones of St Botwulf's, Aldgate. He returned home and was preparing breakfast when the messenger arrived with an emergency call out to Poultry. He tossed down a mug of spiced wine and bolted his bread and salted gudgeon on the run.

London's population was swelling daily and there was a shortage of housing, especially affordable housing. With so much construction and so little space, houses were spreading upwards. Two, three, even four floors. Plus cellars. London had become dependent on construction (as well as trade) to drive its thriving economy but there was also a shortage of tradesmen which meant that unqualified workers were running construction sites. Safety was not considered an issue and one thing there was no shortage of in the Great Metropolis was accidents. Or fires. A single stray spark and a building, an entire neighbourhood was burnt to the ground.

A four-storey conversion had collapsed near the corner of Old Jewry. Bacon had earned a reputation for his skill and dedication and was first on site. There were no physicians to distract with their diagnoses; there wouldn't be – too much blood, too much flesh for a physician's patrician hands to press. A mason had leapt from the roof when the structure gave way. Both legs were shattered and his spine was broken. Twisted bones protruded from torn flesh. The man was in shock. Bacon administered opium with red wine, celandine and helenium. He cleaned the wounds and cut the flesh, enabling him to view the bones. Fortunately, the breaks were clean; Bacon could set the broken legs, but it was the spine that worried him. The man would never walk, let alone work again. Three more surgeons arrived in quick time. Coffin cullies they were called; barber-surgeons who employed boys to tip them of accidents. Bacon ordered them to attend to the other workmen's relatively minor injuries. A labourer who had been buried beneath the rubble was exhumed, his body crushed lifeless. It took Bacon all morning to set the bones and stitch the wounds. His supply of opium was all but exhausted. Bacon sent a message to the nearest hospital, St Thomas of Canterbury at Acre. Porters were dispatched with a pallet.

'He will need more opium,' he told the master builder, 'there's an apothecary in the next street. My fee is one shilling.'

'He's the one who fell. He's the one you fixed,' said the builder. 'Naught to do with me.'

Bacon accompanied the patient to St Thomas's and supervised his admission. The man's distraught wife and four children joined them.

'Best let him sleep,' said Bacon. 'He'll need plenty of this'. He handed her a bottle of the opium concoction. 'I'm sorry, I don't know his name.'

'Stone. Allan Stone. Will he be all right?'

'He'll live.'

'Thank god for that. And thank you, sir. Will he be able to work?'

'What was he? A stonemason?'

'A very good one.'

Bacon shook his head. 'I'm sorry.'

She took the news stoically. 'Alan, my love,' she said, caressing his hand. 'At least you're alive.'

Bacon wasn't sure that was a good thing. God knows what would become of them with no income.

'Your fee, sir. How much?'

'I'll be back to see him tomorrow. We'll sort it out later.'

Exhausted, Bacon made his way to a wine house and ordered a jug of wine. Roast fowl was served and he ordered that as well.

'**A** little more off the sides, I fancy, sir.'

Hoskyns' scissor-work was precision itself. Henry's locks cascaded geometrically either side of a plumb-straight part to a right-angled nape-line. Hoskyns had been trained by the Franciscans from age nine and the Franciscans were sticklers when it came to their tonsures. He then served a term as Warden for the Worshipful Company and had been rewarded with the highest honour – Court Barber.

'As you say, Hoskyns.'

Henry knew he was in for a trying day but for a few minutes he could close his eyes and relax, away from the pressures of government. Henry remained slim, despite his nearly 40 years. His face was angular and austere. His once dark hair had paled to a leaden grey. An austere grey to match his austere grey eyes, his austere habits. And his austere government.

'Last night went well, sir?'

'As well as these things go. Did they keep you up?'

'It was still going about 4 am, sir. Of course, I can't hear the revels from my rooms, but those laurel bushes took a bit of a shaking. Aaah, well, we were all young bucks once.'

The laurels beneath Hoskyns' rooms were often the scenes for trysting on the night of Royal galas.

'Any idea who it was?'

'Not for me to gossip, sir, but I did happen to glance out my window and rather thought I saw my Lord Cumbria.'

'With?'

'No one I recognised, sir.'

That'd be right. Henry had seen Cumbria in action many a time. No doubt Cumbria had returned to the Great Hall to

26

guzzle the free wine. He would have regaled the mercers and merchants with tales from Bosworth and lavished attention on one of their wives. Overcome by the attention a Duke and battle hero (allegedly) was paying her, she slipped behind Hoskyns' laurels with the old goat for a quick 'un.

'I hope they didn't keep you up too long.'

'No, sir. All over very quickly.'

Henry chuckled. A nice little tidbit to spread around. And spread around the Palace it would and quicker than a Cumbria tupping.

'Anything said?'

'My Lord did mention that he was expecting to sit at High Table in the near future.'

Henry stiffened. Cumbria would never take a seat at High Table, not while Henry was alive, and Cumbria knew it. There was no doubt about it, Cumbria and his cronies were plotting a rebellion.

With Perkin Warbeck.

It had to be.

There had been two pretenders to Henry's throne: Lambert Simnel. And Perkin Warbeck.

Simnel had been the pawn in a ruse hatched by the Yorkist Earl of Lincoln. Richard III had locked up and murdered the little princes in The Tower and had decreed Edward Plantagenet the Earl of Warwick his lawful successor but, according to Lincoln, he had liberated Warwick from imprisonment in The Tower; the Warwick that was currently imprisoned was, so Lincoln claimed, not the true Warwick and Lambert Simnel, who, by all accounts bore a striking resemblance to the young Earl was put forward as the genuine Warwick. It was a ludicrous plot, though it did attract a band of followers including, allegedly, Cumbria. Lincoln was defeated and killed at the Battle of Stoke which Cumbria, typically had not joined until he determined the likely victor. Which was Henry himself. To whom Cumbria immediately pledged his loyalty. Henry showed he could be merciful when he wanted and spared the hapless Simnel who was currently employed in the Palace as the Royal Falconer, a position in which he excelled.

And the second pretender was Perkin Warbeck ...

'Are you all right, sir?'

Bloody anxiety.

According to Henry's spies, Warbeck was currently in Scotland. Bloody James. Bloody Scots. Henry was sure James didn't believe Warbeck's claim. Surely he wouldn't support Warbeck? So much for loyalty amongst royalty. James was fucking with him pure and simple.

'I'm fine, thank you, Hoskyns.'

Henry took a deep breath and calmed himself. Henry by Grace of God, King of All England...

'Pity about Naples, sir. Someone should do something about those French.'

'Is that what everyone's saying?'

'More or less. "Sort out those fucking Frenchies." Excuse my French, sir.'

Henry's supposed pacifism was a source of disaffection amongst many of his subjects. None of these flag-wavers were soldiers, none had ever seen a battlefield. He ought to round them up and pack them off to France. See how they liked war then.

'And what would you suggest I do, Hoskyns? Invade France?'

'Well, they are all in Naples, sir.'

Actually, it wasn't a bad idea. France was all but defenceless. Could he raise an army in time? Presumably, the French-hating nobles had hit upon the same idea. No wonder they wanted to confront him.

'I see M. l'Ambassadeur has left for Scotland, sir.'

How did the man know all this?'

'Seems they're all heading up there,' he added.

'All?'

'Senor de Ayala warmed the chair for you, sir. His usual shave and trim.'

'Oh?'

The Spanish Ambassador. With whom Henry was about to meet. To discuss Naples. And he was heading for Scotland. Henry's innards twisted and wrung.

'He said he enjoyed last night. He thought the entremet most amusing, sir.'

Oh, he did, did he? Bloody Cheffie. Who Henry still hadn't sorted out.

'He said he's looking forward to your meeting this morning. Then a spot of packing and he's off to Edinburgh.'

Edinburgh. Henry's anxiety rose like black bile in his throat.

'He spoke very highly of His Majesty.'

'He would, wouldn't he.'

'Er, no, sir. That would be the Scottish His Majesty he spoke glowingly of.'

Of course, he did. Spain was courting Scotland, or, more likely they were courting each other, like a pair of lovers hard at it behind Hoskyns' laurels.

'Very popular, Scotland. Hasn't the Holy Father funded a university up there, sir?'

Yes, Pope Alexander had funded a university in Aberdeen of all places. Rome and Spain were both getting their boots over the Caledonian doormat. Conspiracies. Everywhere Henry looked he saw conspiracies.

What had the court soothsayer said all those years ago: "uneasy lies the head that wears the crown"? Henry had never placed much faith in fortune tellers but this one knew what he was talking about. As much as any advisor, at any rate.

'Shave, sir?'

Hoskyns was getting doddery and Henry wasn't sure he trusted him with a razor in his hand. He had to be sixty which was positively Methuselan for these times.

'Not today, Hoskyns.'

Henry's next meeting was with de Ayala and he preferred the rugged, unshaven look. Show the Castillian bastard he meant business.

'Eyebrows and nostrils could do with a trim, sir.'

'As you say, Hoskyns.'

Satisfied with his cut and denuded of orificial hair, Henry made his way to the Painted Chamber.

'Y our Majesty.'

'Señor de Ayala.'

'May I say, sir, what a wonderful banquet last night. The food, the wine.' De Alaya paused ever so briefly. 'The entremet.'

Cocky Latin bastard. He was a charmer, though, de Alaya. Neatly trimmed hair, courtesy of Hoskyns, beautifully tailored clothes. The man reeked of scent, probably bathed in it. Like most Englishmen, Henry had an aversion to bathing. It was believed that bathing opened the pores to miasmatic infections, so Henry bathed only when necessary and, following the latest medical advice, he forewent bathing completely during summer and winter. He washed his hands and face daily, took mint lozenges for his foul breath and applied scent sparingly.

'I'm glad you enjoyed yourself, Paolo.'

De Alaya smiled his most ingratiating smile. His teeth were blindingly white. Henry's own teeth were almost black. How did the man do it? He must twig after every meal.

'I hear you're going up to Scotland, Paolo.'

'Indeed I am.'

De Alaya had deliberately slipped the information to Hoskyns knowing it would get back to Henry.

'His gracious Majesty, King James has invited me to a wedding.'

Henry glanced at Sir Reginald Bray whose eyebrow rose faintly. They both knew James had no issue at this time. Who would be so important as to warrant an invitation for the Spanish ambassador?

'Oh? Who's getting married?'

'A close friend of His Majesty, a gentleman called Perkin Warbeck.'

Henry's heart missed a beat. Perkin fucking Warbeck. Henry felt the bile gushing through his system. Black. Yellow. Hot blood. Phlegm. The lot.

'Who's he marrying?' said Sir Reginald.

'Umm ... Lady Gordon? Yes, that's the name.'

'The Scottish Lord Chancellor's daughter,' said Bray.

'Yes. I believe so. His Majesty is putting on a tournament in celebration.'

A tournament. Monarchs rarely staged tournaments for anyone less than crowned heads of state. Christ, this was serious. Was James really supporting Warbeck?

'You'll need to supervise your packing, señor,' said Sir Reginald crisply. 'But we do have trade matters to discuss and Naples of course. If we may we'd like to talk about Catherine and Arthur. Ferdinand is rather dragging his heels on this one.'

Henry had long been keen on marrying Arthur off to Catherine, thus uniting the Houses of Tudor and Castille. It would make for a formidable alliance.

'Ferdinand is a doting father who thinks only of his daughter. He feels that both she and Arthur are a little young.'

'They've been unofficially betrothed since Catherine was two, Paolo.'

'Our gracious Queen Isabella feels ten is still a little young, Your Majesty.'

'Not saying they should get married right away, but eight years? Rather a long engagement. What say we set a date?'

'I shall voice your concerns upon my return, but let me assure Your Majesty that Ferdinand has not got cold feet over this marriage.'

Bray wondered if you could drag your heels with cold feet. Yes, you probably could he decided. He also thought that it was Ferdinand rather than Princess Catherine who was playing hard to get.

'But we may have to renegotiate Catherine's dowry,' said de Ayala smoothly. 'Ferdinand feels that 300,000 crowns is a little excessive.'

'**A**ccording to Everson, our man in Naples,' said Sir Reginald handing Henry a missive, 'Naples did indeed surrender without a fight. The Neapolitans have welcomed the French with open arms.'

31

Who on god's flat earth welcomed the French, Henry wondered. Bloody Italians, that's who.

'The French are in bed with the pope,' said Henry sourly. 'The pope is in bed with the Spanish. The Scots are in bed with the French *and* Perkin Warbeck. And Cumbria, Suffolk, Lincoln and the rest are in bed with each other.'

'Conspiracies, sir, are not necessarily grounded in fact.'

'Oh? And what are they grounded in?'

'They're often nothing more than theories, sir.'

'So in theory, they're all in this together?'

'No, Your Majesty. I mean yes. At least I don't ... No, no.'

Charles V of France – aka Charles the Affable had harboured Warbeck before the one had hotspurred it to Edinburgh and the other to Naples. In 1492, Henry, in a rare display of military might had dispatched troops and besieged Boulogne. Charles had caved and handed over 159,000 gold sovereigns. Henry had put one over the Old Enemy and Henry's star had never risen so high. After a century of war England was great again! But that was three long years ago, an eternity in Anglo-French relations and now affable bloody Charles had added Naples to his portfolio, becoming ever more powerful. It was only a matter of time before French eyes turned across the channel. Those 159,000 sovereigns were starting to look small change.

'What are we going to do about James?' said Henry. 'He can't believe Warbeck is the prince in The Tower. Which prince is he supposed to be?'

'The Duke of York, sir.'

'He can't believe it ... can he?'

'He is using Warbeck as leverage,' said Sir Reginald. 'A negotiating pawn which he will happily sacrifice. I don't think anyone truly believes Warbeck's claim.'

'Isn't that worse?'

'That there are parties who would rather a fraudster on the throne than yourself? Yes, I suppose it is.'

Henry had started negotiations with James IV of Scotland to end the intermittent but tedious wars that continued to break out along the borders, but now James was openly supporting Warbeck, putting on a tourney for him no less.

'There's always the old stand-by,' ventured Sir Reginald.

'We don't have a stand-by ... you mean Margaret?'

Princess Margaret. Henry's daughter.

'How old is James? Twenty-two?' said Henry. 'And Margaret's six.'

'A long betrothal, sir. I think we can make it work.'

And it was only a daughter after all. Arthur and Catherine, James and Margaret. One happy extended European family.

'Let's see what the Italians say,' said Sir Reginald.

Henry and Bray met with a succession of Italian ambassadors: Venice, Florence, Milan. None ventured an opinion regarding the fall of Naples. All were looking to Rome to lead the way. The final meeting was with Pope Alexander's special envoy, or nuncio.

'Is there any way we can cancel?'

'I'm afraid not, sir. There's the little matter of Innocent's favour which Alexander has assumed as his own.'

The papal nuncio to Westminster was a priest, one Giovanni de Carbonariis who doubled as the pope's tax overseer and triple-dipped as Alexander's eyes and ears, a spy no less. The Church owned a third (!) of the land in England and collected ten (!) per cent of her income tax. Then there was Peter's pence; a tax of one penny per household which went straight to Rome. So de Carbonariis was a top-shelf dignitary and a ten-course lunch it was: soup to nuts with fish and fowl and hopefully some leftover whale tongue in between. Henry wanted to see the pious bastard squirm. Sir Rowland de Montfort, Commander of the King's Bodyguard announced and ushered him in and John Blanke blew a welcoming alarum on his trumpet.

'You look weary, Your Majesty. Affairs of State?'

Good to see you, too. Cocky, bloody Roman.

'No, all is merry in the House of Tudor, father, let me assure you.'

'So it should be, sire. Your position is secure. Your reign is blessed.'

The talk was idle, small, while the first courses were served.

33

'Whale's tongue. How delicious!' said de Carbonariis.

Henry ground his teeth. That was going to be the highlight of the lunch.

The footmen brought in a pie. Oh, Christ. If Cheffie had baked live fucking birds again ... Fortunately it was dead deer.

'The Holy Father has asked me to raise his concerns regarding church dogma. He fears the Church in England is becoming lax.'

'No heretics in England, father,' Henry assured him.

'The Holy Father is not so sure.'

'What would you have us do?' said Henry. 'Appoint a Grand Inquisitor like Torquemada?'

'Fr Torquemada is doing a wonderful job. Spain is free of heresy.'

'The man is bonckers.'

'Thorough, perhaps?'

Henry knew what was coming next. More or less.

'Alexander would like to appoint a Vatican representative here in England. Just to keep an eye on things. That would require an archbishopric.'

'That's hardly a ringing endorsement of Canterbury, father.'

'We are worried that Sir John is wearing too many hats: Chancellor, Chief Tax Collector and Archbishop of Canterbury are an onerous array of responsibilities. Are there any vacancies, Sir Reginald?'

'The next retirement is probably Blackburn,' said Sir Reginald who was clearly across the matter.

De Carbonariis didn't have a clue where Blackburn was. In fact, Bray wasn't sure he knew either.

'Blackburn ... The Holy Father was thinking Bath and Wells.'

'And who did the Holy Father have in mind for the archbishopric?' said Henry.

'Well, that would be god's will,' said de Carbonariis modestly.

You fat smarmy bastard.

Henry had to think fast. It would mean a papal agent in one of the most prestigious sees in the country. Still, he needed Alexander's support.

'One of the Church's most exalted positions,' said Sir Reginald, coming to the rescue, 'and one which is usually appointed by a committee. Not a standing committee, you understand, but a select committee. I shall have my best men onto it, father.'

'Your best men will select the candidate for Bath and Wells?'

'Not quite. I shall appoint my best men to form a standing committee who will meet to select a select committee who, after appropriate consideration will select a list of candidates which will be returned to the standing committee who will consider the recommendations and compile a shortlist of candidates which will be forwarded to myself who will make a recommendation on the selected candidate.'

'I see ...'

'Which will then be forwarded to a committee to endorse the recommendation. Or, perhaps, not.'

'And when is that likely to be?'

'That would be god's will, father.'

'Of course.' De Carbonariis smiled through clenched teeth.

'Now, father. His Majesty would like you to convey his extreme displeasure to the pontiff for his continued silence regarding France's presence in Naples.'

'A difficult situation, Your Majesty. King Charles does have a legitimate claim to Naples.'

'So do half the crowned heads of Europe,' countered Sir Reginald smoothly.

'I shall convey His Majesty's displeasure.'

The French Ambassador had fled to Edinburgh leaving a single, spotty youth to man the residence. He went by the title of Maître des Sceaux – Master of the Seals and was in charge of dispatching and receiving all communications. In short, he ran the mailroom. Henry was desperate to vent his fury on someone, anyone, but really, what was the point?

'Tell the ambassador I wish to see him the minute he returns,' said Henry, waving the youth away.

'The nobles are still waiting, sir,' said Sir Reginald.

'Oh, all right. Show them in,' said Henry.

There was no ten-course luncheon for the English nobles. No soup, no nuts, no John Blanke alarum. Not even a mug of ale – which Cumbria was quick to note.

'Your Majesty,' said Cumbria, 'as loyal but concerned subjects we demand to know your response to the French attack on Naples.'

'We are aware of the invasion,' said Sir Reginald. 'We have men on the ground in Naples, monitoring the situation and keeping us apprised of developments.'

'France is our sworn, our oldest, enemy. Why are we "monitoring the situation" and not marching on France?'

Because I owe the bloody pope, thought Henry.

'Why wage war when we can work effectively through diplomatic channels?' said Sir Reginald.

'Because we are Englishmen. That's what we do!' Cumbria thundered.

Cumbria's fellow nobles muttered their support for the hawkish northerner.

'Would you challenge your king?' said Henry.

'We are concerned that our oldest enemy grows ever more powerful while we "revel in the pleasures of these idle days, this weak piping time of peace".'

Where have I heard that before, Henry wondered. Barabbas! Had the treacherous little squirt joined the conspirators?

'France is one of our most important trading partners,' said Sir Reginald.

'Trading partner?' Cumbria snarled. 'Alfred and William, and Richard and Longshanks and Henry IV, V and VI – all right, maybe not VI – and Richard II and III – even with his infirmity – would have been half-way to Paris by now.'

Henry heard the mutterings rise a notch. There were six of them; six of the most powerful nobles in the realm. Were they to unite they could raise an army that could topple him.

'France grows stronger as we grow weaker. When will England rise again? When will England be great again?'

'England is great,' said Henry. 'And will continue to be great under my reign.'

Henry called the meeting to a close.

B acon finished his wine and continued on his rounds which were largely follow-up calls, monitoring previous patients. He dressed wounds and removed stitches. One patient, a gilder, had contracted the sweats, the usually fatal illness that had claimed thousands of lives. Many diseases, once contracted, offer immunity. Not the sweats. The poor man had been struck down a second time; high temperature, cold shivers, intense thirst and delirium. Almost as an afterthought, Bacon checked for ulcers but the groin area was clear of both ulcers and the resultant pockes.

'No rash on your chest? Or your arms and legs?'

The gilder shook his head.

Bacon believed that the main cause of disease was the appalling sewage system in London, or rather the lack of one. Few believed him, however. The English study of medicine was based on the ancient texts of Hippocrates (460-370 BC) and Galen (129-216 AD). Whereas European universities such as Bologna, and Paris had advanced the studies of medicine, the English medical system maintained its rigid study of the ancients. The Church had not helped matters by frowning on dissection and the study of anatomy, believing that it violated god's divine creation – ie man. The miasma theory was the major tenet of English medicine. It proposed that disease was caused by miasmata, a noxious form of bad air which arose from rotting organic matter, which in turn created imbalances in the individual's humours – the black and yellow bile, phlegm and blood which make up the human body. The Church was not opposed to these principles, but it was a keystone of Church dogma that disease was God's punishment for sin.

The surgeons were sick of being lumped in with the Worshipful Company of Barber-Surgeons and had long lobbied for a guild of their own. Barbers were able to set their prices and stick to them; unlike the surgeons who were forced to accept whatever they were paid. That a haircut and shave equated to a life-saving amputation baffled Bacon. Membership of the guild entitled the worshipful member to display a column outside his business: a white pole signified a barber, a red pole, a surgeon, a red and white pole a barber-surgeon. Bacon refused to cut hair; he was obsessed with surgery and the human body, its functions and the diseases that afflicted it. A pair of red columns flanked his doorway.

The rise of the Barber-Surgeons was an odd one. The barbers' most regular customers were the various orders of monks whose hair they tonsured. These same monks ran hospitals and tended to the sick but in 1219 Pope Honorius – when not describing how to raise and control demons in his famous grimoire – prohibited all persons in Holy Orders from practising surgery, stipulating that only God could prolong or terminate life. The barbers, skilled with blades, or at least owning them, and sensing a lucrative new revenue stream stepped into the breach, assuming the monks' bloodletting and surgical duties. From the friaries, it was a short step onto the battlefield – and there were plenty of battlefields in the Guild's early years. Many of the nobility wanted their soldiers turned out well.

'If you can't fight like soldiers at least look like fucking soldiers,' the Duke of Lancaster, John of Gaunt had once famously told his troops. As portraits will attest, the Duke sported a full head of locks, lustrous and elegantly styled. Many of the barber-surgeons had returned from battle with a bloodlust and found a life of haircutting thin gruel and turned to the drink. Others had been traumatised, their shaking hand unable to steady a razor. Many had turned the razor upon themselves but things had gone a bit quiet on the battlefield during Henry's reign, Bacon reflected.

Bacon's final call was to tend a joiner who had severed a forefinger. He completed the job efficiently and accepted a groat in payment. The man could afford more, but Bacon was tired and besides, he never haggled.

He bought wine and ham, cheese and bread for his supper then called on his final patient for the day. Sarah Fleece's husband had been an overseer on the docks east of Westminster. He had been crushed unloading cargo. Bacon had attended the accident but could not save the unfortunate worker. The Fleeces had lived frugally but quite comfortably in a neat cottage in Cheapside but with her husband's death, Sarah had been forced to sell up and move to Drury Lane in St Giles, the most wretched borough in all London. She had called for Bacon when she fell ill. It bore all the marks of the sweats and Bacon called to see how she was progressing. The eldest boy, aged perhaps eight, opened the door to his knock.

'Hello, young William.'

'Hello, sir, you'll have to wait, sir. Me mam's busy.'

The four children were spinning a top on the hard-dirt floor. There was no running water or sanitation, of course. A few sticks of furniture had replaced Sarah's previous crafted-in-Camden suites. A curtain partitioned the one room. Bacon was dismayed to hear the grunts and groans of sexual congress. So, it had come to this. Bacon searched his pockets. Four groats. Not a lot of money for a hard day's work. He handed William a coin.

'Share it out. A penny each.'

'We'll give it to our mam, Mr Bacon.'

'You're a good boy, William.'

The curtain parted and a man, face flushed with drink and sexual exertion appeared, securing his breeches. He spat on the floor.

'I've had better,' he said to Bacon, brushing past him.

'Mr Bacon,' said Sarah. 'How kind of you to call.'

The poor woman was humiliated. Bacon, never the most socially adept of men, struggled to find words.

'Oh, Sarah.'

'Don't waste your pity, Mr Bacon. Four mouths to feed. Plus my own.'

'Speaking of which.'

Bacon produced the jug of wine and the food he had bought for his supper.

'Plenty enough for the five of you,' he said.

'No, I won't accept charity.'

'You've paid me, haven't you?' he said abruptly. 'All part of the service.'

It didn't fool her and the conversation was stilted. Sarah's shame did not stimulate conversation.

Nothing to be ashamed of, Sarah, Bacon thought. You've put a roof over your family's head, brought food to the table. You should be bloody proud.

'How have you been, Sarah? The symptoms have cleared?'

She nodded.

'Probably wasn't the sweats then.'

'Except for the headaches,' she added. 'Blinders.'

'I can give you something for them.'

'Strangest thing, Mr Bacon. They only come on at night.'

Bacon's heart lurched.

'Best if I examine you, Sarah.'

She led him behind the curtain. She was clearly embarrassed. Was she this embarrassed with her clients? She lifted her skirt and lowered her drawers.

Oh, no.

The ulcers.

'Lie down, Sarah. I'm sorry, I need to have a thorough look.'

There were half a dozen of them. He gently probed.

'When did you first notice them?'

'Yesterday.'

'Do you have any idea how you got them?'

'No.'

'Any pain?'

'What is it, Mr Bacon? Tell me it's not – '

'No, Sarah, it's not the plague.'

'Or – '

'I don't think it's leprosy.'

'I just want to keep working until my two eldest are in trade. If I can do that we might survive.'

'We'll do our best, Sarah. You must be meticulous with your hygiene. I'll organise medicines at the apothecary in Drury Lane. Send William to pick them up this evening before the bells.'

There was a knock on the door. A man in a ceiler's smock, another client. He had the good grace to look ashamed. Bacon refused Sarah's payment and left thoroughly depressed. London's rich were absurdly rich; but her poor lived desperately. There had been no safety net when Fleece had been crushed to death. And no safety net to save his wife and children.

Bacon was tempted to stop at an eating-house or tavern for supper but he was eager to write up his case notes; he would have to make do with what was in the pantry. Whatever was there, a jug of Burgundy would wash it down. A knight was waiting for him. Not just any knight but Sir Rowland de Montfort, Commander of the King's Guard, Knight of the Golden Fleece, the most celebrated, most idolised knight in the realm. The de Montforts had fought with Henry V at Agincourt and had been granted vast lands and wealth. Sir Rowland was barely twenty-two but was one of the most glamorous members of Henry's court. He had seen no battlefield but had gained fame as a jouster, a peace piping which passed for battle these days. The jousting knights were sporting heroes. Their courage could not be doubted; jousting took a lot of nerve and was damned dangerous and Bacon had been called to repair many a knight's shattered bones. Bacon came only when called. Jousting tournaments attracted a fair number of barber-surgeons; not through compassion for stricken knights but as a means of attracting wealthy clients and bulging their purses. Coffin cullies.

The age of chivalry was long gone according to current opinion, but their stars remained ever high in the firmament. They married nobly of course, but were a licentious lot. 'If it moves, shoot it. If it doesn't move, fuck it. If it stinks throw it on the back of the horse,' was an unwritten addendum to the knightly code, whispered and bantered in the sanctuary of the pre-tourney robing room. But the knights continued to propagate the chivalric myth.

Bacon had never seen de Montfort up close. He was one of the blessed, happy few, all right, Bacon thought. Flaxen hair, creamy, peachy skin. Young boys played at jousts on wooden horses and invariably one boy would pretend to be the heroic Sir Rowland, such was the adulation showered upon him.

'I have been honoured by my gracious monarch with an invitation to display my talents, meagre though they may be, at the forthcoming tilt,' said Sir Rowland. The sporting highlight of the social season was the upcoming tournament which would decide the champion jouster in all England, the King's Champion. Sir Rowland was the hot favourite. 'If God be ever so willing, I may even, perchance, be blessed with the good fortune to vanquish my noble opponents.'

My god, thought Bacon, do they all speak like this? There was an arrogance in the modesty, not an easy trick to pull off. Sir Rowland had practised it since birth. Perhaps it came with the spoon of silver.

'I might put a small wager on you.'

'Put the house on it,' said Sir Rowland, slipping momentarily out of chivalry-speak. He smiled a boyish smile and bowed gracefully, no doubt practised countless times before his cheval mirror. 'But I have a small problem.'

Bacon waited. He had surmised the problem immediately; Knights of the Golden Fleece didn't come to his humble surgery with a head cold.

'Yes?'

'Modesty forbids discourse on such a delicate matter.'

'Down with your breeches.'

'Sir Thomas Metcalfe diagnosed the condition and prescribed an unguent.'

Metcalfe. Unguent. That would be right.

'On the bench and on your side.'

'Sir Thomas said – '

'Knees up to your chest.'

'Owww.'

There is nothing in the chivalric code covering a surgeon shoving his fist up your arse. Sir Rowland did as he was told.

Just as Bacon thought: *fistula in ano*. Loosely translated: a pain in the arse. There was housemaid's knee, sawyer's shoulder and knight errant's arsehole. Like all knights, Sir Rowland had commenced training at seven years and so had spent fifteen years bouncing around on a rock-hard saddle. Coursing, jousting, even recreational riding became agony.

Bacon probed gently.

'Owww.'

Maybe not so gently.

It was a brute of a thing, about as big as a gowf ball.

'Can you fix it?'

'Yes.'

'When?'

'Now I would suggest.'

'Will it, er, hurt?'

'Yes, but not as much as a lance in your breast bone.'

Bacon mixed a tincture of opium and wine. The knight felt clammy and his pulse was quick; nerves probably. He was in dreamland in minutes. Bacon prided himself on his surgical instruments which he designed himself and were crafted for him by a member of the Worshipful Company of Cutlers. Bacon also prided himself on his nimble bladework. It took the best part of an hour to remove the fistula and suture the wound. When the knight awoke, Bacon offered more opium. He also offered to show him the fistula but Sir Rowland, as brave as a lion on the tilt field was a squeam when it came to his own body.

'When can I get back on my horse?'

'At least a fortnight. I'll need to dress the wound regularly and remove the stitches. Where is home?'

'Westminster.'

Of course. Sir Rowland was Commander of the King's Own Bodyguard and lived at Westminster. 'Stay at the Palace. I will place you on my list and visit in two days.'

The knight hobbled from the surgery. Bacon sat in his parlour, poured himself a soothing cup of Burgundy and wrote up his notes. He would need them for follow-up visits with Sir Rowland and the stonemason. And for Geffrey and Sarah. These last two worried Bacon. He couldn't shake the thought that these ulcers were the harbinger of some terrible new disease. He could only hope it lacked the devastating morbidity of the Black Death.

Early in his reign Henry often roamed the streets, talking with artisans and shopkeepers, gauging the mood of his people. He had modified the strategy of late, preferring to invite select individuals to the Palace and pump them for information. One such individual was a town crier called Barrie Vagg whose pitch lay equidistant between Westminster and Holborn. He was born and raised in beyond-the-wall East London, within sound of the St Mary-le-Bow bells. The criers were official employees of London's 25 wards, hired to disseminate news and official proclamations concerning law and taxation amongst other matters. Vagg was both informed and entertaining and spiced the official news with a juicy murder, a titillating item of gossip and one or two of Barabbas's latest sallies.

'The people is not happy about that latest tax rise, Your Majesty.'

'They never are.'

'Thievin' bloody government, they're sayin'. Where does the money go? Look at the state of the roads. Look at the price of bread.'

'What are they saying about Naples?'

'They's wondering why's you don't give them Frenchies a bloody nose, sir.'

Although Londoners had never been so prosperous there remained a significant rump of citizens – either those who had not prospered as well in this new trade- and merit-driven society, or the plain disaffected – flag-wavers all, who supported the dissident nobles and who longed to put the great back in England. The way to do that, they argued was by invading France – or anywhere in Europe, really – and laying waste to it.

'Thank you, Vagg. Make sure you get a chit and hand it into Dunne.' It was worth a sovereign to hear Vagg's thoughts.

Henry conferred with Sir Reginald who conferred with Foxe the Chronicler who conferred with his scriveners who drafted a proclamation announcing that Henry "refused to squander hard-working, tax-paying Englishmen's money on petty squabbles between the French and Italians". This quote would be passed on to Vagg and his colleagues and would be cried throughout the city.

Henry then had Foxe compose a missive to Pope Alexander reiterating his friendship and respect, but suggesting that, having conquered Naples, Charles would not stop there and would soon set his "infect'd eye" (as Barabbas put it) on other Italian states.

'This will do. What do you reckon, Hardwick?'
The land was on Turl Street between Ship and Market Street. There were fifteen colleges in Oxford. Sir Reginald Bray was going to build a sixteenth.

'Prime,' said Hardwick. 'What are you going to call it?'

'Morton wants me to call it Jesus. But I rather thought Bray.'

Henry, Bray and Morton were often referred to as the Holy Trinity with Henry God, Bray God the Son, and Morton the Holy Ghost. Equating his own name with his saviour's did not seem unduly flattering to the vain old man.

'Let's eat,' he said 'I'll show you the plans I've drawn up.'

They made their way to their old college (Merton) which enjoyed a stellar reputation for its kitchen and wine cellar.

Sir Reginald Bray had profited enormously from the enclosure laws by which smallholdings were collated and enclosed for a single owner, thus ceasing to be the people's common land. He had grown doubly rich when he was one of the first to switch from crops to the far more profitable sheep and had become one of the biggest suppliers of fleece to the Merchant Adventurers in London. Bray was appointed Knight of the Garter, one of only twenty-four KGs appointed on Henry's coronation day. He was Chancellor of the Duchy of Lancaster and High Steward of Oxford University, together with a long list of other appointments.

Hardwick could not have been of lower birth. He was the son of a farm labourer who worked Bray's Worcestershire estate and was left an orphan at age six. Sir Reginald took a shine to the boy and paid for his education which culminated in an Oxford degree. Hardwick had graduated dux or near dux in logic, rhetoric, divinity, mathematics, Greek and Latin, history, and law.

Henry had never seen the point in wasting good money on public works but, obsessed as he was with his legacy, he was determined to leave behind something physical, to make his mark – like a dog pissing on a post. Henry decided that he'd put the Europeans in their place and that Westminster and Windsor would be the finest palaces in all Europe. Architecture was Bray's passion. He was not an overtly religious man. You didn't need to be to design churches and Bray had designed much of the interior of the Henry VII's Chapel at Westminster, St George's Chapel, Windsor, St Mary's, Oxford, and now Bray – or Jesus – College in Oxford. Bray's plans for the new college were certainly impressive. Sir Reginald, it seemed, was also pressing to leave his mark and was pissing far and wide.

The Merton food was excellent, the wine even better. The pair decided against pudding and opted for a decanter of the sweet dark wine from Porto that was becoming popular in Oxford.

'Let's talk about your future. What do you have in mind?'

'I'd say head up your new college but that will be years in the building.'

'You were keen on the Church at one time. You could probably make archbishop or even cardinal over time.'

'I've thought about it but I have problems with the dogma.'

'Lost your faith, eh? A churchman doesn't have to believe in god. Most of the good ones don't. We're damn lucky we don't have a Torquemada over here. He'd soon sort out the non-believers.'

'I thoroughly enjoyed my night in Westminster.'

'I rather thought you might. Henry knows how to put on a show. Well, Westminster's the place to be. That's where the money and the power is. I could install you as an advisor. The place is full of advisors but we could always do with another bright young man. And Henry loves self-made men.'

'But surely the monarchy is based on primogeniture.'

'It is. But self-made men are more grateful, more loyal to the crown than the merely entitled. Let me tell you something. There has never been a better time to start a career in Westminster. England is in a state of flux. First of all, the old lord and serf system, the old communalism is breaking down. It is now about commerce. Men trade their skills or their labour for money. The emphasis is no longer the community, but the individual. Merit, not birth is rewarded. Secondly, England is becoming more centralised. London is the true powerhouse of the nation. Look how Henry has glamourised his court. There are very few noblewomen – and noblemen – who don't drool over an invitation to court.'

Bray poured them another cup of wine.

'And thirdly, – and this is between you, me and the wine jug – Henry no longer wishes to reclaim France.'

'What? You mean he's given up on all the lands that H VI lost?'

'I do mean that. We've pulled out of Europe. Militarily. But you didn't hear it from me. Henry believes that money is more powerful than bows and arrows. More valuable than foreign lands. France isn't worth the expense or the bother. A prosperous nation – and England has never been more prosperous – is a happy nation.'

'And its king sits easily in his counting-house. Catchy tune that ballade.'

'Don't sing it in front of Henry or you'll soon be singing hymns in some godforsaken rectory. Up north or the Scilly Isles perhaps. We've planned our international strategy almost perfectly. We have treaties or are at least on good terms with Rome, Spain, Portugal, Burgundy and the Lowlands, Maximilian and the Germans – '

'By which you mean the Holy Roman Empire?'

'We don't call it that any more. Vienna's the capital and the Germans are running the show, so, the Germans it is.'

'As I understand it,' said Hardwick, 'everyone wants our wool so we are trading with all our partners on very favourable terms.'

'Exactly. We're virtually a part of Europe – you didn't hear me say that! – one big happy, trading community.'

'And war would put an end to all that.'

'It would. But we don't say that. We make all the right noises, wave the flag of St George around and all that.'

'But what about the old nobility? They still have the tables closest to the king.'

'We have to look after the old nobles. Take Cumbria. Typical example. Thick as mince. But he's powerful. He could raise a decent army at a single command and there are half a dozen like him. They want a return to the old days. They want to invade France. They want to conquer all of Europe. Madness.'

'I kept hearing rumours about Perkin Warbeck when I was down there.'

'Warbeck has proved a bit of a surprise. Cumbria and Suffolk and all the others are so desperate to get rid of Henry they would happily put a pretender on the throne – *knowing* he's a pretender. He'll be their puppet, of course. Trouble is, politics has become polarised in this country. Old guard versus new. Landed gentry versus urban elite. But the old guard's power is definitely waning.'

'Do you think I have the skills to survive in Westminster?'

'Skills? Most of the Members of the House can barely read or write. They can count the money they've made or know to the inch how many thousands of acres they own. The Council is packed with warriors and loyalists most of whom are quite stupid. It's the advisors that are the clever ones. An awful lot of lawyers are coming through.'

'Have you got anything specific for me?'

'Don't worry, we'll find you something. Be warned, it's a snakepit, Westminster. Always someone shitting on you from above. Fortunately, I only have Henry above me.'

48

Hardwick wondered if snakes could shit on anything from above. Bray poured the last of the wine.

'Of course, Morton ties himself in knots trying to shit sideways, but I have him covered. Do you fancy another jug?'

The following morning Henry met with the Council Learned in the Law, a secretive inner, inner sanctum which comprised Bray and Morton and the knighted – benighted in the view of many – tax collectors, Sirs Richard Empson and Edmund Dudley. Morton was an ecclesiast but as Lord Chamberlain had proven equally adept collecting mammon as saving souls. He had devised the brilliant Morton's Fork which became a kind of Fiscal Holy Scripture. No one – other than the Church and its Holy Orders – was exempted from it: 'If the subject is seen to live frugally,' Morton told his taxmen, 'tell him that is because he is clearly a money saver of great ability, and he can afford to give generously to the King. If, however, the subject lives a life of great extravagance, tell him he, too, can afford to give largely, the proof of his opulence being evident in his expenditure.' The stratagem worked a treat and Dudley and Empson proved able and willing acolytes. They were Morton's chief tax collectors but really, were little more than hatchet-men, venal, corrupt, velvet-collar criminals.

The University of Oxford had added a degree in Commerce and Empson and Dudley's teams had graduated *summa cum laude*. There was not a nook or cranny, a mattress or loose floorboard in the kingdom in which to hide cash from these fiscal bloodhounds. It was, however, dangerous work. Agents were regularly assaulted, occasionally murdered, their bodies thrown in the Thames or the Fleet. Nevertheless, Henry was in good cheer. He always looked forward to the weekly meeting with his taxmen.

'Commerce is flourishing, Your Majesty,' said Empson. 'Memberships of the Guilds are growing rapidly.'

Empson forwarded a document containing the official figure to Henry who thrilled at the numbers.

'The number of apprentices is at record levels. Prices are up at bakers, butchers, poulterers. Wages have nearly doubled over the last century. Which means increased taxation, of course.'

Several more documents were passed around the table to Henry.

'Unfortunately, we have a shortage of labourers and tradesmen which is adversely impacting potential growth,' said Dudley.

'Didn't we discuss bringing in workmen from Bohemia, Morton?' said Henry.

'Indeed we did, sir, but it was felt that English labourers might not accept foreigners taking their jobs.'

'We could tax foreigners at a special rate,' offered Dudley.

Henry nodded, this sounded like a plan.

'An influx of foreign labour would decrease wages and therefore spending, and thus lead to a decrease in collectable tax,' said Empson, who had been briefed by one of his Oxford graduates.

This economics stuff was complicated, thought Henry. Pity. It was a good plan but Henry agreed to shelve it for the minute; he could always resurrect it if gross taxation dipped.

Empson reported that milliners, drapers and jewellers could barely keep up with demand and were clearly undertaxed. One of his agents had noted that citizens were buying beds and pillows in great numbers: it was a new growth industry and could, perhaps, warrant a new tax.

'And there's always curtains,' said Dudley, directing a smirk toward his colleague.

Empson was a notoriously secretive man. If the rumours were true he had a lot to be secretive about. He had acquired sudden, vast wealth and it was widely believed that he took a cut of the taxes he raised. Empson had come up with the idea of placing lengths of cloth across his windows. They became known as curtains, from the Latin, *cortana*. Lady Empson had run with the idea and her colourful curtains and drapes became the rage of fashionable London.

'Eating houses are springing up throughout the City,' Dudley reported, 'and they're proving extremely popular. I suggest we set up a Committee to investigate and tax the hospitality trade.'

He passed Henry another document. All these documents, all these figures, Henry marvelled. He would pore over them later, at his leisure.

Construction was unceasing, Dudley reported. Buildings were being torn down and rebuilt on every street then leased or sold at vast profits. Henry smiled; he could smell a new tax in that one.

'There are many new businesses establishing themselves,' Empson continued. 'Toys and clocks from Saxony and Helvetia, for instance, playing cards from Spain. People become more prosperous and sell off their old goods and chattels to second-hand emporia who resell them at profit.'

'Excellent,' said Henry. This was shaping as a splendid morning's work.

'On the downside,' said Empson. 'Cutpurses, fraudulent beggars, thieves and murderers abound. We could fine the cutpurses and thieves as well as jail them. That would raise revenue.'

'Splendid,' enthused Henry.

Henry thought about raising the matter of the Church which was selling burial plots and requiem masses and making a fortune. No, Morton would have a fit. Perhaps he could raise the tax on coffins ...

'My agents have noted an increase in the number of nightwalkers,' said Empson. Dudley nodded his agreement. The City of London still had a 9 pm curfew. Anyone out after then was clearly up to no good.

'Taverns and brothels, we suspect,' said Dudley.

London had the highest number of brothels and taverns of any city in Europe. It also had the highest number of churches, Henry recalled. Perhaps it was not such a paradox; a visit to one followed by a penitential visit t'other.

'We really should do something about these bawdhouses,' said Morton. It was a sticky situation for the Archbishop/Chancellor; a visit to a bawdhouse was a sin, yet they contributed significantly to the city's economy.

'Perhaps we could legitimise them,' suggested Dudley. 'A Worshipful Company of Bawds?'

Empson chuckled at his colleague's sally. Henry, however, wasn't sure it was such a bad idea. He put it aside for further consideration, perhaps ask Bray to conduct one of his viability studies or whatever he called them.

'We could increase the Watch,' Sir Reginald suggested. 'Have the military train them properly, perhaps.'

The Watch was the sole form of policing and was funded privately by individual neighbourhoods. They were paid a minimum wage and the job attracted an unsavoury bunch of otherwise unemployable drunks and dodderers.

'I don't think so,' said Morton crisply. 'The State is not responsible for policing. The cost should be borne by the citizens. Why burden the Exchequer when it is outsourced at no cost to the Treasury?'

Sir Reginald privately thought that the state might run some services more profitably, but why pick a fight with his fellow Councillor? Both Henry and Bray had their doubts about Morton. He wore two hats – or rather he wore the Archbishop's mitre and the Chancellor's velvet cap and Henry could never figure whether his first duty was to England or to Rome. Three million subjects. How many households was that? More pertinently, how many pence was that for Peter? No. Henry would upset every priest in England and unto the Pope himself should he try to cut a slice of that tasty pie.

'This is all very good, gentlemen,' said Henry. 'But I need to raise capital and I need to raise it quickly. Is there anywhere we can raise the taxes?'

"How much is required, sir?' said Sir John.

'How much, Sir Reginald?'

'75,000 sovereigns, sir.'

Sir Richard Dudley whistled. 75,000 was a *lot* of money. You could wage a war with less.

No one spoke. Henry's subjects were taxed to the hilt. Past the hilt, according to many. The king was bleeding his subjects dry.

'Dangerous, Your Majesty,' said Morton. 'We wouldn't want a *rebellion*, would we?'

That stopped Henry in his tracks, as Morton knew it would.

'What about the Guilds and Companies?' said Henry. 'You said their numbers are billowing.'

'They pay a hefty rate, sire,' said Dudley.

'The nobility?' said Henry.

'We cannot afford to upset the nobles,' said Morton. 'Another rise really would provoke a rebellion.'

'The Merchant Adventurers? God knows, they're practically minting the stuff.'

'According to my *logos arithmos*, sire,' said Empson, whose advisor had developed the actual *logos*. 'Returns on taxation diminish beyond a certain point. The wealthy have money that they freely spend on goods and services. Tax them further and they will have less money to spend. Thus, less goods + less services + less jobs = less taxation + more unhappy citizens.'

'So, you're saying we shouldn't tax the rich?' said Henry.

'Correct.'

'And we should tax the poor?'

'From the middle-classes down. The artisans and the workers have less money to spend.'

But another tax rise on the workers may well provoke the rebellion that Morton warned of. Furthermore, Henry wanted to be remembered fondly. Dammit, he wanted ballades sung about him. Henry called for refreshments. Dudley's heart sank at the sight of such lavish food and drink. It was going to be a long session.

'Fortunately, Sir Reginald and I have come up with a plan,' said Henry. 'Call in the nobles, Sir Rowland.'

Commander of the King's Guard, Sir Rowland de Montfort announced Lords Cumbria, Suffolk *et al* and John Blanke blew a suitably martial alarum. Cumbria's eyes lit up at the sight of the feast: wild boar, fatted calf! And more puddings than you could poke with a pigstick. The nobles tucked in.

'My lords,' said Henry, glancing surreptitiously at some choice words of Barabbas's he had scribbled on a napkin, 'I have noticed of late angry spots doth glowing on thy brows. My Lord Cumbria doth look with such ferret and fiery eyes. I see lean and hungry looks. Men who think too much.' Cumbria looked at Henry blankly. All right, maybe not Cumbria. 'They cannot be made to smile at anything. They are never at heart's ease, whiles they behold a greater than themselves.'

The nobles looked bemused. Damn, they didn't understand a word.

'Put simply,' said Sir Reginald, 'there are many who believe we should attack France. We are not of their number. Not yet at any rate. His Majesty wishes to announce that we are going to rebuild the Royal Navy. Entirely. *In toto*. He who rules the waves, rules the world. Glorious Albion – ' that was better! ' – shall have the finest navy in Europe. Albion shall rule the world.'

That shut them up.

'And how are we going to pay for this?' said Lord Cumbria. 'We will not pay a penny more in taxes.'

Not quite shut them up.

'See my lips?' said Henry. 'See how they move? No. Raising. Of. Taxes.'

Henry's wafer-thin lips angled into the semblance of a smile.

'I repeat my question, Your Majesty. How do you propose to pay for this navy?'

'I won't,' said Henry. 'You will.'

That really shut the bastards up. Cumbria paled. A morsel of fatted calf fell from his spoon.

'Sir Reginald, if you please?'

'Thank you, Your Majesty. As you all know it is illegal to raise armies without Royal Assent. It is also illegal to employ a standing army in the guise of household and estate workers. My Lord Cumbria you have 4,000 men in your employ and sufficient weaponry to arm them.'

'Protection, Sir Reginald. It is my birthright to bear arms. It is written in the – it's written somewhere.'

'You will be brought before the Star Chamber and formally charged on a date to be advised. I believe hanging is the standard punishment.'

Henry helped himself to a cutlet.

'Or ...'

He chewed appreciatively on the cutlet.

'Or?' said Cumbria hoarsely.

'You will pay a fine of 75,000 new and freshly-minted gold sovereigns. Please, drink, eat,' said Henry, savouring a mouthful of Burgundy.

Cumbria was stunned. But not for long, Henry thought. He may be thick-eared and thick-witted but he would not lie back and think of Albion while Henry right royally sodomised him.

A Knight of the Golden Fleece was the apotheosis of the Age of Chivalry, upholding the Code's values of chastity, modesty and honesty. Knights of the Golden Fleece were sworn to show no mercy to infidels and Sir Rowland had vowed to likewise show no mercy – in the unlikely event he ever met an infidel. They lived a friarly, almost ascetic existence, forswearing the sins of the flesh, bedding down in sparse cells or even stables.

Allegedly.

Sir Rowland's palace apartment was sumptuous. The walls hung with Flemish tapestries. The Saracen scimitars and javelins which adorned the walls, however, had been bought from a dealer in Old Jewry. Likewise, the swords, maces and halberds which hung artfully on the wall. A portrait of Sir Rowland mounted insouciantly on Bucephalus, his favourite charger, hung above the inglenook, flanked by sigils and the de Montfort coat of arms. His highly-polished visor with scarlet plumes was arranged just-so on a tallboy. There was a cheval mirror at the end of the bed. Presumably, the first thing Sir Rowland saw on awakening was himself, or himself and whoever he'd invited to his bed.

Sir Rowland lay less than insouciantly on a divan, his breeches around his ankles and Bacon wrist-deep up his arse.

It has to be said that he bore the intrusion with knightly patience.

'Everything all right down there?'

'Healing nicely.'

Infection had not set in which augured well for recovery.

'You've gained a reputation for this,' said Sir Rowland, impeccably mannered as always. 'Did you develop this technique yourself?'

'No. It came from a man called John of Arderne.'

'Can't say I've heard of him.'

'He was a surgeon. He won his reputation on the battlefield about a hundred years ago. A genius at removing arrow heads. The first to treat gunpowder burns. I have all his papers. He also set out a code of conduct. A revision of Hippocrates. No set fees. Charge each according to his means.'

'Yes, well, don't be fooled by this place. Plenty of goods and chattels, but I'm rather light on for cash. You know, Modesty. Frugality. The Code and all that.'

Typical of the nobility, thought Bacon. The rich pay late. The noblesse were all for their oblige as long as they didn't have to pay for it.

How had Barabbas put it? "O, what vile faults look handsome in three hundred pounds a year!" Sir Rowland was on more than three hundred a year and his horses were better fed than many a Londoner.

'Two shillings, thank you, Sir Rowland.'

'As I said I'm a little light on. Can I square up next time?'

'Of course.'

He would have to fight to get his money but if someone didn't want to pay he couldn't force them, Especially someone as exalted as Sir Rowland.

'Oh, um, Bacon? You're not going to tell anyone about this, er, indisposition, are you?'

Neither Hippocrates nor John Arderne mentioned confidentiality, but Bacon had never discussed cases with third parties. He could understand Sir Rowland's concern; a fist-size fistula in your arse hardly fit the popular image of the heroic knight.

'Of course not.'

Bacon made his way across the Great Court. The Tower loomed high, blocking the southern horizon. Surely the young princes imprisoned by Richard III were dead. Yet there was much talk, in circles both high and low, that Perkin Warbeck *was* the young Duke of York and, with Scotland and France's assistance, was raising an army to claim his rightful crown. It seemed inconceivable that such a daft conspiracy could lead to war.

Bacon entered the northern wing of the Palace. The Painted Chamber and The House of Lords lay one way and the White Chamber and the exit lay to the other. Which was which? The corridor seemed to stretch endlessly.

'Halloa! Bacon, is it? What are you doing looking lost and adrift?'

'Hardwick! What are you doing looking so at home?'

The pair were born in the same Worcestershire village, had known each other from short pants to pimples.

'I work here. You?'

'Visiting a patient.'

'Patient?'

'I'm a surgeon.'

'Bacon, I'm so sorry.'

'No need to be. I love the work. I took a degree in Bologna.'

'*Bologna?* Why?'

'No medical schools in England.'

'Physician I could understand, but ... is there money in it?'

'Not a lot.'

'Are you up for a lunch? They do us rather well here and we'll catch up properly.'

They navigated the warren of corridors to one of the several dining halls.

'The kitchen is rather busy, I'm afraid. They've brought workmen in for St Stephen's Chapel – my boss, Sir Reginald Bray, designed the refurbishment – and they're allowing Guild Members to dine here.'

Bacon looked up and saw a team of ceilers installing the oak panels which separated the clerestory windows. They settled on the roast beef. Hardwick chose a wine.

'We're in the middle of a new trade agreement with the Spanish,' he said. 'We're upping their quota of wine. Rather good. From somewhere called Rioja. Keeps the French and the Italians on their toes.'

'What sort of work do you do here?'

'I advise. Personal Advisor to Sir Reginald Bray.'

'Sounds impressive.'

'Not really. Old Edward – the Confessor, that is – had his Lord Chamberlain and his King's Council and that was it. Westminster is awash with officials these days. Army. Navy. Trade. Tax. Roads and Sewers. Duchy of Cornwall. Hundreds of us. At this rate, we'll be running the country soon.'

Bacon paused to enjoy his wine. The ceilers descended their scaffold. The master ceiler's eyes narrowed when he saw Bacon, puzzled as to where he had met him. It was Sarah's client – the embarrassed one. He was presumably a guild member so could easily afford a wife and children as well as regular visits to Sarah.

'What does an advisor actually do, Hardwick?'

'Most of the time I go to committee meetings and take notes. Minute-by-minutes, Sir Reginald calls them. Then I write up the committee's decision – if there is one – and send copies around the various departments. *Memoranda*, they're called. Otherwise, I sit in the snake pit and get shat on from a great height.'

'Can snakes shit from a – '

'In Westminster they can.'

'Are all advisors Oxford and Cambridge?'

'They are. But precious little collegiality. Dog-eat-dog and as I'm the "special" advisor the conversation around the morning jug of mead can be a little frosty. I'm still looking for a niche, a place I can call my own. Meanwhile, I hang onto Sir Reginald's coat tails for dear life.'

'What London needs now is an organised health system.'

'Hmmm,' Hardwick mused. 'Public Health. What, you mean the government pays for citizens' health? No, I can't see Henry buying that.'

The pair parted after their lunch, having committed to staying in touch. Buoyed by the excellent Rioja and the conversation with his old friend, Bacon continued on his rounds. He called at Drury Lane. Sarah's four children were playing at stool ball in the street. They looked healthy and well-fed. She was a good mother, Sarah. She'd been a good wife and homemaker too, until her husband's accident. From the outside, the place looked a hovel. But inside there were fresh rushes on the floor and the walls had been recently re-daubed. He found her, pale and sweaty in her bed. He examined her and found that the ulcers were all but gone, leaving only pockes. A rash covered her torso.

'What is it, Mr Bacon?' She couldn't hide the terror in her voice.

Disease terrified Londoners. More than war, more than the great fires. Those you could see. Those you could flee. But disease was an unknown, unseen assailant. There was no running, no hiding from disease. It struck and left, leaving only death.

'It has some similarities, but, no, I don't think it's the sweats. Nor the plague. Nor leprosy. I don't think so at any rate.'

'Something new?'

'Possibly,' he said, rubbing an unguent on the rash.

'I won't infect you, will I, Mr Bacon?'

The thought had crossed Bacon's mind. Of course, it did.

'No. Absolutely not.'

'Thank god.'

'Have you entertained a client called Geffrey? A gentleman.' He described his friend.

'Entertain? Is that what you call it? I close my eyes, Mr Bacon, and don't look at them if I can help it. I'm not saying no, but I don't remember such a gentleman.'

Bacon was sure she'd remember Geffrey if he had visited her; his tastes were singular – at the very least.

'The "gentlemen" is the worst,' said Sarah as if reading his mind. 'The things they demand and you have to try and please or they'll only go elsewhere.'

The benefits of a public school education, thought Bacon.

'Mam?'

It was the eldest.

'There's a gentleman to see you.'

The lad said it matter-of-factly, without shame or embarrassment. Oh, the innocence of children.

'Thanks, love. Go outside and play.'

'Sarah. I don't know how this disease spreads but I must advise you to stop seeing clients.'

'What will happen to my little ones, Mr Bacon? Five mouths to feed, remember? Go, Mr Bacon, please go.'

The Farrer residence was about half a mile due south. What a difference half a mile makes, Bacon mused as he approached The Strand. Tepper showed him into the sitting-room.

'What the devil are you doing here?' demanded Sir Thomas Metcalfe.

'Seeing my patient.'

'He is not your patient. Neither I nor any other reputable physician has called you. Mr Farrer's condition has deteriorated since your last visit and I am holding you personally responsible. Should you return, I will report you to your guild.'

'How are you treating him, sir? Have you been up all night studying Galen?'

Galen of Pergamon was a brilliant physician and philosopher, but his time was 1300 years previous. An Oxford degree in medicine was based entirely on Latin and Greek and Hippocrates and Galen. Metcalfe was declared the brightest of his year, but this required no great talent; merely a mastery of the ancient languages and a good memory. Metcalfe's faith in the ancients baffled the surgeon.

'Your belief in modernism is sadly misplaced, Bacon.'

Sir Philip Garrick, Worshipful Master of the Barber-Surgeons entered. He carried a jar of fattened leeches.

'I am treating this patient for Sir Thomas, Bacon,' he said, scowling.

Bacon was stymied. Physicians called in surgeons and Metcalfe had called in Garrick as was his right. Bacon retreated, fuming. Garrick was capable enough in his way but he would bow to the Court Physician's wishes.

Bacon made his way home, calling on several of his fellow barber-surgeons. None had treated any patients for this new disease – if new disease it was. He paid a visit to one of the less hostile physicians with whom he had some rapport.

'Genital ulcers? No, nothing. Of course, there could be any number of cases out there. Patients are too embarrassed, too ashamed to admit to something like that.'

And then there was Sir John Morton's decree which, in line with Rome's teachings, had ruled that the plague, the sweats, leprosy were all god's punishment for sin. For those with disease, consulting a physician or surgeon was tantamount to a confession of sin. Bacon stopped at a tavern. Threepence bought him a slice of beef pie and a penny bought a glass of spiced wine.

'Gather ye! Gather ye! Latest. Latest! Gather ye round. Noble fined 75,000 gold sovs! Headless friar found floating in Fleet – Benedictines stay silent. No new taxes! Hear ye! Hear ye! No new taxes'

The tavern's drinkers cheered to a man.

The enterprising Barrie Vagg was supplementing his official Crier wage and taken his crying from his Tower ward pitch to the local taverns. Bacon had not heard about Cumbria nor the taxes, nor indeed the headless friar. He usually learned of the latest news and gossip on his rounds or from his fellow citizens here in the tavern. Vagg concluded with a soliloquy which he attributed to Barabbas. Bacon dropped a farthing in Vagg's woollen cap and ordered a glass of ippocras.

B acon awoke to a knock on the door and a hammering in his head. The latter would be his mixing sack and Burgundy. Always a mistake. And ippocras to finish off!

Liquorish ippocras? Who was dreaming up these exotic new liquours? What was he thinking? The knock on the door was Sarah's client, the Palace ceiler.

'How can I help you, sir?'

'I have an ailment.'

The man was perspiring. His hands were shaking. It could be the drink but Bacon suspected it was nerves. He showed him into his surgery.

'Can you describe the symptoms?'

'Well ... '

'Perhaps you could show me.'

He reluctantly dropped his breeches and Bacon saw his linen underwear was spotted with blood and excretions. Dread hit him in the solar plexus and momentarily he fought for breath. The man's groin and scrotum were flecked with newly-burst ulcers.

'How long have you had them?'

'I only noticed them this morning.'

'Do you know how you got them? Or where?'

He shook his head.

'Any other symptoms?'

'Sweats. Headaches. They come on worse at night. Why night? What's out there?'

The man was terrified. Londoners were brought up on stories of the Black Death. That disease had thankfully died out but the sweats were carrying off people in large numbers.

'I have had a few cases. You may get a rash, gut pain, fevers and cold sweats. But no one has died of it.'

'I am marked for my sins. It's god's punishment, isn't it? That's what our priest says.'

'Have you done anything to warrant god's punishment?'

'I have, Mr Bacon. Drink. Lust. I have lain with harlots.'

Bacon objected to his calling Sarah a harlot, but refrained from voicing it.

'I'm not entirely convinced by the punishment theory of disease. Do you sleep with your wife?'

'I did. But now she is with child. And, well, you know.'

Bacon didn't know. He was unmarried but he assumed sexual relations had ceased during the pregnancy.

Bacon cleaned and lanced the ulcers then dressed them. The symptoms suggested the sweats or leprosy or even the plague. Or was it a new disease? The Black Death had brought terror to London's streets and then pain, misery, poverty and of course, death. Families were broken, ruined. It took more than half a century for London to recover from the plague and its devastating effects.

But if it was a new disease, where did it come from? How did it spread? How did any disease spread for that matter? Through the air? The water supply? Physical contact? Bacon prescribed him a concoction and directed him to the nearest apothecary.

'Do not lay with anyone. Do not allow anyone to touch the affected areas. Avoid contact with anyone who displays the symptoms and that means not breathing the same air. Do not bathe or drink water. Weak ale only. I don't know how this disease is passed and I don't know how it will progress so I will need to see you daily.'

Three cases. Bacon scribbled a note and sent it with a messenger to Ralph Howard Esq at the Barber-Surgeons. He waited for the return message, completed surgery for the day then headed for his guild which was housed at the Barbican.

Like Bacon, Howard was a surgeon who did not barber. He was the Warden and therefore the highest-ranking, pure surgeon in the Worshipful Company of Barber-Surgeons.

'I ran into Sir Thomas Metcalfe at an Apothecaries' dinner last night, Bacon. You've ruffled a few feathers.'

'We share a patient, warden.'

'Not according to Metcalfe. He is the one man you don't want to cross, Bacon. He could destroy your career. And stymie our hopes for a guild of our own. If we are ever to get a Royal Charter we need the physicians' support and the Court Physician is the last man we need to upset.'

'Yes, warden.'

'Now, it is my understanding that Sir Thomas had first dibs on this patient.'

'The patient himself called me. I had no idea Metcalfe was attending him.'

'I should be able to smooth things over with an apology. Unfortunately, he also complained to the Master. Membership of the Barber-Surgeons confers respectability, Bacon. The barbers could vote to expel we surgeons. You have managed to upset both the Physicians and the Barbers. If it comes to my supporting them or you, I will support them. I must put our fellow surgeons' careers above yours.'

'I understand.' Bacon knew the Warden's arguments were just.

'Physicians diagnose. Apothecaries dispense. Surgeons treat. That is the way of the world.'

'Yes, warden.'

'Now,' said Howard, holding up Bacon's scribbled note. 'What's all this?'

'I think there may be a new disease in London.'

He had his attention now. Bacon described his patients and their symptoms.

'I thought it might be the sweats but I'm beginning to think it may be a form of leprosy.'

'Three cases? Is that all?'

'So far.'

'Has anyone died?'

'No. But it's a nasty illness and Geffrey Farrer is in a bad way.'

'Diagnosis is physicians' work, Bacon – '

'I tried to tell Sir Thomas. He refused to listen.'

'No, Bacon, we cannot encroach on physicians' territory.'

'But what if this is a new leprosy? Or plague?'

'If it is then the physicians will diagnose and we will treat. As per usual.'

'But *I* discovered this.'

'Vanity, Bacon? I will pretend I never heard that.'

For a moment Bacon wondered if it was vanity. After all, what medical man didn't want to discover a new disease? Find its cure? It was akin to Colombo's discovery of the New World. Or Henry's ambitions for Westminster Palace. Or even Charles' invasion of Naples. Respect. Achievement. A legacy.

'Look, I will alert our members and have another word with Metcalfe. If the numbers increase we will talk again.'

I t was four o'clock of the morning when Tepper hammered on the door.

'He's raving, sir. Ranting. I fear he's gone mad.'

'Sir Thomas has barred me,' said Bacon.

'There is talk of Bethlem, sir.'

Bethlem was a terrifying prospect. Londoners feared its name almost as much as the Black Death.

'Let me get dressed.'

Bacon grabbed his bag. A wagon and pair was waiting outside. With London's narrow potholed streets to negotiate, it wasn't much quicker than walking. They did, however, brush past a zealous Watchman without having to explain.

The valet showed Bacon into the parlour where Geffrey's wife and distraught parents waited.

'He's raving like a lunatic,' said Sir Andrew. 'What has he got? Our only son and we daren't see him. Is he infectious?'

'What does Sir Thomas say?'

'Burnt blood and a bad case of boils,' said Farrer.

'Metcalfe is a pompous fool,' Lady Farrer muttered.

'He is the Court Physician, dear.'

'Which only serves his vanity.'

'I will need your permission,' said Bacon.

'You have it,' said Lady Farrer simply.

Sir Andrew nodded reluctantly, curtly.

Geffrey lay perfectly still in his bed, talking quietly. He was oblivious to Bacon's presence. Bacon felt his pulse. Rapid. His brow was far too hot. The ulcers were mere pockes now but his chest was covered in dozens of reddish-brown sores. His mouth was ringed with the same. Bacon cleaned the sores and applied an unguent. He peered into Geffrey's eyes. They were bright, almost luminous. Bacon felt he could see the Holy Spirit within them. All the while Geffrey talked quietly to someone, or something. On a higher plane? Who was he talking to? God himself?

Geffrey was no scholar but he was speaking flawless Greek. And there was another language – Aramaic? The language of Jesus. Geffrey had never learned Aramaic, probably, never seen it.

' – and I will strike her children dead. And all the churches will know that I am he who searches mind and heart, and I will give to each of you according to your works ... '

Where have I heard that, Bacon wondered. Come on, man, you read a term of theology at Bologna. Revelations, that was it. Geffrey talked fluently, cogently, dissecting, interpreting, analysing The Book of Revelations. The intellectual flights made sense yet were beyond Bacon's understanding.

Geffrey seemed in no pain but Bacon gave him opium and henbane. 'He's not mad,' he told the exhausted parents, waiting in the sitting room. 'You need not worry about Bethlem.'

'If he's not mad, what is he?' said Farrer.

'If I didn't know better I'd say he was fired with divine inspiration.'

'Divine inspiration? Is that the best you can do?'

'I'm sorry. I don't know what possesses him. I best get back to my patient.'

Sir Andrew nodded.

'It might be wise to call his confessor," said Bacon.

'You will stay with him?' said Lady Farrer.

'Of course.'

At first light, Geffrey awoke. He shook his head as if to clear it.

'Halloa, Bacon? Up for a night on the town?'

'I'd love that, Geffrey.' Bacon humoured him.

'We had some wonderful times, didn't we, Robert?'

'We did.'

Bacon and Geffrey had been friends on and off since Bacon's return from Bologna. Bacon had once imagined himself in love with him, imagined that the love was reciprocated. It might have been briefly but Geffrey loved company. Varied company. And Bacon was a solitary man.

Geffrey held out his hand. Bacon hesitated, fearing the disease's spread but he clasped his friend's hand. He felt his pulse flutter.

Geffrey's eyes dulled as the Holy Spirit – if that is what it was – departed. Bacon knocked on the parlour door.

'I'm so sorry.'

Lady Farrer sobbed. Sir Andrew was silent in his grief but his body wracked. Beatrice had apparently retired.

'We were good friends for many years,' said Bacon, searching for and failing to find appropriate words. 'He had ... an adventurous spirit. A zest for life and all its experiences.'

'Thank you.' Lady Farrer dried her tears.

'Is there anything I can do?'

'Nothing,' said Sir Andrew. 'Thank you for coming. Go through to the kitchen and have cook prepare you breakfast.'

'I'm not sure if I'm contagious. No need to put your servants at risk.'

'Oh, yes, of course.' Farrer hadn't considered the servants. He wouldn't, thought Bacon.

'I'll let myself out,' he told Tepper who had maintained a night-long vigil.

'Thank you, sir.' Tepper struggled to find the words. 'Your friendship ... I think he loved you, sir. In his way.'

'Thank you.'

The front door closed. On a friendship. On a life. Bacon paused. He was one of those men who have difficulty expressing emotions, yet for whom tears come easily. You're in the wrong profession, he told himself.

'I expressly forbade your seeing my patient.'

Bacon was too weary for words.

'If his condition has deteriorated ...' Metcalfe saw the priest hurrying towards them. 'You've killed my patient. I will have you expelled from your guild, Bacon. I'll have your scarlet column removed.'

'A fuck to you, Sir Thomas.'

Bacon called in at a tavern for breakfast and a glass of sack then returned home hoping to collapse in his bed. Instead, he returned to a waiting room of patients.

2. After the Manner of Egypt

It had been a trying day for Henry.

He had Sir Reginald fire off several missives to the pope and had not received a reply. He had dispatched his ambassador in Paris to voice his displeasure to the French chancelier, the grand maître and the grand chambellan at Charles's court and had received the reply: 'Sa majesté est en voyage d'affaires ...' Away on business! He sent an envoy to Naples to meet Charles in person only for the French king to tersely inform him that he had claimed Naples through his grandfather, Charles VII (Charles the Victorious – bah!) who had married Marie of Anjou of the royal Angevins, Naples's ruling family until 1442. More than fifty years previous! Henry was outraged: Charles's claim on Naples was about as legitimate as Henry's on England. No! Perish that thought ... Meanwhile, the French remained in Naples and there were rumours of a French attack on Genoa. Henry didn't know who he loathed more – the arsey French or the brick-shitting Italians.

'What say you, Hardwood? You're an Oxford man. What will Charles do next?'

'It's, er, Hardwick, sir. I don't know King Charles, sir, but given the ease of victory, I suspect His Majesty has rather got a taste for it.'

Snail-eating, garlic-munching swine.

'How old is he?' Henry snarled.

'Charles? Twenty-four, twenty-five.'
'And his queen?'
Anne of Breton.
'Seventeen.'
And Henry was almost forty. Fuck. That marriage had united Brittany and France in one powerful and wealthy alliance. Henry felt he was being out-manoeuvred all over Europe. And he felt old. He'd thought about asserting himself. Taking a young mistress, perhaps, buying some sleek new steeds to course. Dammit, he liked sitting in front of a fire, felt slippers on his feet, a ledger or a copy of the Domesday Book on his lap.
'So, what is Charles thinking, lad, what next?'
'Florence is without her own army,' Hardwick speculated. 'She relies on mercenaries − French mercenaries − for protection,'
Oh, fuck.
'And then Milan in all probability,' said Sir Reginald.
'Charles has no claim on Milan ... has he?'
It would take a week and a roomful of experts to untangle the various claims European royals had on each others' kingdoms, thought Sir Reginald.
'I don't think so, sir,' he said. 'But young Cesare Borgia − '
The pope's psychotic little boy.
' − has designs on Milan and Charles and Borgia are getting quite chummy.'
'So, assuming Charles takes Milan, what can we expect?'
'Duke Ludivico − '
Lucky Ludo of Milano.
' − is a man after our own heart. Milan is prosperous. Agriculture, metal, silk. He is one of our trading partners. But if Charles takes over he will probably transfer the Milanese trade to his allies, Habsburg and Burgundy.'
Damn. That would put a dent in the coffers, hitting Henry where it really hurt. Bloody Germans. And Margaret of bloody Burgundy. Widow of Charles the Bold of Burgundy, former Duchess of York, sister of Edward IV and Richard III. Margaret would support *anyone* against Henry. She'd once said she'd support Mehmed the Conqueror, the antichrist,

the *muslim* ruler of the Ottoman Empire, such was her blind hatred of him. If only she'd been on Bosworth Fields with that misshaped brother of hers ... Actually, Henry was beginning to wish he'd never stepped foot on Bosworth Field. He had quite enjoyed his exile in Brittany – nice food, nice weather – until, in a rush of blood, "the hectic in my blood" as Barabbas would have it – he decided to overthrow Richard.

Henry's news that evening was a little better. He sat in his gown and slippers in front of the fire, a modest glass of Madeira at his side and the Domesday Book which he had taken to learning by heart on his lap.

'Rutland. Tixover, Tolethorpe, Whissendine. Aaah, yes, Whissendine. Witewell: Countess Judy and Herbert from her. Church, mill. Witewell estate: 600 acres, manor house and eight tithed cottages, 18 out-buildings, 427 sheep ... '

A knock on his door. Henry sighed. What now?

Henry's valet announced Sir Reginald Bray and Nicholas Hardwick.

'What is it, Bray?' said Henry peevishly.

'A missive from our man in Rome, sir.'

'Well, what does it say, man?'

Bray tore through the ambassador's seal and scanned the letter's contents.

'It would appear that the ease of the French victory has unnerved the Holy Father ... he believes that Charles is looking towards Genoa and even beyond ... Alexander has decided to form an alliance and has invited Milan and Venice, Spain and the Germans to join him.'

'Quite the super league,' said Hardwick.

'Alexander is calling it the Holy Alliance,' said Bray.

'He would, wouldn't he?' muttered Henry. 'Still, it'll stop Charles dead in his tracks.'

'It will balance French power,' Bray agreed. 'But in Charles's present mood it may lead to all-out war.'

'Sometimes I wish the Europeans would just blow each other to bits,' said Henry.

'Not good for trade, sir,' Bray reminded him.

'Pity we don't make arms,' said Henry. 'All the wars going on. Hmm ... look into it, Bray. An arms trade would be worth a fortune.'

'I should point out, sir,' said Hardwick, 'that the Holy Father has declined to ask us to his super league.'

'Oh.'

'I fear we may lose our voice in Europe,' said Hardwick.

'Oh.'

For the first time, Henry contemplated the consequences of not sitting at the European high table.

'I have no idea how history will judge Henry, but believe you me he is one of the smartest monarchs to ever wear the crown.'

Bray and Hardwick were relaxing in Bray's chambers over a goblet of Porto.

'Henry's goal – under my direction of course – is to reduce the power of the nobles. He's executed most of the dissident ones, confiscated their wealth and seized their lands. The wealth went into treasury and helped balance the books. The lands were granted to loyalists. And he hasn't replaced those he executed. The number of peers dropped from 57 to 44. The consequence? More loyalists and fewer dissidents. Titles have never been more valuable or more sought after, further bonding the recipient's loyalty to Henry. The lesson to be learned?'

'Stick fat with Henry.'

'Exactly. Henry prizes loyalty above all else – and that includes talent and intelligence. Especially talent and intelligence.'

'He doesn't want men who think too much?'

'Exactly. Loyalty covers a multitude of sins. Yes, I know there are those who consider Morton and I yes men. Not true of course. Compromise is an art, Nicholas.'

'I'll bear that in mind.'

In fact, Sir Reginald was a yes man. He carefully weighed every proposal, every item of information, before presenting it to his king in a manner likely to please.

'There are numerous paths to the summit, my boy. But there are three fast tracks. One: the Exchequer. Dream up some new taxes and you'll be Henry's golden boy. But Dudley and Empson have closed up shop on that one. The second is diplomacy: dealing with problems like Charles whilst simultaneously developing trade markets.'

'And third?'

'Putting out spot fires.'

'Spot fires?'

'Disputes. That flare and disrupt. Local ones, in the main. The current situation is complex. On the one hand – let's call it the left – there is London to which money and power are increasingly flowing. The merchants, the guilds, most Londoners, they all want peace. London has never been more prosperous. Change suits them. On the other hand – call it the right – there are the landowners, the nobles. The loyal ones grow richer with each generation. Others cling to the feudal spirit and hang on to their land by their eyebrows. They would rather burn Europe to the ground than trade with her. They are still powerful but are losing influence at court. Some even have this rosy view of the Age of Chivalry, long gone of course. However, their hawkish spirit still has the power to inspire or inflame.'

'Agincourt. Once more for Harry! Wish not a man from England god's peace!'

'He's very good, that Barabbas.'

'And the nobles are averse to change?'

'Exactly. Broadly speaking they are allied to the Church.'

'Who also wish to preserve the status quo.'

'You're a quick learner, Nicholas. Now, as things stand the great powers of Europe are Spain, France, the Germans and England.'

'And Rome, of course.'

'Of course. We have slipped down the ladder. Fifth of five. Propping up the table. And the St George-wavers don't like it.'

'So if Charles takes the rest of Italy his eye will turn – '

'To us. Henry wants to build up the navy, to protect the merchant fleet as much as anything. But we need the nobles in time of war. Because, to put it bluntly, they've got the guns.'

'So, Henry has to stay sweet with the nobles.'

'Indeed. As long as the old nobles don't openly revolt he can't confiscate their lands. But to keep them happy he has to give them more land.'

'Enclosure. He has to enclose more common land to give to the new nobles to keep them on-side. Which upsets the peasants.'

'Precisely. Personally, I'm all in favour of enclosure. The average English peasant couldn't find a hay bale in a barn. But, Cumbia and his chums are playing a smart game too. They say Westminster is the enemy. They claim they are one with the common people. When common land is taken off the peasants, the nobles blame Henry, even though it is the nobles who are getting the land.'

'And the people swallow it?'

'Most times. Then the nobles pay their workers just enough to keep them in food and ale and fill them with tales of "this noble breed" and the peasants fall it for it.'

'Occasionally they don't. Occasionally, they revolt.'

'True. But Wat Tyler and the peasants' revolt was over a century ago. Of course, we try telling the people they've have never had it so good.'

'And they fall for that too?'

'Yes, but it's *true*.'

'You know Henry's problem? He doesn't think anyone likes him. All kings have their enemies, that's a given and Henry has his share. But it's true no one much likes him. And he's obsessed with dissidents, high and low. And now he's fretting because the pope hasn't invited him into this super league of his.'

'Europe always seems to cause us problems.'

'Too true. They're always laying claim or siege to some duchy or state. Trouble is, we need Europe for trade. We more or less depend on them.'

'Sounds a bit tricky, this diplomacy. No spot fires to put out?'

'Patience, Nicholas. There will be.'

THE GREAT POCKES

Like his king, Bacon had had a trying day. Geffrey's death had hit him hard and he had slipped into melancholy. His work briefly lifted him until he received a message summoning him to a hearing at the Company Hall that afternoon.

His final patient was a Dominican novitiate. The lad's scalp was nicked from his first tonsure. He was sixteen so had been admitted late to the order, probably at his family's insistence.

'How can I help you?'

'I need something for boils.'

'Let's have a look at these boils.'

The lad was embarrassed. Bacon felt a presentiment. There were four ulcers on his groin and upper thigh. A mild case, perhaps?

'How long have you had them?'

'A week.'

'Any pain?'

'Headaches. It's strange – '

'They're worse at night.'

The lad nodded.

'What is it, Mr Bacon?'

'Do any of your family have the symptoms?'

'No.'

'Your order?'

'I don't think so. It's not been mentioned.'

That possibly eliminated air or water as a conductor of the disease. Possibly. There were symptoms of the sweats, the plague and leprosy. Or it may be some variant on one of the three.

'Have you had physical contact with anyone?'

'No.'

The boy was lying.

'I know you have.'

'Once. Only once.'

Bacon waited.

'She was my betrothed. Before my parents made me take Holy Orders. We lay together on my last night.'

First time. Probably last time.

'But we didn't, you know, do it.'

'But you lay naked? And she pleasured you?'

'Yes.'

'Did she have the ulcers?'

'No!'

'You mean you didn't see any.'

The lad shook his head.

'I've sinned, haven't I? I'm being punished.'

'I shall have to examine her.'

'No. Absolutely not.'

Bacon cleaned the ulcers. He prescribed opium and henbane for the pain. There was no cure for leprosy or the plague or the sweats. Concoctions containing gold, leeching and bathing in virgin's blood were common treatments for leprosy. Anabas shit – climbing fish excreta – was another one mentioned in the texts. He had searched his texts and found that mercury frictions and theriac had proven the most effective in the fight against the Black Death. The cure rate was not high but remained the best. It might work ...

Theriac, or mithridatium, was developed by the Zoroastrians who reportedly experimented with drugs on prisoners-of-war. The wonder drug spread through India and along the Silk Road and ingredients were added or substituted along the way.

'Ask your herbalist at the monastery for theriac.'

'I can't do that. He will ask questions.'

'All right, I will get some for you.'

He tried to obtain the young woman's name but again the lad refused.

Bacon had always purchased his herbs from a Benedictine monastery in Moorgate. He studied the salve in its pot.

'Can you tell me what's in it?' he asked the friar.

'It's a secret best keep between god and ourselves, Mr Bacon.'

The friars guarded their secret recipes. Benedictines refused to share them with Augustinians who refused to share with Franciscans.

The bell of the nearby St Bartholomew's tolled. Five o'clock. He was late for his hearing with a lengthy walk before him. He arrived at the Company Hall, hot and breathless.

The beadle shook his head and frowned.

'I thought this was an informal enquiry.'

'Best think again, Mr Bacon.'

He entered the committee room and saw Sir Philip Garrick and Ralph Howard, the Worshipful Master and the Warden respectively, and various company office holders seated at high table. Sir Thomas Metcalfe had been given the due honour of a seat with them. Several worshipful members, seated in the gallery, were along for the show.

'Glad to see you could make it,' said the Master drily. 'Let us proceed. You have been charged with a Breach of Etiquette, Mr Bacon. Do you accept the charge?'

'No, worshipful master.'

'Noted. Sir Thomas?'

'On the night of the sixth inst., I arrived at the Farrer residence to call on Geffrey Farrer, a patient of mine. I discovered Mr Bacon in attendance. I had not called Mr Bacon – '

'The patient called me.'

'Do not interrupt Sir Thomas's testimony, Bacon,' snapped the Master.

'I did not prescribe the concoctions or salves with which Mr Bacon was treating the patient and I immediately noticed a deterioration in Mr Farrer's condition.'

'That is not true, Sir Thomas.'

'Mr Bacon!'

'Did you diagnose the patient, Sir Thomas?' asked a peer surgeon, a kind of defence counsel as per the Company's rules on formal enquiries.

'The patient had contracted a mild form of the sweating disease.'

'Not a fatal contraction?'

'No, the sweats is not always fatal, as we all know. The patient was progressing toward full recovery.'

'But then the disease took a fatal turn?' said the defending surgeon whose name was Heckstall.

'Following Mr Bacon's intervention, yes.'

'You cannot prove beyond all doubt that Mr Bacon's treatment caused the patient's death, Sir Thomas.'

'No, I cannot,' Metcalfe conceded reluctantly. 'But, I, sir, am the Court Physician with thirty years' experience. This whelp is not a physician. He is a mere surgeon and barely out of swaddling. Furthermore, as everyone here knows, physicians diagnose. Surgeons treat.'

There was no getting around it.

'And should surgeons hope to gain the Royal Charter for a guild of their own,' Metcalfe reminded them, 'they had best remember it!'

'Thank you, Sir Thomas,' said Garrick. 'Mr Bacon, do you have anything to say in your defence?'

'Worshipful Master, gentlemen, with all due respect to Sir Thomas I am not convinced the patient contracted the sweating disease.'

There was a sharp collective intake of breath. The Royal Physician turned a bright shade of mauve.

'I believe we may be dealing with a new and potentially fatal disease.'

The worshipful members collectively exhaled. Nothing terrified – or excited – medical men more than a new, unknown and potentially fatal disease. Metcalfe's mauve hue darkened to puce; nothing enraged a respected physician more than a claim of misdiagnosis.

'At the very least this is a variant of another disease,' said Bacon defiantly.

'A variant of the sweats? As Sir Thomas has suggested?' said Ralph Howard, hoping to appease the physician.

'Possibly. Though not probably.'

'How many cases, Bacon?' Howard asked.

'Four.'

'Hardly an epidemic,' snapped Sir Thomas.

'All bearing the same symptoms?' said the Master.

'Yes. Well, no. It starts with ulcers.'

'Always?'

'I think so. I haven't always been called in at the start. Pockes were all that remained by the time I examined some patients. As the disease progresses sores and a rash develop.'

'In all cases?' said the Master.

'No. Well, it's too early in the case of two patients. Headaches. High temperature. In Farrer's case, he developed a form of insanity.'

'Like the falling disease?' said the Master sarcastically.

'Epilepsia, yes.'

'And this "disease" spreads how?' said Metcalfe. 'Miasma?'

'I haven't ruled out miasmata. Nor air nor water as yet. Physical contact certainly.'

'Like leprosy?'

'Yes.'

'So it could be a new form of leprosy?' said Ralph Howard hopefully.

'Possibly.'

'Come now, man,' spat Sir Thomas. 'Falling sickness? The sweats? Leprosy? You don't know what it is. You don't know how it spreads. You haven't a clue!'

'That will be all for now, Mr Bacon. We will discuss the matter and you will be informed of our decision in due course.'

Bacon exited the Company Hall. He was shaken by the hearing. Time for a bite to eat and a glass of wine before the curfew bells. The charge was serious; if found guilty, he faced expulsion. This would not prevent his practising surgery but it would irreparably damage his career.

'Oi, Bacon?'

Heckstall caught up with him.

'Mr Heckstall.'

'No need to thank me for all my efforts defending you.'

'I'm sorry. Thank you.'

'I am on your side, you know.'

'I didn't think anyone was on my side.'

'I'm probably the only one. May I walk with you?'

'If walking with me doesn't ruin your career. Oxford?'

'Cambridge.'

'Oh, yes. So I see.'

Heckstall was wearing an enamel pin enscribed: "Round Earth Society".

'How did a Cambridge Radical end up a surgeon?'

'Because he *was* a Cambridge Radical. And two years studying surgery in Paris.'

They discussed their experiences at their respective universities.

'There's a wine house along here,' said Heckstall. 'Food's not bad and the wine's tolerable. They sometimes put on an entertainment. Minstrels or mummers.'

There was a minstrel who sang plaintive ballades and strummed a lute.

'How do you think it went?' Bacon asked.

'The hearing? Not good. Sorry. Sir Thomas is a formidable enemy. And he has Garrick on his side. You may be lucky and escape with a censure.'

'Or I could be expelled.'

'You know, Bacon, you really are your own worst enemy. You think attack is the best form of defence. You really should try to be more conciliating.'

Heckstall fetched a bowl of pickled eels.

'Tell me more about this disease.'

'The common symptom is the ulcers in the groin or on the genitals.'

'Male and female?'

'Yes. The number and severity may vary but the next stage is typified by reddish-brown sores across the torso and limbs. Fevers are common to all. Usually headaches, some report abdominal pain, but the pain either appears or increases dramatically at night.'

'How do you explain that?'

'I can't.'

'Does it strike randomly?' said Heckstall.

'The Strand. St Giles. Cheapside. Farringdon. Random enough for you?'

'What is the causal link? Bodily contact?'

'I think so. But I can't rule anything out at this stage.'

'So, it's most likely leprosy, the plague or the sweats. Or a variant.'

'Most likely a variant, a *mutandum*.'

'A mutant. You make it sound like some hellish devil's spawn. You know the Church will say it's God's guiding hand.'

'Like some apocalyptic horseman, chasing down sin? No, I don't believe it.'

'Neither do I,' said Heckstall.

'I believe it's a new disease.'

'You'll need a bigger sample size.'

It was a morally perilous situation; wanting more cases, but hoping they didn't materialise; needing more suffering for some in order to find a cure for others.

'Oyez. Oyez. Listen-ye, listen-ye. Nun has baby. Names Jesus the father!'

The surgeons listened to Barrie Vagg's entertaining telling of the news. They threw farthings in his cap. Bacon and Heckstall finished their mug of sack.

'I have rather an interest in new diseases. Do you mind if I follow you on your rounds?'

There was no doubt Heckstall was an intelligent man. A second opinion could prove useful.

'I'll see you tomorrow, Heckstall.'

'The day's half fuckin' over,' Cumbria roared at the unfortunate stable boy. The Palace stables were at their busiest at dawn, preparing horses for military routines, hunting parties and recreational riding.

Cumbria had left his wife sleeping. She wouldn't arise before ten. She wouldn't ride at all today, being far too busy choosing cloth and design for a fitting with Queen Elizabeth's dressmaker, no less. Silk and satin, brocade and lace, pearls and gold thread. Christ almighty. *150 sovereigns* for a fucking dress. He'd almost whacked her one when she told him. Wholesale slaughter of the stags on Richmond Park wouldn't go near quelling his anger. He waited impatiently while the marshal assembled the party of grooms and pages and prepared a string of coursers, palfreys and packhorses to transport Cumbria, his party and equipment on the journey to Richmond.

The Richmond road was well-travelled but rough and rude nevertheless. Prince Arthur and his instructor, Sir Rowland de Montfort, were along for the sport; Henry's eyes and ears, no doubt.

'Hup, Sir Rowland,' he called impatiently as they approached Wimbledon. Rowland was normally the most nimble of riders, Cumbria grudgingly conceded, but he was uneasy in his seat today. What was wrong with him? He had thought about a wager for the King's Championship but he wouldn't stand a chance, not with a seat like that.

He met Suffolk by Pen Ponds. It was an open meeting; a couple of nobles out in the fresh air, killing a few wild animals for sport. Young Arthur along, all above board. The pair conversed in short, cryptic snatches.

'I've received a message from Margaret,' said Cumbria.

'Which one?' said Suffolk.

'You know which one,' muttered Cumbria.

'There's quite a few Margarets. Margaret of – '

'Margaret of York.'

'You mean Margaret of Burgundy.'

'She's the same one, isn't she. She offers unwavering support and ten thousand men.'

Good old Margaret. She was pushing 50 now but the old battleship was still firing on all guns, still determined to destroy her brother, Richard III's murderer and hellbent on restoring a Yorkist to the throne.

'Good. Very good.'

'And James awaits our word in Edinburgh.'

'Splendid.'

Suffolk didn't sound enthusiastic.

'What's wrong with you, Suffolk? A chill in your balls?'

'No, no not at all ... have you paid the 75,000?'

So that's what he was nervous about.

'No. Never. I am just the start, Suffolk, and I won't be the last. You may well be next. And then Devon. And then Somerset. Unless you remain *loyal*, of course.' Cumbria spat the word.

'We advise caution, Cumbria. Patience.'

'While France takes all of Italy. Take patience and we are doomed, Suffolk.'

'M'lord,' a stalker appeared and pointed.

A stag grazed at the edge of Sidmouth Wood. A beauty. 14-points at least. Cumbria's artillator selected an arrow and handed him his bow. Cumbria pictured Henry's head on the stag and fired.

L ady Cumbria hurried to the rooms which the Cofferer of the Royal Household had allocated the Cumbrias. She wished to change before dining with Queen Elizabeth and assorted noblewomen. She was barely 25 years of age and so not much more than half her husband's age. She drank only moderately and applied all the fashionable unguents and creams and so had retained her looks and figure. Many women younger than herself had lost both to childbirth. She was surprised to find her husband, who, furious at the lack of support from his fellow nobles had taken out his anger on a herd of hapless deer and returned to Westminster, leaving the rest of the party to return with a wagon brimming with dead animals.

'I thought you were staying at Richmond.'

She sounded disappointed. Uppity sow, thought Cumbria.

'De Montfort's indisposed. Typical of these poncey young knights. A hard day's hunting is beyond them. Thank god he wasn't at Bosworth.'

The Lady Cumbria said nothing. That her husband would disparage a knight as lauded, as brave and chivalrous, as handsome as Sir Rowland was ironic, given Cumbria's nickname – Which Way Cumbria, which he'd earned because of his habit of joining battle only when he had gauged the likely victor.

83

'Do you fancy a spot of dinner?' he said, another form of sport on his mind.

'No, thank you.'

'Why? What are you doing?'

'I'm otherwise engaged.'

Cumbria's petulance rose. His first wife had been his social equal – she was his cousin after all – and although no great beauty – "as ugly as a capful of monkeys' arseholes", he would quip – she had shown him due respect. The Lady Alice, on the other hand, young and beautiful though she was, ranked below him according to the obscure laws which governed the nobility's social ranking, yet showed no deference. Of course, there was the extremely generous dowry. But so there should be – her son, if there ever was one – would be an earl, dammit.

Cumbria grabbed her wrist. He'd give her a black eye; it wouldn't be the first time. See how she enjoyed her dinner then.

'You will eat with your husband and be glad that he asks you.'

She slapped his jowling cheek.

'If you think I'm giving up dinner with Her Majesty and Ladies Berkshire, Buckingham and Sussex, you, sir, are quite mad.'

Cumbria was too shocked to respond.

'Have you received any dinner invitations from His Majesty? No? A summons for 75,000 sovereigns, of course. I have been reliably informed that her Majesty has approved my appointment as Queen of the May.'

Fuck.

Cumbria had received no ribbons, no medals, no black rods nor white staves since, well, Bosworth. And yet this daughter of some minor arriviste, some pissant *mercer,* had been invited centre stage to one of the grandest social occasions of the year.

'Enjoy your dinner, dear,' he said meekly.

'I shall. By the way, where did you get to after the last gala?'

'Oh, umm, you know. A couple of mugs of wine. A few billiards with the lads.'

'You were spotted behind a laurel hedge with a draper's wife. At least, they thought it was you. It was all very brief apparently.'

Heckstall joined Bacon at the surgery the following morning and they breakfasted on ale and a scramble of eggs.

'I can't read a word of this, Bacon.'

The surgeon's notes were meticulous, but his scribble was indecipherable.

'So the apothecaries tell me.'

He translated the notes.

'In summary,' said Heckstall, 'the symptoms vary and the outcomes are inconsistent. We don't know where the disease originated and we can only surmise how it spreads.'

'Correct.'

'Is there an incubation period?'

'Between infection and the appearance of the ulcers? We don't know.'

'If this disease takes hold there will be terror on the streets.'

'Black Death revisited. You think we might have learnt something from the plague. As it is we've learnt nothing. We're not remotely prepared for an epidemic or even another outbreak of plague.'

'Couldn't agree more,' said Heckstall. 'We all knew there'd be another epidemic one day.'

Heckstall was easy-going, intelligent and witty and Bacon was glad of the company as they set off on his rounds. They first called on Allan Stone and his wife. The mason was in a pitiful state. He had lost use of his limbs and was confined to a paillasse. He required continuous doses of opium and henbane for the pain.

'Better off dead,' he said. 'That's not pity talking. There's plenty like me and we're all better off dead.'

Bacon left more opium and henbane and Mrs Stone insisted on paying.

'We'll sort it later, Mrs Stone.'

'Best take it while you can, Mr Bacon. We'll have to sell up,' she said. 'We can't afford to stay here.'

'What will you do?'

'I worked as a seamstress before we married. I have friends in the trade. I'll take in sewing. Dresses. Curtains. There's good money in curtains these days. I'll make enough to scratch by.'

The surgeons made their way to Farringdon. Darley's cottage was made of stone rather than daub and wattle. The walls were plastered and the floor, freshly rushed. In these boom days of construction, a master ceiler was a good provider.

'How are you, Darley?'

'Not good, Mr Bacon. Thankye for comin'. I'll be needing more of that theriac,' he said. 'But it's Janey, my wife, I's worried about. I think she has the disease.'

Jane Darley lay in their bed. She was heavy with child.

'Mr Bacon's here, love. You three, outside and play,' Darley ordered their children.

'We shall have to examine you, Mrs Darley,' said Bacon abruptly.

'I'd rather you didn't,' she said modestly.

'We are sorry, Mrs Darley,' said Heckstall, 'but we cannot diagnose your illness without a proper examination. I promise there'll be no pain and we'll be as quick as we can.'

'Very well.'

Bacon was impressed, indeed envious. Heckstall was soothing and quietly confident. He invited trust, in contrast to Bacon's abrupt, embarrassed, bed-by manner.

An angry red rash, ugly with sores, spread across her arms and torso.

Case Number 5.

'We'll have to examine the genital area,' Bacon said. Soothingly and professionally, he hoped.

'No!'

Not so soothing, perhaps.

'Please, Mrs Darley,' said Heckstall. 'It will take but a minute. You know, I've lost count of the number of honey-pots I've seen over the years.'

She smiled.

How did he do it, Bacon wondered. Heckstall quickly examined her.

'One, two ... five ulcers,' said Heckstall.

'Fevers? Chills? Nighttime headaches?' said Bacon.

'I thought it was the child. What is it, Mr Heckstall?'

Bacon decided to let his colleague get on with it. He was so clearly better with patients.

'I cannot lie to you, Mrs Darley. We're not sure.'

'Will my baby be all right?'

'I'm sure he will,' said Heckstall. 'Or she.'

'Oh, I'm hoping for a boy. Life's so much easier for boys, I reckons.'

Heckstall cleaned her ulcers and gently rubbed her with theriac. He gave her opium and she soon slept. They gathered their things and moved into the parlour.

'How is she?' said Darley.

'She has the disease,' said Bacon. 'You'd best tell her all.'

'I'll never forgive myself.'

'Mr Darley, you said you had had no physical contact with your wife.'

'Perhaps I was wrong. I do drink, god forgive me. I'm sure the last time was before them ulcers appeared. Mebbe not. You'll find a cure for her, won't you?'

'We'll do our best,' said Heckstall.

'Send a message boy if there's any change in her condition,' said Bacon. 'Or yours.'

'Three shillings, thank you, Mr Darley.'

'Three shillings?'

'That includes the previous visit and the theriac for the both of you.'

'Of course, of course.'

The surgeons headed south-west toward St Giles.

'We have our causal chain, Heckstall. Sarah. Darley. Mrs Darley. Physical contact.'

'Steady, Bacon. They share a common well, so we cannot discount water. And these drains – it may yet be the miasmata. We need proof. And what of Geffrey Farrer? And the novitiate? Where did they get it?'

'And have they passed it on?'

It was a chilling thought.

They approached Sarah's Drury Lane cottage. The door was open and a man and his lad were loading a cart with furniture.

'Who are you?'

'Landlord. You looking to rent?'

'Where's Sarah?'

'She's gone.'

'Where?'

'Bethlem.'

The Priory of the New Order of Our Lady of Bethlem or St Mary of Bethlem or more commonly, Bedlam.

Bacon felt his tripes roil.

'What happened?'

'One of her "clients" did a runner. Said she'd been possessed. Neighbours called in a priest and it was off to Bethlem. Lucky she wasn't owing no rent.'

'Where are her children?'

'How do I know? St Giles, I guess.'

The almshouse.

'I must go to see her,' said Bacon. 'Don't come if you can't face it.'

'I'll come,' said Heckstall. 'I haven't had the pleasure of Our Lady of Bethlem.'

They headed due west to the parish of St Botolph which was in Bishopsgate just beyond the wall.

For a house of God, Bethlem was a hellish sight. Its walls had blackened precipitately, its doorway suggesting a pathway to damnation more than salvation.

Neither surgeon had stepped inside Bethlem's walls before but the horror stories they had heard were soon realised. A prioress handed them to a warder who showed them to a cell. It was perhaps twelve feet square with ten women within. Some were chained to a wall, moaning or screaming at unseen demons. Others were naked and covered in their waste.

Sarah sat in a corner, serene, talking quietly, earnestly. Bacon recognised the light in her eyes.

'To see the world in a grain of sand, and to see heaven in a wild flower, hold infinity in the palm of your hands, and eternity in an hour.'

'They have visions. Perhaps it is a form of divine madness. Hopefully, it's only temporary. Geffrey Farrer was the same.'

'It won't be temporary if she stays here.'

'Why is she here?' Bacon asked the warder.

'She's fuckin' mad, in't she?'

'Who says so?'

'The physician says she's a lunatic.'

'Rubbish.'

'Who are you? A fuckin' surgeon, that's all. She is possessed by Beelzebub. "The Lord will smite you with madness and with blindness and with bewilderment of heart".'

Bacon demanded to see the prioress.

'One of them do-gooders, are ye? Think ye know best.'

He reluctantly led them back to her office.

'I insist you release her into my care.'

The prioress considered but a moment before agreeing, happy to relieve herself of an inmate.

The warder grunted as he unlocked the cell door. He was loath to let her go, apparently considering the inmates his personal chattels.

'She'll be back,' he snarled. 'They always comes back.'

Bacon and Heckstall returned to St Giles with Sarah. The children had been taken into the workhouse at St Giles-in-the-Fields. It was a degrading existence, but better her children were with their mother and better the workhouse than the asylum.

'My children,' Sarah said, roused from her mysterious reverie, 'where are my children?'

She held tight to her four children, refusing to let go.

For Bacon, it was a glimmer of hope in another sombre day.

'H
ow did Barabbas describe it?' said Sir Reginald. '"Like gentle rain from heaven".'

Henry ground his teeth. 75,000 sovereigns! Tantalisingly in touch. He could smell it, could feel his coffers swell!

'"It becomes the throned monarch better than his crown".'

Henry glared at Hardwick. He hadn't heard that one either. He rarely listened to any of Barabbas's fancy new stuff – not unless it was accompanied by a glissando of his fruitiest eructations.

'How much mercy do we show?' said Henry through his grinding black teeth.

'I would suggest reducing the fine to 5,000 sovereigns.'

'No!' Henry felt faint.

Sir Reginald knew Henry wouldn't like it but he had considered his proposal carefully.

'Your show of authority has silenced the dissidents, but for how long? Margaret continues to rally support. Our agents say she is talking to France. And James is still offering protection to Perkin Warbeck. We need the nobles.'

'How much will my navy cost me?'

Bray passed him the costing estimate.

'Fuck me!' Henry closed his eyes and opened them again. All those zeroes ... Really?'

'You want the finest navy on earth, sire.'

'Couldn't we get the Portuguese to build the navy? Fine ship-builders the Portuguese. I'm sure they'd be much cheaper.'

'We don't want to upset the Worshipful Shipwrights, sir. A very powerful guild.'

'And it sends out a message that English craftsmen are inferior to European,' said Hardwick. 'Which will upset the flag-wavers.'

'I can't raise taxes again, man. Where am I going to get the money?'

'I've had our men onto it.'

'Very well, Bray. Call in the bloodhounds.'

Dudley and Empson entered looking uncharacteristically gloomy.

'I'm sorry, Your Majesty,' said Dudley. 'We have looked everywhere and cannot find anything.'

'We will have to raise taxation,' said Empson.

Henry groaned. A tax rise would incite the commoners; commissioning the Portuguese to build his navy would inflame the shipwrights and insult god-knows-how-many other guilds; and the fine had provoked the nobles. Stymied.

Hardwick cleared his throat.

'I realise taxation is not within my field of expertise,' he began. He saw Dudley and Empson turn cold hard eyes upon him. Best tread carefully here, lest the taxman's toes get in the way. 'But, almost one hundred years ago Edward I – '

Henry scowled. Edward, Hammer of the Scots. He knew how to deal with the bloody Scots.

' – granted tax exemption to the stannaries of Cornwall.'

Hardwick saw Dudley and Empson's minds ticking.

'Could we not revoke this exemption? You would honour your pledge not to raise taxes, sir. Nor, strictly speaking, is it a new tax. It is an old tax restored.'

It was a masterstroke. Why should the tin miners be exempt? Cornwall was the least educated, and per capita, one of the poorest counties in all England and thus ill-equipped to challenge the new tax. Cornwall was also a long way away. Almost another country. And full of pagan Celts. The rest of England could care less; as long as they weren't taxed, so the revoke would not be unpopular. Furthermore, there was no Duke of Cornwall to rage against the tax. Actually, there was; the Duke of Cornwall was a title traditionally given to the monarch's eldest son. Arthur was unlikely to raise any objection.

'Well done, Hardwood,' said Henry.

Dudley smiled. He bowed to Hardwick and doffed his feathered cap. High praise indeed.

'I've recused myself,' said Heckstall, waiting for Bacon outside the Company Hall.

'Bad news, is it?'

'I fear the worst, but you never know.'

The main chamber was packed with worshipful members. Word of Bacon's charges had spread. Quicker than the plague, Bacon reflected sombrely. He had hoped his brother surgeons might support him but his hopes were dashed as he scanned their stony, or even hostile faces.

'On the first charge,' said the Master, 'in that you treated a patient in the care of Sir Thomas Metcalfe, the committee has found you guilty.'

A murmur of approval rippled around the room, followed by a chorus of cheers. In the battle lines drawn by Sir Thomas Metcalfe, the Company almost to a man supported the Court Physician. Someone – probably Sir Philip Garrick – had been lobbying hard, Bacon realised, shocked at how political the situation had become.

'On the second charge, in that you exceeded your professional duties by firstly, diagnosing Geffrey Farrer, our esteemed colleague's patient in contravention of his directives – '

Metcalfe was seated at the committee table, silently hostile.

' – and secondly, in that you prescribed concoctions without physician's instructions, you have also been found guilty. Finally, as regards the most serious charge, the charge of mispractice – '

The silence was oppressive. Short of murder, there was not a more serious charge than mispractice.

' – in that your diagnosis and treatment contributed to the death of a patient. We find the case not sustained due to insufficient evidence. This is not to say you have been found "not guilty", Mr Bacon. There have been calls for you to forfeit your membership of the Company. We have elected to exercise leniency and issue you with an official censure. This is, of course, a greater punishment than a reprimand and any future misdemeanour will result in an immediate revoke of your membership. Do you have anything to say in response?'

Bacon was tempted to argue. He was sure he had done no wrong.

'A very fair hearing, master.'

'You will apologise to Sir Thomas.'

Bacon hesitated. He hated apologising to a bully, a pompous relic, a man as out of his time as the ancients but without their wisdom.

'I sincerely and unreservedly apologise, Sir Thomas.'

Metcalfe was unappeased.

'You have done both your personal and your colleagues' reputations irreparable harm. I think it safe to say that your worshipful brothers' hopes for a Royal Charter have received a major setback. I say with confidence that there will be no support from the physicians for His Majesty's indulgence.'

Metcalfe nodded curtly at the Master, rose and departed.

The Master banged his gavel, calling the hearing to an end.

Eyes were averted, backs were turned as Bacon made his way from the hall. Heckstall was his only colleague to offer condolences.

'Best you could have hoped for really.'

'Care for a drink?'

'I have my patients, Bacon. Good luck with it. Head down, bum up. Don't make waves and you'll soon restore your reputation.'

'I can't sit back and do nothing, Heckstall.'

'What do you propose to do?'

'You know what Aristotle says: in order to understand a phenomenon you must trace it to its origin.'

'This is a disease, Bacon. Is tracing its origin even possible?'

Bacon shrugged.

'I don't know.'

'Good luck, Bacon.'

Bacon decided against the mug of sack as welcome as it would be. As always, he took solace in ministering to his patients. He made his way to Westminster.

'I'm rather tied up, Bacon. I have archery lessons with young Arthur and Harry.'

'One final check for infection, Sir Rowland.'

'Nothing to worry about. Sir Thomas has it in hand. His finger on the pulse as he says. Your services are no longer required.'

Metcalfe had got at his patient.

'As you wish. Perhaps you could square your account. Six shillings, thank you.'

'I'm not sure I have my purse with me. Not to worry. Rowland de Montfort is always good for an account. But, sorry, have to run.'

How many more patients might refuse to pay? How many more might Metcalfe poison with his malice? He made his way across the great court toward the north gate.

'Fie, Bacon,' said Hardwick. 'Why the glum looks?'

'A ruined career. An empty bank balance.'

'Tell me about it over a spot of lunch. Wednesday today. Brown soup and roast beef. That should cheer you up.'

'You always seem to be at lunch when I call here.'

'We work as we lunch, Bacon. Damnably hard. Eight till six. Half an hour for morning mead. A couple of hours for lunch. Half an hour for afternoon sack. No more than we deserve. Non stop. Allez, allez, allez!'

'You're doing well then?'

'Henry is pleased with me. He likes my honesty and my analysis of the European situation.'

'Well done.'

'And I helped draft the new Stannaries Tax.'

'I hope you're not planning a new tax on surgeries.'

'Per wound stitched? Per limb amputated? Interesting ... No ... not yet.' He laughed. 'A joke, Bacon.'

'Sorry. I'm worried, Hardwick,' said Bacon as they tucked into their soup; brown Tudor with enlivening slivers of ox heart and pig's liver. 'I could do with your advice, I believe there's a new disease on the streets.'

The tender young liver turned to stringy offal in Hardwick's mouth. A hundred years after the Great Plague and the mention of disease still struck fear into a man's heart.

'It's a nasty one,' said Bacon.

'How nasty?'

'Ulcers. Weeping sores and rashes. Fevers and chills. Headaches and gut aches. Blindness and insanity.'

Hardwick pushed his soup away.

'And contagious.'

'How contagious?' said Hardwick, discreetly retreating in his chair.

'Enough.'

'A plague would be a disaster.'

'A million souls taken in the last plague, they say. And a horrible death.'

'Yes, well, there is that of course. I was talking about the economy.'

'Economy? οἶκος,' said Bacon. 'νέμομαι. Household management?'

'We can't live without our Greek, can we Bacon? Some Augustinian came up with the expression and we've adopted it. National household management. Tax, expenditure, trade. Everything. Economy. An epidemic could bring down the entire οἶκος νέμομαι.'

Hardwick sensed a spot fire about to spark. Which could turn into a raging conflagration. Which could lay waste to the realm. Unless it were nipped in the bud.

'Can a spot fire be nipped in the bud, Bacon? No matter. We must take this to Sir Reginald.'

'Right. Well, I'm ready.'

'Steady on.'

'I thought you said it could bring down the entire οἶκος νέμομαι.'

'Yes, but we can't disturb him at *lunch*. He'll be back in his chamber in an hour. Or two.'

Bacon fidgeted as Hardwick lingered over a second jug of wine before they returned to Hardwick's office. Sir Reginald finally appeared. He ushered them into his chamber.

Bacon repeated his story.

'How many cases?'

'Five.'

'Five's a bit thin. How many deaths?'

'One.'

'One?'

'The Great Plague began with one death, Sir Reginald.'

Bray paused to consider the matter. Another plague would be disastrous for the economy, for the country as a whole. Henry would not like it, not one little bit.

'What do the physicians say about this?' said Bray. 'Tom Metcalfe hasn't mentioned it.'

'Sir Thomas does not share my opinion, sir.'

Good, thought Sir Reginald. If there is a plague, I can always pass the blame to Metcalfe.

'I'm not sure what you expect us to do,' said Bray, liverish following his substantial lunch. 'You're not a physician. You're a surgeon. How long have you been practising?'

'Six years since I graduated from Bologna, sir.'

'Bologna? What's wrong with Oxford? Or Cambridge at a pinch.'

'Neither has a faculty of medicine, Sir Reginald.'

'Metcalfe has been around forever,' Bray said curtly. 'He's the king's own physician. Henry will never believe you over the Court Physician. Sorry, there's nothing I can do.'

Hardwick showed Bacon out.

'He cuts to the quick of things, that's why Henry relies on him.'

'Hardwick!' Bray shouted.

'I'd best go.'

They parted with promises to stay in touch but Bacon doubted they would see each other again. Hardwick returned to Bray's chambers.

'Your first duty is to screen people like that.'

'Sorry, sir.'

'I'm not sure what your friend wanted. Money?'

'I don't think so, sir. He's genuinely concerned.'

'Go and see the court astrologer if you're worried. See what he says.'

'Perhaps I shall, sir.'

'Fortunately, we didn't take it any further. Henry hates having his time wasted. Waste his time and your career will float down the Fleet like any other turd.'

'Thank you, Sir Reginald.'

'Sorry, Hardwick. We're all a little edgy at the moment,' said Bray reflectively. 'There's a funny mood in London. No one is ever satisfied with their lot. The common man has had his first taste of prosperity under Henry but they want more. The economy is a strange beast – the more you feed it, the stronger it grows. Yet ... '

'The bigger they are, the harder they fall, sir.'

'Barabbas?'

'No, sir. I rather think it was me.'

'Another plague would be a disaster. Do you think there's anything in it? Or is it just some surgeon out to make a name for himself?'

'I'll consult the soothsayer, sir.'

T he Abbey was packed with Merchant Adventurers, the Mayor of London, palace officials and courtiers, and office bearers and members of the Worshipful Company of Mercers which was the premier livery company in London, first of the Great Twelve Livery Companies and ranked first in the order of precedence. The Mercers were paying their respects to their former Master, Sir Andrew Farrer, on the death of his only son.

Sanctus, sanctus, sanctus/Dominus Deus sabbaoth.

Hardwick accompanied Sir Reginald Bray as His Majesty's official representative. Sir Thomas Metcalfe, Masters and office bearers of the other Great Liveried Companies and a contingent of Hospitallers of St Thomas of Canterbury at Acre, aka the Knights of St Thomas, attended in their white robes.

*Pleni sunt caeli et terra gloria tua/*Hosanna in excelsis.

Sir John Morton, Archbishop of Canterbury, cloaked in the black and purple vestments of the requiem led the service.

Benedictus qui venit in nomine Domini/Hosanna in excelsis.

Geffrey would have enjoyed the spectacle, the drama of it all, Bacon reflected.

Bacon did not usually move in such exalted circles, though he was a long way from the inner circles, seated as he was at the end of the farthest pew. The Abbey was cold enough but Sir Thomas Metcalfe had spread his poison and the cold shoulders and icy stares had rendered the atmosphere frigid. Following the interment, the congregation assembled at the Hospital of St Thomas of Acre which headquartered both the Hospitallers and the Mercers.

He hoped for a quick drink with Hardwick and cornered him at the bar.

'Is Farrer the patient who caused the bad blood between you and Metcalfe?'

'Yes.'

'He was a friend?'

Hardwick looked distinctly uncomfortable in Bacon's company.

'A good one. Though we didn't see so much of each other these last few years.'

'Any more deaths?'

'No. But the toll will rise, Nicholas. I'm sure of it.'

'I'm sorry, Bacon. I can't take it back to Sir Reginald. We'll catch up some time for a glass of sack,' he said vaguely. 'Excuse me.'

And so a friendship dies, Bacon reflected. He watched Bray introduce his protégé to a bevy of dignitaries. He watched them move around the room chatting to the highest and mightiest of the great metropolis. He envisaged Hardwick in a few years; Lord Chamberlain to King Arthur perhaps? Why couldn't he make friends and influence strangers like Hardwick? Or make friends as easily as Geffrey for that matter?

'Libera me, Domine, de morte æterna, in die illa tremenda,' he sang softly. Deliver me, O Lord, from death eternal in that awful day.

He saw Beatrice Farrer and joined the line of mourners offering condolences.

'I wish I could offer more than words,' he said.

'I ask no more, Mr Bacon.'

'Then may I ask you – can you spare me a few minutes?'

She looked reluctant but agreed and they moved to a quiet corner.

'This is a terrible disease, Beatrice, and I'd like to know where it came from.'

'You think I would know?' she said icily.

'Were you and Geffrey close these last few months?'

'Geffrey had little time for his wife and children, Mr Bacon, but you knew that.'

'There must have been some physical contact?'

'None.'

'But surely there were meal times?'

'Our lives were quite separate.'

'And you are quite well? None of his symptoms?'

'I did not lead the type of life my former husband did, Mr Bacon. If you'll excuse me – '

'Did he do anything, go anywhere new or unusual before the illness?'

'You would know better than I, Mr Bacon. Geffrey sowed and thus he reaped.'

Bacon called in at the Fleet St tavern on his way back to Cheapside. He had no rounds to complete so took solace in a veal pie for supper and offered a toast to Geffrey with a jug of Burgundy. He thought about another jug but opted for an ippocras.

'Liquorish or honey, sir?'

'One of each, my good man,' he cried, ' my fine, stout fellow.' Bacon was getting very drunk. What the hell, the brew was washing down nicely. He was also getting maudlin. His stalled career, the absence of love in his life, the loss of an old friend. Perhaps he ought to go on a pilgrimage – Camino de Santiago. Or Santiago de Compostela. Whichever was the longer. Or maybe join a penitent order. A daily flogging might sort him out.

'Halloa, sir.'

'Mr, er?'

'Vagg, sir. Barrie Vagg.'

'I didn't recognise you out of your uniform. Do you bring good news, Mr Vagg?'

'Well, sir, I have heard a whisper. Unconfirmed, like.'

'Yes?'

'France is about to invade Genoa, sir.'

Bacon tried to digest the news. Damn, that ippocras was strong!

'That would be bad news, surely.'

'It's like your glass of ippocras, sir. Is it half-full or half-empty? It all depends. There is those who think it's bad for trade and there is others who consider it a good excuse to give the Frenchies a good thumping.'

'Can I tempt you to a glass? Hiquorish or ... I mean liquorish or – '

'Why, thankee, sir. The honey if I may.'

'Two of each, my sturdy man,' he cried, pushing the empty cups aside. 'Where do you get your stories, Mr Vagg?'

'I sniff 'em out, sir. I'm a bloodhound when it comes to news, Mr Bacon. That particular tidbit came from my source down the docks. All the European news comes through the docks, sir.' Vagg drained his cup of ippocras and smacked his lips. 'Otherways, Watchmen is a good source. And then there the ordinary folk. People tells me things. Things about themselves, things about their neighbours. Let me tell you something about the crying game, Mr Bacon. People love to hear their names. Everyone likes their time in the sun, sir.'

'I've got a whisper for you, Mr Vagg. A plague is descending upon us.'

'I did used to include a daily scripture reading but it didn't play well. Daily horoscopes, now they play well.'

'No, Mr Vagg, this plague is amongst us already.'

'Holy hell.' Vagg held up one hand and swept dramatically. He lowered his voice half an octave. '"It walks amongst us". How many dead, sir?'

'One.'

'Not much of a plague then, sir.'

'My good friend, Geffrey Farrer – '

'The Merchant Adventurer? Sir Andrew Farrer's son? Let me tell you something about the crying game, Mr Bacon. People love to hear about famous names. Especially if it involves sex or scandal. The pleasure derived from another's misfortune. There should be a word for that, Mr Bacon.'

' – my good friend died of this disease, Mr Vagg.'

Bacon wiped a maudlin tear from his cheek.

'Are you drunk, Mr Bacon?'

'Never! Well, maybe a little. Strong stuff this ippocras. Let me remind you – The Great Plague began with one death.'

'Is it disfiguring? Like that elephant disease.'

'Elephantiasis. No. Armpit swelling, sores and ulcers.'

'I can't sell swollen armpits, Mr Bacon.'

'On the genitals.'

'Now you're talking!'

'Blindness. Madness. And death.'

'That's more like it!'

'You must emphasise the safe disposal of human and animal waste and hand-washing.'

Vagg's stories had often been compared to human waste but Vagg shook his head.

'Won't play, sir. No one's interested in sanitation.'

'We have a sacred duty, Vagg, we surgeons and criers. We must prevent the spread of this disease.'

'I already has a sacred duty, sir, and that is selling the public my stories.'

B acon awoke the next morning with a headache cleaving his skull and a tongue pasted to the roof of his mouth.

He shuddered at the thought of ippocras. Never again! The previous night's events slowly returned. Oh, god, he hadn't, had he? He staggered out of bed. His waiting room was full. He quickly mixed a dose of opium, sack and butterbur which served as breakfast, attended to his patients, imbibed another, stronger dose and made his way to Vagg's lunchtime pitch by The Tower.

'Headless Body in Bed! Wife Blames Satan!' Vagg cried.

'Thank god for that,' Bacon muttered as Vagg described the gruesome scene.

'Fear the Reaper. Fear for Geffrey Farrer, his young body blanketed in boils and reeking pustules,' Vagg cried. 'Join him on his descent into madness, this flower of English youth, blind, unable to move as the reaper's blade descends, ending his last agonized days on earth.'

Oh, fuck.

'Death stalks us all. Who will be next? It may be you.'

Vagg knew how to sell a story. Bacon consoled himself. It would soon be all over the city.

'Or you. Or you! You look doubtful, ma'am. Let me assure you my source is a prominent man of medicine, Mr Robert Bacon.'

Oh, fuck. Bacon fled. Surely Sir Thomas Metcalfe would not hear about this and neither would the Worshipful Master. He returned to his surgery to find a line of patients stretching as far as distant Bread St.

Sir Thomas Metcalfe did not waste his precious time at the crier's pitch. But Lady Jenefer did. She met friends who likewise enjoyed a lurid story and the daily horoscope before repairing to a hostelry for an invigorating glass of prunellé.

'I suppose it could have been Satan,' she told her husband over lunch, 'though I strongly suspect it was the wife herself.'

Sir Thomas's attempts to ban conversation at table had fallen on deaf ears, though his wife was anything but. He chewed stoically on his devilled sweetbreads.

'You didn't tell me anything about a plague, dear.'

'Plague? There's no plague. What are you talking about, woman?'

'There is a plague, dear. Mr Vagg said so. It must be true.'

'Who is this Vagg? A crier? What would he know?'

'Mr Vagg quoted a prominent Cheapside man of medicine.'

'Bacon,' he spat.

'Sweetbreads, surely, dear. I'll talk to cook.'

Sir Thomas rose, leaving his sweetbreads to congeal on his plate. He ordered his valet to fetch his cloak and brush his cherry-red velvet chaperon. Thus dignified he hurried to Monkwell Square, there to confront the Worshipful Master.

Bacon's skill and diligence were recognised by his patients but his practice had never been so busy. He lost count of the number of patients he treated. He lanced boils and ulcers, treated chicken pox and assorted rashes all because of his patients' mistaken belief – courtesy of Barrie Vagg Esq – that they had fallen victim to the new plague. He spent most of the day in surgery then set off on his evening rounds which culminated in a call to the Church of St Giles-in-the-Field. There he found Sarah in a tight embrace with her terrified children. Her limbs were paralysed; her eyes were sightless. Bacon was perplexed. The theriac had alleviated the worst of the body lesions but her deterioration had been so rapid. Yet at one stage he had hoped she might recover. He blamed himself for not prescribing a mercury friction. He stayed with her through the night and administered theriac hourly and, in a last-ditch attempt to save her, sent for mercury. She burned with fever; her body wracked with pain. Bacon recognised that she had reached the *krisis* point: the disease would soon take her. Or she would survive. Bacon could do little more than pray. William, her eldest prayed with him.

As dawn approached her eyes opened; her body became very still.

'I'm so very thirsty,' she said.

William fetched watered-wine for her. Bacon almost wept with relief. He had at least managed to save one patient. He waited for the morning bells then returned home shortly and found a message summoning Robert Bacon to a formal hearing at the Barbican at 5 pm the following afternoon.

H

enry normally enjoyed his weekly meeting with Barry Vagg. Not today.

'How the fuck did Barrie Vagg know before I did that France is about to invade Genoa?'

'The invasion is unconfirmed, sir,' said Sir Reginald. 'Our agent in Naples says Charles is *readying* his forces for a *possible* invasion.'

Henry fumed. Charles the Affable? Charles the Bloody Idiot more like it. The Medicis were mad. Ferdinand was burning his own citizens left, right and centre courtesy of Torquemada and his witch-hunts. Maximilian was several groats short of a sovereign. And as for Cesare Borgia ... Talk about an unholy alliance. Lunatics all.

'Is the French Ambassador back from Scotland?' said Henry.

'I have taken the liberty of summoning his Excellency, sir,' said Hardwick.

'Send the swine in.'

The French Ambassador swept in wearing an engaging smile and a cloud of scent.

'Your Majesty.' He bowed in a single, fluid movement. All grace and elegance. Smarmy bastard.

'How was Edinburgh, M. l'Ambassadeur?'

'Wonderful, Your Majesty. The Scots are so friendly, so hospitable – '

Christ, thought Henry, *no one* had ever said that about the Scots.

' – the wedding was magnificent. The bride, so beautiful and M. Warbeck? A fine figure of a man. A natural leader.'

Henry was tempted to smite him across the chops.

'What's this I hear about Charles invading Genoa?'

'Pah! Absurdité. Faux news, Your Majesty. Our glorious King Charles harbours no ambitions regarding Genoa.'

Which means Charles had probably invaded already.

'You can guarantee that France will not go to war elsewhere in Italy?'

'Well, circumstances can always change,' said M. l'Ambassadeur. 'And Charles does have claim over certain Italian territories.'

'Charles thinks he has a claim over every inch of fucking Europe,' snapped Henry.

'As Your Majesty is aware,' said M. l'Ambassadeur slyly, '*all* claims can be disputed.'

Henry flushed. Sir Reginald stepped in, fearing that Henry really might smite the Frenchman one.

'We don't want our European friends at war with each other,' he said diplomatically. 'Think of the cost and the bloodshed.'

'You fear a powerful France?' said the ambassador. 'There is no need for fear. We are allies. Remember Étaples? We have a treaty.'

Which isn't worth the parchment it's written on, thought Henry.

'And regarding Naples? We have the support of the pope,' he added smugly.

'Perhaps the Holy League will have something to say about that,' said Sir Reginald.

'We are both in the same boat vis-à-vis the Holy League. Neither of us has been invited.'

Henry dismissed the Frenchman. The French were cocking their snook at the old enemy, there was no doubt about it.

The nobles will not be happy, thought Hardwick. Or will they? Naples might provide a cause to rally support around.

'I'm beginning to think we're better out of Europe,' said Henry. There, he finally said it. And didn't it feel good!

'I couldn't agree more, sir,' said Bray. 'Unfortunately, we're rather dependent on Europe. Our major trading partners are all there. Our wealth, our economy depends on the Europeans.'

It was tricky. Sticky. India was too unreliable, China too far away. Spain had the New World all tied up and the Ottomans were a closed shop thanks to Richard and his lion bloody heart. Europe was their closest neighbour. Really, there was no one else.

'Bray. Hardcore. You're my advisors. Advise.'

The advisors sat silently.

'Perhaps I should sack the lot of you and appoint Barry Vagg Chief Minister. He at least seems to know what's going on.'

Bacon arrived at the Dominican monastery in Carter Lane. He was shocked to see the novitiate in the throes of the *krisis*.

'Did he lose his sight? His hearing?'

'No,' said the prior.

'No paralysis? No hallucinations?'

'No. Will you bleed him?'

This particular Dominican chapter were not mendicants. Like all Holy Orders they were forbidden to spill blood but they did not cultivate herbs nor mix their own concoctions.

'I'm not sure that will do much good.'

He applied theriac and, in desperation, a mercury friction, but the lad passed within the hour. Bacon was stunned by the speed of it. He displayed few of the symptoms. Did the lad have an underlying condition which exacerbated the illness? How could he hope to grapple with such an unpredictable disease?

When Bacon answered the summons to Monkwell Square he was met with the now familiar icy stares and open hostility. The committee comprised the Worshipful Masters of the Barber-Surgeons (Sir Philip Garrick) and the Apothecaries, the Surgeons' Warden (Ralph Howard), and Sir Thomas Metcalfe, representing the physicians. They were already assembled at their bench.

'Do you deny that you are – and I use the term advisedly – the "prominent Cheapside man of medicine"?' said Metcalfe.

'I have never described myself as such, Sir Thomas.'

'Do you deny that you are responsible for the quote "a plague has descended upon us"? And "death stalks our city"?'

'Mr Vagg has a way with words, Sir Thomas.'

'You deny you were responsible for Mr Vagg's information?'

'No. I alerted Mr Vagg to the situation. I believe it is our duty – '

'Our? You do not speak for physicians, sir.'

'Nor our worshipful members,' said Sir Philip Garrick.

'No, I speak for myself.'

'You have no need of your worshipful colleagues' support, Mr Bacon?' said Sir Philip.

'Do I have my colleagues' support, master?'

The Master smiled grimly.

'It has come to my attention,' said Sir Thomas, 'that a second patient of yours has died, Mr Bacon.'

'Yes. He died of the disease.'

'I put it to you that he died because of your mispractice.'

'He died of the disease.'

'Did you bleed the patient?'

'No.'

'Urine? Stools?'

'No.'

'Did you determine the balance of his humours?'

'No.'

'What proof do you have of this disease?' demanded Metcalfe.

'We could exhume the body,' said Bacon.

'You would violate a holy burial to press your spurious claims?' Metcalfe thundered.

Bacon knew he could not.

'No, Sir Thomas.'

Ralph Howard provided the only defence.

'Bacon is a young surgeon making his way. He is an idealist – '

'He is a disgrace,' Metcalfe roared.

'Let us put this down to the enthusiasm of youth. Let us not destroy a promising career.'

Bacon was dismissed from the committee room only to be called back within five minutes. The Warden looked downcast. Bacon knew his career was cooked.

'We consider this a reprehensible error of judgement,' said the Worshipful Master. 'You have spread untruths which have caused unnecessary panic and a loss of public confidence in our collective professions. It is tantamount to professional negligence. We will never know the true circumstances of the unfortunate novitiate's death. Nevertheless, we have no choice but to order your expulsion from the Company. You will remove the scarlet column from your premises immediately or we will remove it for you. You may go.'

It was a painful walk back to Cheapside. Bacon would not endure the indignity of having Company-appointed workmen remove his column and did so himself. The loss of the Company's imprimatur, the earned right to display the scarlet column brought fresh pain. It didn't mean he couldn't practise. But he would lose prestige which mattered to him and income which did not.

Only proof that this was a new and virulent disease would restore his reputation and he determined to find it.

The bells of St Mary's tolled 10 pm. One hour past curfew.

The streets of London were deserted. Or should be. Bacon thought he had left his Nightwalking days behind him but, he admitted, he still got a thrill darting down side-alleys, creeping through the shadows. He hurried east to Wormwood St. The Mitre was a former tavern turned gentleman's club in a cul-de-sac off the main thoroughfare. Most gentlemen's clubs were located west of Cheapside. But not the Mitre. Bacon knocked on the door. A slot opened and a familiar face appeared.

'A long time, sir.'

'A very long time, Wilf.'

Bolts were drawn and the door opened. The ground floor comprised a wine shop and tavern and served everything from the finest Burgundies to the weakest ales. Food was available. A pair of minstrels in satin gowns, make-up and wigs performed bawdy laments to a packed audience of men.

Behind the tavern were more discreet rooms for smaller parties and above, three floors of chambers, where, for a tariff, members could stay the night.

Bacon ordered a cup of Burgundy. He saw several familiar faces. It was a varied crowd. A few nobles and merchants. Youths, some rude boys from the docks, soldiers, sailors and a pair of young black African men.

'Did you hear about Geffrey, Wilf?'

'I did, sir. I'm most sorry.'

'Did you see him in here much these last few months?'

'Yes, sir. Regular like. But then ... not so much. He was very ill, sir?'

Bacon nodded.

'I'd like a room, Wilf.'

'Of course. And a jug of Burgundy? Anything else, sir?'

'No.'

'That's very restrained, sir.'

Bacon showed him a purseful of coins.

'I'd like to talk with anyone who met Geffrey in the last six months. It is most urgent, Wilf.'

The rooms were clean. The linen regularly washed. As they should be, for the rooms weren't cheap. Bacon poured a cup of wine and waited for a knock on the door. He was nineteen or twenty; a fair, slim young man. Just like Geffrey. Which is how he liked them, the narcissist.

Bacon asked the familiar litany of questions and learned that the youth had stayed several nights with Geffrey over a period of some months. The relationship finished three months previously. Bacon insisted on examining the young man.

'I have paying customers, sir.'

Bacon paid him. He displayed no symptoms.

'When did you last see him?'

'Two months, no more.'

There were two more lads. Neither displayed the ulcers nor the rash nor traces of the pockes. Neither had seen Geffrey in several months. However the disease was passed, Geffrey must have contracted it within the last two months.

'Can I offer you anything, sir?' said the lad. 'Anything at all?'

Bacon was sorely tempted. Once, surely once was not too much?

'Can you ask Wilf to see me, please?' he said thickly. 'And to bring me a jug of Burgundy?'

The lad left. Wilf knocked on the door.

'Anything wrong, sir?'

Bacon told him about the disease and described the symptoms.

'I haven't seen it, sir. There have been rumours though. And one lad a couple of weeks ago. One of the regulars complained said his lad was bleeding and demanded his money back.'

'Who was he?'

'The regular? Or the – '

'Both.'

'I can't give you the regular's name, sir. You know that. Respectable man, married.'

'People are dying, Wilf. I probably know him. It will go no further. I'm a surgeon. You have my word.'

'Mr Norris, sir.'

Bacon knew him. Sir Edward Norris. Highly respected. Very wealthy. Former Worshipful Master of the Merchant Taylors.

'And the lad?'

'He came up from the docks. Rotherhithe, I think. Didn't catch him.'

'He was a dock worker?'

'No. A sailor. A lascar. Worked the European ports. London-Cadiz. London-Naples. Thought he could make a bit of extra brass.'

'Any other information?'

'He was popular. You know the lascars with their tricks.'

Geffrey would like the tricks.

'Will, I don't know how this disease spreads but it is contagious. And it's a killer. I'm sorry, Wilf, I think it's best if you close up shop. At least for a little while.'

'We're not doing anything illegal, sir.'

It was true. Homosexuality was not illegal, though there were many, Sir John Morton, in particular, who were lobbying to criminalise it.

'You know what the religious fanatics will say. They burn catamites at the stake in Europe. We don't want that here. And if Morton believes the disease originated at the Mitre he'll attaint your property and all your wealth.'

'You wouldn't be planning on telling anyone, sir?'

'Wilf, close your doors, at least until we find more about this disease.'

'As you say, sir,' said Wilf quietly before leaving.

Bacon was suddenly worried. Wilf was a former seaman, both in the King's navy and with the Merchant Adventurers. He was a reserved man but could restore order amongst the most unruly and there had been a number of suspicious deaths associated with the Mitre; sexual misadventures which had been hushed up. Bacon left the room. He heard footsteps climbing the stairs and, panicking, returned to his room. He flung open the windows as a pair of Wilf's toughs entered.

'Hoy.'

Bacon clambered through the window and dropped to the street, wrenching his ankle. He suppressed a cry of pain and hobbled westwards, keeping to the backstreets and alleys.

'Huer!'

Watchmen. Two of them. An older man and a young bruiser. Bacon ran as best he could.

'Get him! Huer! Huer!'

The younger man gave chase. Panicked, Bacon took a wrong turn and ran into a blind alley.

'I'm sorry. My name is Robert Bacon. I'm a surgeon on call to a patient.'

The older Watchman joined his colleague.

'Says he's a surgeon.'

'Where's your tools then, surgeon?'

'They weren't required.'

'Bawd creeping, I'll warrant.'

He would have to pay them. He reached for his purse which was hidden in the folds of his cloak. Too late. He saw the short, thick pikestaffs tucked in their waistband.

'Please. I'll pay.'

'But we're the sporting types, surgeon.'

'We loves our sport.'

They whaled into Bacon with the zest and enjoyment of true sportsmen. Bacon could do little but protect his face and genitals. They beat his calves and thighs expertly, then onto the kidneys and back, arms and shoulders. They spared his head.

'Ugly enough as it is.'

'I fair enjoyed that.'

They cut his purse and left him in the alley. He raised himself to his knees and then to his feet. Every step was agony and he stopped frequently to gather his breath. He felt the two fractured ribs. He was lucky they hadn't punctured a lung.

He finally made it home and dosed up on opium. He applied arnica to the bruising. Several of the Mitre's members were nobles, he reflected. Judges, a King's Councillor, and wealthy and powerful merchants. None would admit to being a member, but these were men Wilf could call on and they were enemies he could do without.

Sleep was elusive but the opium finally wove its narcotic spell. The nightmares were vivid and featured Geffrey and Will and past fleeting encounters in the Mitre, and in these nightmares, he contracted the disease. He was blind, his limbs were paralysed. He was unable to move and his body and face grew covered in hideous boils and ulcers.

Her Majesty, Queen Elizabeth spent half her waking hours, each and every day, at fittings with her dressmaker. It was tedious but it was her royal duty after all. Her ladies-in-waiting entertained her and whiled their time gossiping and reading poetry. HM was no romantic but her favourites included Robert de Borron's Arthurian poems and the unknown Pearl Poet's Patience and Sir Gawain. When in a saucy mood she enjoyed a spot of Chaucer. Of late her courtiers had taken to reciting snippets from Barrie Vagg's cries. Each morning a lady was dispatched to Vagg's Tower pitch and returned to amuse HM and her court with the latest juicy tidbits. Tales of lust, murder and witchcraft were favourites. The daily horoscopes were also popular. Lady Cumbria felt duly honoured when she was added to the rota.

'I'm not sure this story is suitable, Your Majesty,' she said.

'Nonsense. The unsuitable ones are the best.'

The ladies duly savoured Vagg's vivid, if nominally redacted account of illicit sexual liaisons between prominent members of London's high society.

'The man deserves an honour,' said HM. 'Services to – does it qualify as literature? No matter. I'll tell Henry to add him to the list.'

Over supper with her husband, Elizabeth would relay a digest of Vagg's news and views.

'Plague? Is that what you said, dear?'

'Yes, Henry, there is a plague amongst us.'

For a *hupokhondrium* like Henry, any mention of disease had him heading for the Royal privy, bowels a-quiver. Damn. He had been so het-up over Genoa that he hadn't taken in Vagg's full story.

'Were you aware of this new plague, Bray?' said Henry, at their morning meeting.

'One hears whispers, sir,' said Bray cautiously. 'Where did you hear news of a plague, pray tell, sir?'

'The queen. Who heard it from one of her ladies. Who heard it from Barrie Vagg.'

'Yes, well, sir, I wouldn't believe everything one hears on the crier's pitch. Mr Vagg has been known to rank the entertainment value of a story above its veracity.'

'So there is no plague?'

'I have been made aware of an ailment, an indisposition, on the streets.'

'Is it serious? Is it fatal?'

Sir Reginald Bray was blessed with many gifts and an eidetic memory of meetings was one.

'Five confirmed cases, Your Majesty,' he said, repeating Bacon's numbers.

'Deaths?'

'One death, sire. Geffrey Farrer.'

Henry scuttled to the privy to settle his churning stomach and then called for Sir Thomas Metcalfe.

'Bowels are regular, Your Majesty?'

'Could set the clock by them.'

'You're not forgetting to study your stool.'

'Every day.'

'Urine is clear?'

'Yes.'

'A strong and steady stream?'

'Torrential. Well, not as strong and steady as it used to be. I'm pissing five, six times a night, man. Drives me bonckers.'

'I'll order a special concoction for you, sir.'

'What's in it?' said Henry who liked to keep abreast of the several concoctions he ingested.

'A combination of marshmallow root for the nighttime pissing and goldenrod for the weak flow.'

'What? One herb to make me piss and the other herb to stop me pissing. How does that work?'

'Trust me, sir, I'm a physician. The herbs do not oppose, they are complementary. For a man of your age, sir, your humours are in excellent balance.'

'So I haven't got this plague, Metcalfe?'

'Where did you hear of a plague, Your Majesty?'

'A most reliable source. Are you sure this is a boil? And that rash I sometimes get?'

'There is no plague, sir. Fiction. Fakery.'

'But Barrie Vagg says it came from "a prominent Cheapside medical man".'

'Bacon is a young surgeon, sir, eager to make a name for himself. He has been expelled from his Company for gross professional misconduct.'

'Oh.'

THE GREAT POCKES

Like many *hupokhondria*, Henry's relief was tempered by a mild disappointment that a life-threatening illness was a false alarm.

'**M**y first case, Bacon,' said Heckstall, barely containing his excitement. 'Ulcers. Rash and sores. Nocturnal headaches.'

The news was not welcome. Nevertheless, Bacon was pleased to see him. It was gratifying to know he wasn't totally ostracized. But he couldn't deny the frisson of excitement he felt at Heckstall's news.

'A textbook case. Who is it?'

'Male. A churchman. Plays the organ and composes for St Martin-in-the-Fields. 22 years of age, a bit of a prodigy apparently. But one other symptom – deafness in one ear – which is what brought him to my surgery.'

Deafness. Baffling.

'Do you mind if I examine him with you?'

'Not at all.'

'Are you all right?' said Heckstall as Bacon limped with him toward St Martin's.

'Nothing,' said Bacon, 'a minor fall.'

Bacon asked the patient his usual questions. The musician had heard rumours of the disease which had amplified since Vagg's story and he was terrified. He had no idea where he had picked up the disease or when. He was unmarried and could recall no physical contact of any sort. He flatly denied visiting bawdhouses.

They warned him of the dangers of drinking water and any sort of physical contact and, after much discussion, prescribed theriac.

'Do you believe him about the bawdhouses?' said Heckstall.

'I don't know. We cannot categorically rule out that the disease is air- or water-borne.'

'Do you have a name for it?'

'It always leaves pockes. The Pockes? Let's hope it doesn't turn into The Great Pockes.'

'I remain active in the Company,' said Heckstall. 'I'll ask around. We can't be the only medics seeing cases. I also know a few friendly physicians.'

'Unlike me.'

'You're too insular, Bacon,' said Heckstall. 'No one doubts your ability but you're too abrupt with people.'

Bacon knew only too well his failures at social intercourse. The lack of intimacy, the burden of his secret which he struggled to contain emotionally and physically took its toll in all his daily encounters.

'There are few records detailing the progress of the Black Death,' said Bacon, changing the subject, 'but notations indicated localised clusters and spikes and an acceleration in the death rate.'

Heckstall interviewed his contacts and colleague over the following days.

'Eight cases,' he reported, 'three deaths.'

'How many people must die before we're believed?' said Bacon.

'No clusters,' said Heckstall, 'no causal link, no tie to a single origin. It's pointless taking it to the Company until we have more evidence,' said Heckstall. 'Besides, Metcalfe has Garrick cowed.'

'Howard is sympathetic.'

'Yes, but he's desperate for that Royal Charter and he won't get it if the Companies blackball us.'

The surgeons decided to pool resources.

'My surgery is big enough for the two of us,' said Bacon. Heckstall readily agreed.

'There must be a causal link,' said Bacon. 'The pockes cannot progress by mere chance. Surely?'

Heckstall wasn't so sure. The disease had proven baffling in all regards so far. Why not mere chance? Maybe it was god's will after all ...

'This disease must form a chain,' Bacon continued. 'We'll have to track the patients.'

'And trace it back to origin.'

Eight cases. Three deaths. How many more had been misdiagnosed as the sweats?

116

'It's a big job,' said Bacon. 'And not always paid. Look, you don't have to continue with this.'

'We could do with help.'

'I think I know someone.'

A lad called Lowther, barely out of his apprenticeship had knocked on Bacon's door recently, looking for a position.

'What's wrong with your current position?' Bacon had asked.

'All I do is cut hair. All day long. The occasional stitching or some kid breaking his arm.'

Bacon had no work at the time but the lad seemed keen to learn. He called him back to the Cheapside surgery. The lad was delighted to jump shop.

The three surgeons sat at day's end to compare notes over a glass of wine – or ale for Lowther – and meals which had been ordered from a local eating house. Patterns remained slow to emerge over the next few weeks. Sixteen patients. Four deaths. Some married, some unmarried, one married couple.

'Have you noticed something strange?' said Heckstall. 'No children are infected.'

'You're right,' said Bacon checking the notes. 'Check the ages of our confirmed cases, Lowther.'

'Eighteen to thirty-six.'

'No children then.'

'And here's another thing,' said Heckstall. 'Almost no one has infected anyone in their household. Not parents, nor siblings, nor servants.'

The Black Death had wiped out entire families, entire neighbourhoods in extreme cases. It had not discriminated on gender or marital status; it had taken babes in arms and the elderly in their dotage. This disease was apparently discriminating, which made it all the more frightening. Disease could not possess intelligence, could it? Yet it was taking healthy men and women in the prime of their lives. Was there some form of Providence directing the disease – god as the Church insisted? Or Satan? Or, more terrifying still, was there a human agency?

Deploying disease as a weapon of war was not a new phenomenon; its use dated back to 600 BC at least. Could one of England's enemies – the French? – be responsible? Poisoning water wells, for example?

Bacon called on Edward Norris, former Worshipful Master of the Merchant Taylors, member of the Mitre. Like many of the Mitre's habitués, Norris had sequestered the Mitre and that part of his life which centred on it from his respectable daily activities. Norris tried to cut him but Bacon finally cornered him on The Strand.

'I will follow you until you speak with me, sir.'

'What do you want?' Norris hissed.

'I'm looking for the lascar.'

'I have no idea what you're talking about.'

'I'm talking about ulcers, sores and rashes. Blindness, insanity and death.'

'Can't help you, sorry.'

'You had this lascar removed from the Mitre.'

'I refuse – '

'Sixteen deaths, Mr Norris. And rising rapidly. You may be next, sir.'

Norris paused for thought.

'All right, man. Be quick.'

Bacon described the symptoms.

'Yes. Disgusting they were.'

'Did you and he – ?'

'No.'

'So you don't have the symptoms yourself?'

'How dare you? No!'

'Do you know where I might find this lascar?'

'What sort of pervert are you, Bacon?'

'This disease is contagious and it is lethal, Mr Norris. The victims include your neighbour.'

'Geffrey?'

'Geffrey.'

'No, I don't know where you might find him. Down the docks, I presume. He was very cagey. A matelot.'

'Up in London to earn some extra money.'

'I assume so.'

'Thank you, Mr Norris. If you hear anything of this lascar will you let me know?'

They parted. Norris was his best hope and it had failed. The docks were full of foreign sailors. How could he hope to find a lascar, last known whereabouts Rotherhithe, in a city of London's size?

L owther provided the breakthrough. They were wading through the case notes yet again.

'Here's something funny. There's four bangtails among this lot.'

'Bangtails?' said Bacon.

'Bawds, Mr Bacon. You're not married, you must have been to bawdhouses.'

Bacon wasn't sure how to answer that. He had been to the type of bawdhouse which Lowther was refer ring to; an experience which only served to confirm his sexual preferences.

'I don't think we can blame prostitutes, Lowther,' he said finally.

'Four out of twenty-eight,' said Heckstall. 'That's not such a high number. Most of our patients are in the poorer areas. Less hygienic.'

'Just sayin',' said Lowther.

But Lowther's observation struck a chord.

'No children,' said Heckstall.

'No older folk,' said Bacon.

'Or siblings.'

'You don't think – '

'I *am* beginning to think ... ' said Bacon.

Bacon and Heckstall left Lowther in charge of the surgery while they re-interviewed or in some cases cajoled information from their patients.

It took the best part of a week but they traced backwards from known victims. The results were frightening: more than 80 cases were linked in various causal chains. Eighteen dead.

'Sex,' said Bacon.

'Fornication,' said Heckstall.

'Fucking,' said Lowther. 'Wotcher know?'

'Unmarried fucking,' said Heckstall.

'The Church will say it is the sin and the punishment in the one act,' said Bacon. 'The Wrath of God. They'll have a field day.'

'We cannot say that it is spread exclusively through copulation,' said Heckstall cautiously. 'Physical contact may be enough.'

'Hygiene, or lack of it, may play a part,' said Bacon. 'We can't totally rule out miasma.'

'We have to take this to the Company,' said Bacon. 'Will you come with me?'

Heckstall hesitated.

'I'm sorry. I shouldn't have asked.'

Such a move might jeopardise Heckstall's career. Their theory was too radical for the conservative Company and Bacon had more than his fair share of enemies.

'No, I'll come,' said Heckstall.

Even with Heckstall's charm, even with the compelling facts and figures, the surgeons' pleas were not well-received.

'We cannot get involved,' said Garrick tartly, 'leave it to the physicians.'

Bacon and Heckstall waylaid Sir Thomas Metcalfe outside his practice on The Strand.

'Fornication? Of all the absurd notions. You are bringing the entire medical profession into disrepute. I will have your careers for this.'

The Worshipful Company of Barber-Surgeons duly passed the matter on to the physicians. The physicians, led by Sir Thomas Metcalfe, consulted their classical texts and declared that miasmata arising from the foul vapours in Houndsditch, Smithfield and St Giles were responsible for the transmission of the disease.

'At least they've admitted there is a disease,' said Bacon.

It was a glum surgery, with only Lowther providing any cheer.

'I could only get evens on Sir Rowland for the Championship,' he gloated. 'Still, that's double my money.'

'What money? You haven't got any,' said Heckstall.

'Me worldly riches,' said Lowther, 'which, in my case, amounts to four shillings and a groat. Soon to be eight shillings and two groats.'

'When is the Championship?'

'Next Saturday,' said Lowther. 'What a night that'll be.'

The revels which accompanied the Championship were legendary. The tourney drew huge crowds. Tens of thousands of Londoners congregated in the tilt fields at Whitehall and its surrounds. The eating houses, taverns and grog shops did a roaring trade. And so did the bawd houses ...

'I have to see Hardwick,' said Bacon.

He hurried to Westminster, scribbled a note and handed it to the sentry.

'This must get to Mr Hardwick. Lives depend on it, soldier.'

Hardwick made his old friend wait but finally, reluctantly, appeared.

'Sex,' said Bacon.

'Pardon me?'

'The pockes is spread by sexual intercourse, Hardwick.'

'You can't be serious.'

'You must stop the tourney.'

'Now I know you're not serious.'

'I have 80 documented cases. Eighteen deaths. Blindness. Deafness. Paralysis. Insanity. Need I go on?'

'Are you sure of this?'

Bacon offered his files which were several inches thick.

'Some files you've got there. Sir Reginald loves files. The thicker the better. Let's see what he says.'

Sir Reginald listened patiently.

'Sir Thomas insists he has the disease in hand,' he said. 'But nice files,' he added admiringly.

'Can you give us a minute, Bacon? Eighteen deaths, Sir Reginald. A spotfire. Which could easily turn into a conflagration. Another Black Death.'

'It will decimate the economy,' said Sir Reginald, paling at the thought.

In the end it was the case files which swung him. Years of writing files had trained Sir Reginald like a Derby-winning

121

colt. He had both the speed and stamina to produce lengthy reports on, for example, the legibility of reports quilled by goose feather as opposed to raven feather, but this facility did not extend to reading files which he delegated to underlings.

'You shall have to burn the midnight lamp, Hardwick.'

Hardwick put in an all-nighter and despite Bacon's illegible scrawlings he finished the notes by dawn's light. He presented his report to Sir Reginald over a heart-starting mug of mead and Cheffie's special poultry breakfast (whole panfried larks, smoked fowl and scrambled quails' eggs).

'Splendid report, m'boy.'

'Thank you, sir. What are we going to do with it?'

'Nothing.'

'Sorry?'

'We shall do what we always do with files such as this.'

'Which is?'

'File it.'

'But – '

'No buts, Hardwick. Henry is a *hupokhondrium*. If he reads this he'll seal off the Palace. He'll lock the City gates and the people will be furious. It'll be the Black Death all over again but a hundred times worse. The reigning monarch during the Black Death was Edward III, a military man, a great warrior. Edward's royal seal has him sword drawn, seated on a charger. Henry's seal has him sitting on the throne. Edward was revered. Henry, alas, is not even popular.'

'He deserves better,'

'He does but Edward most certainly did not. He was known as Edward the Bankrupt around the Palace, for obvious reasons. But King of the Seas is the one that stuck.' Bray shook his head sadly. '*Kharisma*. Even the Greeks couldn't understand it.'

'What do we do about Bacon? He has his patients' welfare at heart.'

'Your friend is an idealist? Idealists are dangerous. No, I will not close down the city. I will not jeopardise the economy.'

'Could we perhaps support his investigations?'

'How might we do that?'

'Financial support, sir?'

Sir Reginald choked on his panfried lark.

'Use *government* money to fund *public* health?'

'It seems a small investment, Sir Reginald. Say, a hundred sovereigns? If we can extinguish the spot fire before it becomes a conflagration?'

'Hmm. And if it turns into a plague, we resurrect the files, say we didn't want to panic anybody and we're on top of it ... Ever tried prising a hundred sovereigns from Dunne's iron grasp? A hundred groats for that matter. Very well.'

Sir Reginald clutched the lapels of his jacket and thrust his jaw forward. His voice sank half an octave to a throaty growl.

'We face a foe as dangerous, as implacable as the Black Death, but we face the enemy foresquare. We grasp the nettle, Hardwick, no matter how painful, we display courage, our forefathers' spirit and resolve. Albion will not be cowed by perfidious disease.'

'Is that a yes, Sir Reginald?'

Sir Reginald inclined his head imperiously.

Hardwick sent a message to Bacon, summoning him to the Palace.

'Your evidence is persuasive but not quite compelling,' said Bray. 'I cannot take this to the king.'

'I'm sorry, Sir Reginald, but it is my duty to alert my fellow citizens.'

'You will not talk to the criers, sir. Should you do so, I will have you arrested and placed in The Tower.'

'I will welcome a trial, Sir Reginald.'

'The Tower is full of men who died waiting for trial.'

The reference to the murder of "the little princes" was quite clear.

'However,' said Hardwick. 'Sir Reginald and I have devised a plan.' Which he outlined for Bacon. 'How do you suggest we proceed, Bacon?'

'Aristotle says: if we are to understand a phenomenon we must trace it to its origin. We track the disease to its source.'

'You will proceed discreetly,' said Sir Reginald. 'Word must not get out. There will be no panic on the streets of London.'

'One hundred sovereigns?' said Mr Dunne. 'Do I know you?'

'I am Sir Reginald's personal advisor,' said Hardwick. 'We met at a palace banquet some months ago.'

Dunne looked at Hardwick with open hostility. He read the document again as if looking for some evidence of forgery. Dunne was the Master of Court Accounts, responsible for dispensing cash for day-to-day palace administration. He ruled his fiefdom from a gloomy chamber in the bowels of the Palace.

'One hundred sovereigns? "Office expenses"?'

'Yes, Mr Dunne.'

'What sort of "office expenses" run to a hundred sovereigns?'

'Umm ... I don't know. I am but a humble advisor. Look, it bears Sir Reginald's signature.'

Dunne studied the signature carefully. The line behind Hardwick was growing with impatient suitors bearing chits.

'For fuck's sake, get on with it, Dunne.'

'Yes, Sir Edmund. Sorry, Sir Edmund.'

Dunne reluctantly countersigned Hardwick's document. He counted out the cash and with a final display of resentment handed over the money.

'Thank you, Mr Dunne.'

Sir Edmund Dudley watched Hardwick hurry from the cashier's office.

'Two hundred please, Dunne.'

'The Treasury account, sir?' said Dunne, lowering his voice. 'Or your personal account?'

'Personal.'

Dunne quickly drew up a chit.

'Hardwick was it, Dunne? Bray's advisor.'

'Yes, Sir Edmund. One hundred sovereigns for Office Expenses, would you believe? I shall write a note to Sir Reginald.'

Dunne countersigned the chit and handed over the two hundred sovereigns.

'Wife having a birthday, Dunne?'

'Already had it, sir, thankee for asking. My daughter's getting married.'

Dudley pushed a sovereign back across the counter.

'A small contribution to her dowry.'

'Thank you, sir.'

Dudley returned to his chamber. The taxman stood foursquare in the Morton camp, of course, but had spies throughout the Palace including a minor official in Bray's office. He ordered the official to keep an eye on Hardwick. He doubted Hardwick was fiddling the accounts but Dudley liked to know what Bray's men were up to.

The official had a quiet word with the guards, one of whom reported that Hardwick had met with a man called Robert Bacon and had handed him a purse.

Containing one hundred sovereigns no doubt, thought Dudley. Strange.

The death toll continued to rise but, given London's sprawl beyond the city walls, its rapidly growing population, and the degrees of separation between cases, 30 deaths went largely unnoticed. The vast majority of Londoners soon forgot about Vagg's "plague amongst us". It was a slow news day in the capital and Barrie Vagg despaired of finding a newsworthy lead. Vagg was known to embellish the truth, but he did take pride in the veracity of his cries; despite their sensational nature, he always checked his facts. He decided he might have to invent a lead item when he spotted Alfred Lowther in a Cheapside tavern.

'Aren't you Bacon's offsider? Looks like your killer plague is just another ailment,' he said.

'That's where you're wrong, Mr Vagg. This disease has a number of unique features.'

'Such as?'

'My lips are sealed, Mr Vagg.'

In Barrie Vagg's experience "sealed lips" usually meant a stoncker of a cry.

'Ale is it, Lowther?'

'Don't mind if I do.'

Vagg returned with the drinks.

'I've been talking to some surgeon friends and they say you lot are manufacturing this pockes thing. Trying to make a name for yourselves.'

'Oh, if you'd seen what I've seen, Mr Vagg.'

'Oh, and what have you seen then?'

Lowther took a long draught of his ale. Unwise perhaps, given he had already sunk half a dozen tankards.

'Well, there's the way it's spread.'

'How is it spread?'

'Sex.'

'You mean ... '

'Fucking.'

Slow news day or not, fact or fiction aside, Barrie Vagg knew he had a belting lead cry. He scurried to Bacon's surgery.

'Is it true, Mr Bacon, that the pockes is spread by the act of copulation?'

'Who told you that?'

'Sources, Mr Bacon. Can you confirm that the pockes is passed by the act of sexual congress?'

'The disease is passed by means of physical contact – '

'Fornication.'

'I didn't say that – '

'Can you confirm that the disease is passed by the act of sexual intercourse, Mr Bacon?'

'I cannot confirm – '

'You refuse to confirm?'

'I cannot comment – '

'Can you deny the allegation?'

'I can neither deny nor – '

*

'The disease is passed by … I'm not sure I can say it,' said Lady Cumbria, attempting to reiterate Barrie Vagg's morning cry.

'Act it out, dear,' said HRH, who was modelling the new ensemble she had commissioned for the King's Championship. 'I do love charades.'

Lady Cumbria decided this was probably a worse option.

'Sexual intercourse,' she whispered.

HRH's inner circle gasped then tittered.

'Really?' said HRH. 'I wonder if it's true.'

'It came from Barrie Vagg.'

'It must be true.'

The queen's couplings had become all too infrequent in recent times, and those few had done little to unbalance her humours, she reflected. She was in perfect health, couplings or not.

'Should we be worried?' she said to Henry later, over lunch. Henry was in a foul mood. He had hosted a banquet the previous evening with mixed results. Cheffie had prepared a spectacular fourteen-course menu. The wines were superb. Henry had chosen the music, some of his favourite choral pieces but these had fallen rather flat. All they wanted to hear were bloody minstrels and Robin bloody Hoode. Cheffie had not provided an entremet; rather he had carved a replica of Westminster Palace from butter which had melted as the night progressed. Will Kempe the Elder told some new jokes which went down well and John Blanke had performed wonderful new alarums but the star of the show, Barabbas, had declined calls to exercise his melodious arsehole, instead reciting his new work:

Barabbas had composed soliloquies for Henry's predecessors, Henry's IV, V and VI, Richard's II and III and now King fucking John.

'Barabbas,' said Henry. 'Ever thought about putting together a few words about me?'

'Can't say I have, Your Maj,'

Saucy midget was getting too big for his size 1 boots. He'd be writing about Arthur or even Young Henry one day and skip him completely. Henry the Overlooked.

What surety of the world, what hope, what stay,
When he who was once a king, and now is clay?'

'Worried about what, dear?'

'This sex plague, dear.'

Henry paused, a tasty morsel of leftover lamb brains in black butter suspended inches from his parted lips. He wondered what he might have missed.

'Sex is not illegal, dearest one. Magna carta and all that.'

'You're not listening, Henry. Not a plague of sex. A sex plague.' She repeated Vagg's cry, somewhat embellished in transit via herself and Lady Cumbria. Henry paled. He had been known to lock the Palace gates over a single case of grippe. He lived in fear of the sweats, leprosy, or a return of the Black Death. Foxe the Chronicler believed these anxieties stemmed from insecurity which in turn arose from the illegitimacy of his claim to the throne. Foxe also pointed the finger at Henry's father whose continual absences on some battlefield or other contributed to his son's anxieties. Whatever, disease scared the holy ghost out of Henry.

Henry summoned an immediate meeting of the full King's Council.

Sir John Morton was a conflicted man. Two hats are a burden few men can bear. When wearing the black velvet cap of His Majesty's Lord Chancellor he swore fealty to Henry, King of all England. When he wore the gold and sky blue mitre of the Archbishop of Canterbury he swore allegiance to Alexander, the Bishop of Rome. He was dismayed when Alexander had declined to invite England into the Holy League. It was a blow to the nation's, and, he had to admit, to his own prestige. The pope did not trust him; he was wary of England's independent and rebellious spirit. Alexander believed that if there were ever a challenge to his authority, if ever a nation was to split from the Church it would be England. In his more reflective moments, Morton conceded, there was a streak of exceptionalism to the English character.

In such reflective moments, Morton wished he had a full-blown heresy to prove his mettle to the Holy Father. The Fraticelli, the Michaelites, and especially the Lollards had all taken root in England over the centuries and been ruthlessly stamped out by Morton's predecessors. Morton had not had a whiff of heresy; had never savoured the heretic's burning flesh.

Morton made his way to the Painted Hall and joined his fellow members of the Council.

'I've got a palaceful of advisors,' Henry spat. 'I am up to my apricots in experts. And I find out what's going on in my own kingdom from Barry fucking Vagg! Thirty deaths! And not just any deaths. 'Blindness. Insanity. Flesh-eating pustules the size of stoolballs!'

Henry looked to Sir Reginald. Bray kept an open file in front of him at all times and discreetly buried his head in its contents at moments such as these. Less prepared courtiers studied their fingernails or adjusted their cuffs.

'Well?' Henry thundered.

Silence.

'Metcalfe, you are the Court Physician. What say you?'

'London is awash with disease Your Majesty. This is but a minor variation on the sweating disease.'

'No it isn't. It has a name,' said Henry. 'According to Barry Vagg, it is called the pockes.'

'To paraphrase Barabbas. The sweats by any other name shall smell so foul.'

'According to the prominent Cheapside medical man, "large gatherings and physical contact should be avoided". What say you?'

'According to the disgraced Cheapside medical man, sire,' said Metcalfe. 'Completely unnecessary, sir. An overreaction which will only cause panic on the streets.'

'But surely we need a cure, Sir Thomas.'

'Oh but I have a cure, sir. There are a number of unguents with proven efficacy. And if worse comes to worst there's mercury friction.'

'Mercury? You want the patient to rub himself in *mercury*?'

'Precisely, sir.'

'But surely that will kill him.'

'It may, sir, indeed.'

'What if this pockes turns into another Black Death?'

'The person responsible for the propagation has caused some of these deaths himself. His theory is discredited and he has been expelled from his worshipful company.'

Sir Reginald looked up sharply. He wished he'd known that before doling out 100 gold sovereigns.

'But you do not deny that people are dying.'

'The death of a few peasants is a small price to pay. I have the matter well in hand, Your Majesty.'

'You'd better hope so, Sir Thomas. Court Physician is not necessarily a job for life. Court Apothecary, can you give us something to ward off this disease?'

'Of course, sire. But I can only dispense what the Court Physician prescribes,' he said, smiling cheerfully at Sir Thomas.

Wonderful.

'Can one of you answer a simple question: is there a plague amongst us?'

Silence.

'Zorima, you are the court astrologer.'

'Er, well, Your Majesty. Currently, we have Saturn in the sign of the scorpion and Jupiter in the house of Mars.'

'Is that bad?'

'Very bad.'

'So, we do have a plague?'

'The movement of the stars in their celestial orbit is a very precise but complicated procedure, Your Majesty. The amount of information I need to process and analyse will take time – '

Henry sighed.

'I should appoint Mr Vagg's astrologer. He at least will give me a straight answer.'

In fact, Henry had appointed Barrie Vagg's astrologer. Zorima was earning an extra two shillings a week as The Old Magus, turning out daily predictions for the cryer.

'Sir John. Can you cast any light on the situation?'

'I have not heard anything about this new disease. My priests and parish councils have reported nothing. The Church's position *re* disease is quite clear: all disease is god's punishment for sin. London is awash in sin, so, a plague is possible.'

'Possible? Probable? Unlikely? Highly likely?'

'These are words that do not appear in holy scripture, sir. I would be violating the boundaries of my position were I to attempt an evaluation of the probability – '

Experts.

'Sir Reginald, you said it was nothing to worry about.'

'A great deal of information crosses my desk, sire. Matters of public health are of the gravest concern to me and I regard my responsibilities with the gravity that such a lofty position entails. However, I am reliant on certain court officers to supply me with official documentation detailing the specific nature of any outbreak which threatens – '

'Jesus Christ on his holy wooden cross, Bray, did any of you know that – ' Henry tried to remember Elizabeth's exact words – '"Death's grim visage sweeps the city, his ravening eye seeking his next victims?" Sir Reginald?'

Bray considered the matter. His colleagues studied their boots or wiped dust from their collars and tried to look inconspicuous.

'Not in so many words, Your Majesty, but, as you know, sire, a great deal of information crosses my – '

Advisors.

'Will someone tell me if there is any fucking truth in Vagg's cry?' said Henry.

'As I understand it, Your Majesty,' said Bray, 'the "prominent Cheapside man of medicine" has "refused to confirm" that sexual intercourse is responsible for the disease.'

'Doesn't refusing to confirm actually mean confirming?' said Henry.

'No, sir. No,' said Bray, unconvincingly, given he had used the same tactic himself.

'So, refusing to deny – does that mean he refuses to deny. Or refuses not to deny?'

'Well,' Bray began thoughtfully.

Experts.

Lord Cumbria had remained silent. He had been humiliated by Henry's imposition of the 75,000 sovereign fine and even more so by its reduction. In a rare flash of strategic insight he said:

'Will Your Majesty be cancelling the King's Championship, given the contagious nature of this terrible disease?'

There was a brief, stunned silence. No one had ever credited Cumbria with political foresight before. Henry saw his advisors bow their heads and purse their lips thoughtfully. Those sitting at the king's table knew the licentious nature of the Championship revels and immediately saw Henry's dilemma; cancel the Championship and perhaps save lives but be seen as cowardly in the face of a mere disease. Or hold the tourney, sacrificing lives on the altar of the economy. Either way, it was a win for Cumbria and his fellow dissidents.

'Simple question,' said Henry. 'One word answer. Should the Championship be cancelled?'

Silence.

'Sir John?'

'If it be God's will, sire.'

'And is it God's will?'

'God's will is unknowable, sire.'

Of course.

'Zorima?'

'Good chance of sunshine, sire.'

'I'm not interested in a weather forecast. What about this disease?'

'It is truly written in the stars, but deciphering and interpreting – '

'Sir Thomas?'

'The "prominent man of medicine" is nothing more than a charlatan, Your Majesty. He is motivated by both vengeance and the hope of glory.'

'That is not answering the question, Sir Thomas. Sir Reginald, should the tourney go ahead?'

Bray looked wise and thoughtful. He gently batted the stoolball back to the bowler.

'Our first duty is the protection of our citizens. The tourney will promote physical contact and perhaps the disease.'

'The tourney is a boon to local business,' said Sir John, wearing his Chancellor's cap. 'Livelihoods are at stake.'

'Hear, hear,' Dudley and Empson cheer-led.

'Badly needed taxation will be lost.'

'I hear you, Sir John,' said Sir Reginald. 'Likewise, the economy must be protected.'

'That's it? What's it to be, Bray? My subjects' health? Or My economy?'

Sir Reginald scribbled notes, playing for time.

Henry scanned his Councillors' faces. Deep in thought, undecided. As indecisive as Which Way Cumbria on Bosworth Field. Unlike Cumbria Henry was a student of history and knew the horrors of the Black Death. The shortage of labour in the realm would only get worse in an epidemic. Tax revenue would fall, endangering Henry's plans for reviving the navy. Henry's grand statement – Windsor and Westminster Castles which were already months behind schedule – to build the finest palaces in Europe would remain unrenovated. A killer disease bred doubt and instability; Henry's divine right would be further questioned. Ethelred the Unready's lack of preparation cost him a kingdom. Would Henry the Ill-equipped suffer the same fate?

'Someone? Anyone? Hardcock? What should we do?'

All eyes swivelled on Hardwick. Every fibre in Hardwick the court official's being screamed "obfuscate"! Let the *status* remain *quo*. But if he was decisive now his star would rise as

133

surely as Zorima's constellations. He turned to Sir Reginald's expert training for inspiration.

'Nothing, Your Majesty.'

'Nothing?'

'The tourney is one of the most popular events on the calendar,' said Hardwick. 'It unites all London, rich and poor, high-born and low. It provides an opportunity for His Majesty to meet with his people.'

Well, that wasn't going to happen this year. Not with disease on the streets.

'Cancelling the tourney will threaten people's livelihoods,' Hardwick continued. 'Inn-keepers. Taverners. Food vendors. Costumers. Fettlers. Blacksmiths. Cancellation will be a massive blow to the local economy.'

'And put a huge dent in public morale,' said Bray, joining in enthusiastically.

'And in the royal coffers,' Hardwick continued.

'Moreover,' said Sir Reginald, 'it will damage the crown's prestige and make Your Majesty look weak and fearful.'

Everyone held their breath and waited for their king's judgement.

'At last. An opinion. Thank-you, Hardcock. Are we in agreement, gentlemen?' said Henry.

'Aye. Aye.'

'Aye,' said Cumbria, after the briefest of hesitations.

Lord Cumbria felt depressed. Cancelling the Championship would have damaged Henry's standing amongst his people, perhaps irreparably. And he would have to steer clear of the bawdhouses for the tournament's duration which had to be a first. He soon cheered up when his associates congratulated him on his political acumen – political acumen! He wasn't sure what it meant but he knew it had to be good and, as Suffolk pointed out, if the disease were to ravage London post-tourney it would create the febrile – febrile? – conditions conducive to rebellion. He returned to his apartment in buoyant mood and burst into his wife's chamber. A maid was divesting her of her Queen of the May gown. Good, it would save him doing it. Mind you he wouldn't have minded shredding the garment even if it did cost 150 sovereigns. He loosened his breeches.

'Be gone!' he shouted at the maid.

'Stay where you are,' said Lady Cumbria defiantly.

Whooah, thought Cumbria, if you want a spectator to the sport ... He moved toward his young wife.

'You would spread fatal disease?' she said.

'What?' She sconed him with a pewter candlestick.

'Infect your wife with your filthy disease, would you?' she cried.

'Oww! I have no disease ... '

She threw the candlestick for good measure.

'You would assault the Queen of the May? I will tell her Majesty.'

'Oww.'

Cumbria retreated to a sitting room. He opened a jug of French brandy. He nursed the egg-sized bump on his forehead and his wounded pride. With his breeches already *in situ* around his ankles, he began a rigorous self-examination but, beyond a fresh nest of some tiny, invasive lifeform, he found nothing.

Desperate to relieve himself of sacfuls of seminiferous fluid he prowled the corridors in search of a maidservant but, alerted by their mistress, the entire female staff had fled.

Cumbria retired to the library and found a dictionary, but, unable to spell acumen was none the wiser. He took solace in a second jug of brandy.

Henry was known in palace circles by many names: Henry the Miser, Counting House Henry, Stay at Home Henry. But Henry's miserly gamekeeper turned profligate poacher when it came to pageants and tourneys. Grand they were. Awesome *and* awe-inspiring. History and religion, spectacle and sport came together to dazzle his subjects and frank his divine right to rule – even as many were beginning to question it. Even the most cynical looked forward to a big day out.

Henry dealt with the incipient epidemic by ignoring it; pretend it wasn't there and it would go away. England would not be cowed by a minor ailment like the pockes and Henry would be seen to cock a snook at the disease and the naysayers.

At noon the pageant wound its way from St Martin-in-the-Fields through the cheering crowds of commoners to the tiltyard at Whitehall. Henry and Elizabeth had decided to theme the pageant as the Crusades. Knights and nobles, bowmen and halberdiers played the part of Richard's brave crusaders or Saladin and his Muslim barbarians who were as fodder to the Englishmen's courage and superior military skill.

Henry spared no expense. Brilliantly coloured banners bearing seals and heraldic symbols fluttered in the gentle breeze with thousands of flags of St George. Tudor roses festooned the hundreds of marquees in which trestles buckled beneath the weight of food and drink. An escafout with seating for two hundred was erected for Henry's inner circle and the cream of London society mingled in the cordoned Royal Enclosure.

Outside the tiltyard, there was wrestling and archery, and games of skittles, stool-ball and football to entertain the commoners. All London joined together to celebrate their very Englishness by drinking prodigious amounts of ale and wagering money they could ill-afford to lose, then engaging, or at least attempting to engage in "lewd and licentious acts manifold", as Foxe would have it. Ale and mead sellers and pie, whelk and eel vendors did a roaring trade. So did the bawdhouses.

The highlight of the pageant was the joust which was contested by sixteen knights who competed for the title of King's Champion. Each was led by a silver chain secured to the sedan chairs of sixteen of the court's fairest damsels who were borne on a circuit of the tilt field by four hewn and hefty young members of Henry's elite troops, the King's Own Guard. The Guards were hand-picked for their athleticism and skill with weaponry. They were kitted in snugly-tailored uniforms, carried a halberd when on duty and wore their sabre at their hip. They became known amongst the Westminster ladies as "the Sabre Rattlers" and their unofficial motto was "play up! Play up and fuck like Rattlers"!

Lady Cumbria, the Queen of the May, and Sir Rowland, Commander of the Guard, led the parade the length of the tilt run before presenting themselves to their King and Queen. The King's Champion would present the plume from his helm to the Queen of the May at tourney's completion. Queen Elizabeth would crown the Champion with a gold garland.

Barabbas adapted "The Song of Roland", an epic poem about Charlemagne and Richard and their wars with the Saracens. Minstrels accompanied jongleurs who sang the epic – all 4000 lines of it – to the crowds. About 3000 lines into the epic, the minstrels who had been drinking since breakfast time had forgotten their lines, but the nobles were equally drunk and no one seemed to notice.

Barabbas was a kind of de facto Master Of Revels. He had composed a few lines specially and performed them before the Royal Box.

> *This story shall the good man teach his son/And Crispian shall ne'er go by*

'Oh Christ,' muttered Henry. 'Not fucking Agincourt again.'

All in all, it was quite the jamboree, one of the best in his reign, Henry reflected, as knights lined up to joust. There is no formal document which describes the Knight's Code of Chivalry. It is more an agreed and accepted moral system. It originated in France with the heroic exploits of Charlemagne and his paladins. It was fostered in England largely through Geoffrey of Monmouth and his written history of Arthur and his fabled knights. And that's what chivalry was in England: a fable. The Code had a set of commandments: to fear God, to protect the defenceless, to forego pecuniary reward, to respect the honour of women. But no one took any notice, especially the one about the honour of women.

The tilt is scored in arrows which are awarded for hits on various parts of the opponent's armour. Forfeits – or broken arrows – are deducted for, for example, lancing a knight's horse. Fourteen knights (and a dozen steeds) had been eliminated (euthanised) before the final two faced off. The score was eight arrows apiece as Sir Walter Sentjohn in his famed red and white and Sir Rowland de Montfort in his storied blue and gold bowed to Henry and Elizabeth and to Lady Cumbria, Queen of the May. Their squires offered refreshing cups of mead and adjusted their helms and visors. There was a dramatic pause and a hush fell over Whitehall. Sir John stroked his mount's neck. Sir Rowland tucked at his codpiece. The knights spurred their mounts and charged and 100 stones of human and equine flesh and almost as much again in weapons and protective equipment hurtled along the tilting lanes. A thousand throats opened to the heavens and roared as one. The knights cocked their lances. At the last minute, Sir Rowland feinted and swivelled. His lance pierced Sir Walter's breastplate, skewering the unfortunate jouster and catapulting him from his steed. The crowd erupted. Coffin cullies rushed toward the stricken Sir Walter.

Sir Rowland cantered his horse back to the Royal Enclosure. He removed his helm and bowed to his King. Henry and his two sons raised their swords in salute. The knight bowed again and sank to one knee before the Queen of the May.

'My lady, I pledge my loyalty and my love to you. I forsake my life to protect and honour you,' he announced in his mellifluous tenor.

'Aaaaaahhh.' Five hundred fair English ladies sighed. A number swooned.

'I am your humble servant and I await your pleasure.'

More thumps as drunken English noblemen forgot to catch their swooning wives and daughters.

Lady Cumbria garlanded her knight with a gold chain and, in an impromptu gesture, removed a garter from her shapely thigh and presented him with it.

'Arise, Sir Knight, accept this as a symbol of your allegiance and servitude.' She smiled coyly as she grasped his hand and the enclosed garter. 'You will await my pleasure,' she added in a hoarse whisper. Sir Rowland gulped. Lady Cumbria had gone off-script.

He did not have to await long.

The sexual activities of the ladies of Westminster were regulated by palace life. It was a given that they might be called on to sexually favour assorted dukes, earls or barons if it furthered their husband's standing at court. Westminster careerists spent more hours attending the king's needs than stoking the home fires and there was only so much needlepoint a woman can do. At least they didn't have to fuck boring old Henry. He was strangely content with his wife.

All London enjoyed the Championship. While the men watched the tilts and the wrestling and discussed politics many a fair Westminster lady slipped away with a handsome young knight for a discreet Sir Roger. And so, as the festivities drew to a close, and after the Royal Party had departed for Westminster, elaborate and courtly dances of seduction were enacted by the country's knights and ladies. Nobles' boudoirs, or failing that, their carriages, or failing that, a convenient alleyway, wall or hedgerow rattled like no other night. Even that wily old Greek, Zorima with the aid of a flattering (and totally false) soothsay managed to get his end away with a minor royal's handmaid.

Lady Cumbria was a married woman and knew she shouldn't, but she was Queen of the May but the once, and traditions must be upheld. She followed Sir Rowland to the stables where he was attending Bucephalus with a palm brush. She pinned him against the stall.

'Madam, the chivalric code.'

'Fuck the chivalric code.'

'I am honour bound to preserve thy honour, m'lady.'

'Enough of the formalities. Out with it.'

She tied one end of her souvenir silver chain to a post and wound the other end around his throat.

'M'lady,' he gurgled.

She deftly lowered his breeches and felt the first stirrings of knightly desire. She sunk to her knees to further enflame his desires.

'Good evening,' she said calmly to a stable-boy, come to investigate the disturbance. 'Nothing to see. On your way.'

At least that's what the boy thought she said, her mouth being rather full.

Sir Rowland gritted his teeth and silently mouthed the Chivalric Code and Lady Cumbria felt her knight detumesce. Of the hundreds of knights in England, she had chosen the only one who actually practised the Code.

Angry, but still highly aroused, and stimulated by half a gallon of finest Kentish mead, she recalled an amusing play she had recently seen. One of the mummers had fallen under a magic spell and upon awakening fell in love with the first person she encountered. Lady Cumbria vowed to do the same. The first person she encountered she almost didn't see. He was as dark as the night. The court musician, John Blanke. She took him in the middle of the tilt field and then on the stool-ball pitch. Then in an alleyway off Whitehall and in his lowly chamber in the Palace.

'Whew,' she sighed contentedly as she collapsed into her bed. It was one of the last good nights of sleep she enjoyed for the morning illness began within days. John had not been firing blanks.

The inhabitants of Westminster Palace rattled mightily on the night of the King's Championship. Some did so within the confines of the marriage bed. Most did not. Curiously, in what Foxe described as a unique form of "social mobility", most of the couplings did not occur *within* the classes: male nobility coupled with scullery maids; females with soldiers of the guard. Foxe believed that the English upper-class male felt intimidated by females of his social equivalence. Furthermore, it was the only time English ladies enjoyed a fulfilling sexual experience. In keeping with Foxe's theory, many a noble Englishman attended the lowly bawdhouses of St Giles and Aldgate. Thus, did the pockes breech the defences of the English nobility.

Having enjoyed one of his irregular, albeit brief visitations with his queen, Henry retired to his chamber where he spent an engaging hour with the Domesday Book. Cheshire: Hatton, Heswall, Hooton ... Unlike most of his subjects he had not over-indulged alcoholically and awoke refreshed. Inspired by the previous day's heroics he decided on a morning canter around the park and set out for the stables. Thinking he might borrow Sir Rowland's mighty Bucephalus, he looked in at the stall and saw Sir Rowland on his knees, secured by a silver chain to the stall post, his cobalt breeches around his ankles. His face and his *glans* were swollen and were matched in a shade of brilliant purple. The champion's garland lay askew across his golden locks. One of Henry's tutors had introduced him to Boccaccio as an adolescent but Henry had believed such tableaux existed only in a depraved Italian's overheated imagination.

The groomsman fetched the stable-boy.

'Who was here last night, boy?' Henry demanded.

'M'Lady Cumbria, Your Majesty.'

Lady Cumbria. The fact might prove useful.

Foxe did not chronicle Sir Rowland's death though there is an entry in his diary on this date and is curiously annotated: αυτοασφυξία? – *auto asphyxia?*

Regardless, Sir Rowland's Championship reign was the shortest in jousting history.

The first great wave landed in the weeks following the tourney. Bacon and his colleagues were overwhelmed by the number of infections.

'We still don't know the most effective treatment,' said Heckstall.

They divided their patients into three groups: the first received the mercury friction; the second, theriac and the third received both. Word soon reached Sir Thomas Metcalfe. A mendicant friar who mixed him a concoction of wine, leek and laurel berry for his gout casually mentioned that theriac supplies were running dangerously low.

'Theriac? What's that?'

The friar told him.

'A young surgeon is using it to treat the pockes. He's ordering it up in buckets.'

'His name wouldn't be Bacon, by chance, would it?'

'It would.'

Metcalfe's network of apothecaries, friaries, physicians and barber-surgeons soon told him that Bacon and his two assistants had set up a kind of *clinicum* and were specialising in treating the illness. Metcalfe strode down to Cheapside and saw with his own eyes that the scarlet columns had been returned to the doorway. He barged into the surgery.

'You, sir, are not a member of the Worshipful Company, yet you display the Company column.'

'Mr Heckstall is a worshipful member, Sir Thomas,' Bacon explained. 'And Mr Lowther will one day join him.'

This was a ticklish situation for Metcalfe. Bacon was within his rights to practise with his worshipful colleague. He invited the Masters of the Barber-Surgeons and the Apothecaries, and the Prior Warden of the Herbalist Friars to lunch in one of London's finest eating houses. The party enjoyed their potted shrimp, best end of lamb, custard tart and a ripe west country cheese, splashed down with Burgundy, red and white, and a carafe of Oporto wine.

'This Bacon has upset citizens with groundless diagnoses. Diagnoses, I might add, which are not his to make.'

'He really ought to face charges,' said Sir Philip Garrick.

'I haven't completely dismissed that option,' said Metcalfe. 'There is not a scintilla of evidence suggesting an epidemic. Consumption is contagious. The ague, quinsy, the common cold – all are far more contagious than this illness.'

'Didn't Geffrey Farrer die of it?' asked the Prior, whose own priory had supplied Farrer's theriac.

'Bacon's misdiagnosis cost young Farrer his life. He found a few boils in a private area and concluded that this was a lethal new disease. Bacon seeks glory. He believes he will find fame by curing the disease. Such men are dangerous.'

'Hear, hear.'

Following lunch, Metcalfe ordered the remaining supplies of theriac within the City walls. It had achieved limited success treating the plague, but if Bacon was right and it did work, Metcalfe was damned if he was going to miss out. The drug was for his patients, he reasoned, and, his patients being the ruling class upon which king and country depended, his action was justified. He dispatched emissaries to the apothecaries insisting that Bacon's prescriptions be dishonoured and ordered all physicians not to refer patients to the *clinicum*.

Metcalfe concluded his campaign by calling on Sir John Morton in his chambers in the Palace. In the politics of the court, one was either in the Bray camp or the Morton camp and Metcalfe stood firmly in the latter. Conservative. Traditional. Sir Reginald Bray was too much a modernist for Metcalfe with his army of liberal advisors.

'Bacon is overstepping the mark. He believes he can cure this plague.'

'So a plague is visited upon us, Sir Thomas?'

'Only in the, er, narrowest sense of the word, Sir John.'

'And who is this Bacon?'

'He is a Humanist, your Grace.'

'Humanism!'

Humanism, a system of thought based on rational reasoning and which valued human endeavour above divine intervention had sprung up during the so-called Renaissance. Mathematics. Chemistry. Astronomy. And now surgery. In Morton's book, it was one step, one tiny step short of heresy. There were heretical whisperings that the earth was round, that Jerusalem – as was claimed in the Holy Bible – was not the centre of the earth, and that this round earth revolved around the sun. In his mind's nostrils, Morton smelt the heretic's burning flesh. Not for the first time, the Archbishop of Canterbury wished he had a Torquemada to stamp out these heresies once and for all.

'This disease is god's punishment for sin, Metcalfe.'

'Absolutely, your Grace. No doubt about it.'

'And this surgeon does not believe the Church's teachings?'

'Alas, no, your Grace. He is hoping to find the origin of the disease and eliminate it.'

This was playing God in Morton's holy book.

'Thank you, Sir Thomas.'

Morton dismissed the physician and pondered the situation. One tiny step? No! This was heresy. Morton alerted his network of agents and within days learnt that Bacon was a regular visitor to the Palace. He had treated Sir Rowland de Montfort. Had the Champion's unorthodox demise anything to do with Bacon's treatment? Was it some sort of Humanist ritual? Bacon had also met with Bray's latest advisor – Hardacre, was it? Bray was of a liberal persuasion; he regularly forsook mass and rarely took the sacraments. What was he up to? Morton was an Englishman to the depths of his soul and to the soles of his holy, sandal-wearing feet. He knew Henry hated paying the Church the vast amounts of taxation it collected and the one thing Morton feared above all else was that Henry wanted to split from Rome. Should Humanism take root in England Alexander might demand his resignation. Bacon must be stopped before the disease of heresy spread.

'They're out of theriac,' said Heckstall.

'The Franciscans? As well as the Augustinians?' said Bacon. It was possible, given that deaths and infections were steepling.

The monasteries had discovered a kind of loophole in the Church's "punishment for sin" dogma. The monks had borrowed and adapted the doctrine of signatures from the ancients. The doctrine argued that disease was a punishment from God, but that in His infinite mercy He had provided herbs and plants which could cure or at least alleviate disease. The herbs resembled that part of the body affected by the disease. Skullcap was used to alleviate headache; birthwort, which resembled female genitalia was used to treat illnesses during pregnancy. As luck would have it, the signatures were only visible to the faithful ie the monks and some were very expensive. The monks grew their own herbs and blended their own concoctions. It was a lucrative trade but supported the good friars in their charitable works.

'I'll go to the Dominicans.'

'Not a drop,' said the herbalist at Greenwich Blackfriars.

'You had plenty a week ago.'

'Not any more, my son. I am sorry.'

'Who ordered all your stock?'

'I'm not at liberty to say.'

The surgeons scoured London.

'The Knights Hospitaller must have some,' said Bacon. 'Have you been to Clerkenwell Priory?'

'None,' said Lowther.

'We'll have to go beyond London,' said Heckstall.

'Who's left? The Cistercians?'

The nearest Cistercian herbalist was at Stratford Langthorne. It was eight miles east of Cheapside, a fair distance, but the prior agreed to supply them with theriac.

No sooner had that been sorted than the apothecaries refused to supply them with necessary concoctions and frictions. Of course, if they were prepared to pay a little over the odds ...

Given many of Bacon's patients came from the poorer classes, this extra expense drained the clinic's finances. Bacon, as always took solace in treating his patients. His rounds took him past Drury Lane.

'Halloa, Mrs Stone. What are you doing here?'

'We live here now, Mr Bacon,' she said, pointing at Sarah's old cottage. 'We've had to adapt.'

'Are you well otherwise, Mrs Stone?'

'We get by. I've been meaning to call on you. It's Allan. Come in, Mr Bacon.'

Allan Stone forced a smile. He was confined to his old armchair, one of the few sticks of furniture they'd managed to save from Cheapside.

'Are you out of pain?'

Allan shook his head.

'I'll get you something for it.'

The mason had lost weight. He had been a robust twelve stones when working, now he was barely nine. His hands were shaking and excretion was difficult, often painful. His breath was laboured.

145

Marian Stone had set up a bench, surrounded by lengths of material.

'I'm running up curtains. There's quite the demand.'

'You make a living?'

'Just. Most of our money goes on medicines. But I'm putting a little aside to buy my own material. I fancy in a year or two I might be able to open a little shop.'

'That's wonderful news, Mrs Stone. It's a credit to you.'

She offered him a glass of ale which he accepted.

'Where are your children?'

'With my sister. She and her husband are childless and their cottage is so much bigger.'

'And he works. He provides.'

'Don't talk like that, Allan.'

'Mr Bacon? A word with you?'

'No, Allan. Don't listen to him, Mr Bacon.'

'I'm a drain. An extra mouth to feed. Please, Mr Bacon, an extra dose of that opium of yours.'

'I'm sorry, Allan. I've taken a sacred oath. I can't.'

It was desperately sad. Bacon finished his ale. He turned to go.

'Your family loves you, Allan. They need you.'

Bacon was torn. Allan Stone might hang on for months, possibly years, but he was wasting away and in pain while he did so. Bacon made his way to St Botwulf's and explained his dilemma in the quiet of the confessional.

'Thou must not kill, It is written. You will condemn your soul to hellfire for all eternity,' he said. 'You have sinned for merely thinking of it.' he added before imposing a hefty penance.

The morning bells had barely rung when the first patients arrived. Bacon left Heckstall and Lowther to attend morning surgery. He went to the small room in which he mixed their concoctions. Opium was a given. Thereafter he was spoiled for choice: belladonna, hemlock, foxglove. He decided on monkshood or wolfbane as it was also known. Its lilac, hood-shaped blooms were quite beautiful. Its roots were deadly. He crushed the root, pasted it with opium and diluted it with a little wine.

The choice was simple: he could continue treating Allan Stone, but were Stone to die by his own hand he would condemn himself to damnation. But, if Bacon administered his concoction, he was guilty of murder. Effectively, he was trading his own soul's place in hell for his patient's. He made his way to the Stones' cottage via St Botwulf's.

'Try this, Allan, it should help with the pain,' he said. 'I have brought father here with me. I am sure taking this medicine in a state of grace will improve its efficacy.'

'Thank you, Mr Bacon.'

Was Stone aware that he was about to take poison? Perhaps.

'Let me pay you, Mr Bacon,' said Marian.

'Next time, Mrs Stone.'

'But my little business is doing so well. I shall have my shop in no time.'

'That's wonderful news. Let me know when it's up and running.'

It was a short walk to the St Giles almshouse so Bacon decided to call on Sarah. He was met with a great commotion.

Sarah lay on a rude paillasse, surrounded by her distraught children. Her skull was cleaved. She was unconscious and close to death. The brain had bled. There was a giant clot in the frontal lobe. Bacon had never attempted surgery this delicate and dangerous before. He cleaned the wound and cleared the fragments of bone as her family held hands and prayed. He chose his finest blade and cut; prising, teasing the clot from the healthy tissue.

'A new candle, please.'

The procedure lasted nearly two hours and Bacon had no idea what damage he had done, nor how or if she might recover. Speculation was futile, however. Sarah fought valiantly but the trauma was too great and she passed.

Bacon was close to tears. She had been so near to a full recovery from the pockes and now this. He held hands with the family as the priest intoned the last rites.

'Please let me know the funeral arrangements,' he told the priest. 'I will foot all expenses.'

A crowd had gathered outside and were fêting a Watchman.

'Does anyone know what happened?' said Bacon.

'Ask old Alf here,' said a local resident, plying the Watchman with a mug of ale.

Alf had heard Sarah's cries and seen a man emerge from the almshouse. It was the murderer's misfortune to catch the off-duty Watchman the one day he wasn't blind drunk. Alf had stuck out a foot, the man had tripped and cannoned head-first into a stone wall. The man believed Sarah had infected him with the pockes and, outraged, he had taken his revenge.

How many more innocent victims, Bacon wondered, how many innocent women would be blamed for the disease's spread?

B acon handed his card to Tepper and waited for his return. His call was unannounced and he expected to be sent packing.

'Mrs Farrer accepts your condolences, sir and asks if it is urgent.'

'Tell Mrs Farrer, it is.'

Tepper finally returned.

'Mrs Farrer agrees to see you.'

Tepper led him to the sitting-room.

'Good afternoon, Beatrice.'

'Mr Bacon. What is so urgent that you would call on me without notice?'

She clearly wasn't in the mood for chatter and didn't offer refreshment.

'Geffrey contracted the pockes, Beatrice.'

'The sweats according to Sir Thomas.'

'It wasn't the sweats, Beatrice. Sir Thomas has finally conceded that there is a new disease in London.'

'Whatever disease took Geffrey, it was God's punishment.'

'Perhaps. But we need to stop its spread.'

'If he has helped pass this disease then I am sure his punishment will last for eternity.'

'I'm sorry to ask you again – but did you and Geffrey have normal sexual relations?'

'I wouldn't know what constitutes normal sexual relations, Mr Bacon.'

'Did you have *any* sexual relations?'

'Is this pertinent to your enquiry?'

'The disease is transmitted through the sexual act.'

'So I have heard. And the disease is fatal?'

'It killed Geffrey.'

'Our relations all but ceased following the birth of our second child. A few times when he was drunk, perhaps.'

'How long ago?'

'Months ago.'

'Six months? Twelve months?'

'Somewhere between. Should I be worried?'

He described the symptoms.

'No. I have none of these.'

'Incubation periods vary, but I think you may have escaped it, Beatrice. But if you show any of these symptoms, please send word to me.'

She nodded.

'One more question. Have you ever sought comfort outside your marriage?'

'I refuse to dignify your question with an answer.'

'Please, Beatrice. This may save lives. This disease is highly infectious. We could be talking another plague.'

Beatrice rang the bell. The interview was terminated.

Tepper showed him to the door.

'Mr Bacon? The master was well, sir, until two months afore, when he returned in a right state.'

'Agitated? Or injured?'

'Beaten. He said he met someone in Rotherhithe.'

'Geffrey was the first known victim. So, where did he get it from?'

'Aristotle notwithstanding, your chances of finding the origin of this disease are negligible,' said Heckstall.

'I have no other suggestion.'

Bacon was terrified of going to Rotherhithe. He had only been there once. With Geffrey. The Black Swan was a tavern, outwardly indistinguishable from dozens of others which lined the docks. It served ales and an extremely potent brandy which was smuggled into the country via French caravelles. This was illegal of course but so was opium trafficking and dealing in contraband goods, both of which activities took place on its premises. Many young men had collapsed under the distillate's influence and had woken to find they had been violated while unconscious. It was that sort of place. It served no food.

Geffrey thrilled in violent sexual encounters with muscular sailors and had suffered – enjoyed? – cracked ribs, a broken collarbone, a snapped tooth, amongst other injuries. He had returned to The Strand on several occasions, bruised and contused. Bacon thought it degrading and the place horrified him. He never returned. Until now.

The stench was terrific. The structure of the building, its very foundations were steeped in piss and sweat and shit and male sex. Bacon could feel the malignancy which hung in the air. If there was such a thing as miasma this was the place to find it. He ordered a calming brandy.

'I came here once with a friend. Geffrey.'

The taverner, a husking brute of a fellow said nothing. Bacon put a shilling on the counter.

'He's dead.'

The taverner didn't blink an eye. Death was cheap on the Rotherhithe docks.

'A new, highly infectious disease took him. It may prove as lethal as the Black Death.'

The taverner was listening now.

'It's spread through sex.'

Listening closely now.

'I'm looking for a lascar.'

The taverner shrugged.

'I know he comes here,' Bacon persisted.

The taverner ignored him and served another customer.

Bacon moved around the room asking after the lascar, only to hit a wall of silence.

'Information has to be worth something,' said a gnarled old seaman.

'Two shillings if I find him,' said Bacon.

'Anything else on offer?' said the seaman, grinning toothlessly.

Bacon ordered another brandy. He rapped his knuckles on the counter.

'May I have everyone's attention, please. There is a new and fatal disease on our streets. I am trying to trace its origins. My name is Robert Bacon. I am a surgeon.' He described the symptoms and how it was passed. 'If you or anyone you know has this disease please talk to me. I may be able to help.'

No one took up the offer.

'Or come and see me at my surgery on Cheapside.'

Bacon downed his drink. No point staying. If these men wished to see him they would come.

He was heading for the door when hands tore at his hair and clothes, hauling him into the middle of the room. One brute pinioned his arms while the other cut his purse and threw it on the counter. Bacon saw a ring of faces: some emotionless, others leering or grinning. The cutpurse tore at his breeches. How many of them would line up, he wondered. He screamed. The brute punched him in the solar plexus, the liver, the kidney. Finally, two blows to the face.

'Enough,' said the taverner.

Bacon thanked his God – at least he was spared the ultimate violation. They threw him into the street.

Bacon vomited. He coughed and spat blood. He'd be pissing blood for days. He hauled his breeches up and tried to stand but couldn't. Passers-by ignored him.

'Sodomite,' a crone hissed, and spat at him.

Bacon crawled then found the strength to rise. He would never beat the bells home. The journey was one long, painful stagger. The streets were deserted, no help in sight. He heard the bells ring. He was a mile from home.

'Oy. Huer. Huer!'

Bacon leant against a shopfront.

'I've been robbed,' he told the Watchman.

'What do you expect, out after curfew.'

'Help me to Cheapside. Two shillings awaits you.'

Two shillings bought a lot of ale. It bought him safe passage home.

'Bacon? What in damnation?' said Heckstall, aroused by the Watchman's demands for his two shillings. He helped his colleague to a divan and paid off the Watchman. He examined Bacon and washed his wounds. One eye was fully closed. The bruising to his face was almost pitch in colour.

'Are you in pain?' said Heckstall.

'Only when I laugh. Of course I'm in pain.'

'Broken nose. Cracked rib.'

'Ouch.'

'Bruised kidney.'

'You're good, Heckstall. You ought to be a surgeon.'

'Very droll, Bacon. I'm worried about that eye. I'll fix an arnica press.'

'Arnica's on Metcalfe's embargoed list.'

'Damn! Potato and cold compress. Do we have any eyebright?'

'A little.'

'And Bald's?'

Bald's was a salve made from garlic, onion, wine and ox gall. Most surgeons kept it on hand for the eye infections that arose from fistfights and street brawls.

'Yes. And opium. Please.'

'This is the second time, Bacon. What are you doing, where are you going to warrant such beatings?'

The opium induced sleep, but not the usual pleasant dreams. Bacon slept the sleep of the damned, haunted by visions of dockside taverns, flaying fists and sexual violation.

B acon pissed blood for three days. Heckstall didn't press him on the source of his injuries. Black bile, according to the Ancients, is secreted by the kidneys and causes melancholy. Bacon was certainly depressed. Yellow bile is secreted by the liver and causes irascibility. Bacon was beyond irascible. Perhaps the physicians were right; perhaps the theory of humours was right. He reread Galen. It was tosh, he was convinced of it. And there was no reference to the pockes.

'I can mix you some nightshade and blessed thistle for the black bile,' said Heckstall.

'To hell with your black bile.'

'That'll be the yellow bile talking.'

'Not funny, Heckstall.'

Lowther appeared in the doorway.

'In case you two hadn't noticed, we have a full surgery and a line half-way to Epping Forest.'

After a long day in the surgery, the three surgeons compared notes.

'We know that sexual intercourse is the primary means of infection,' said Bacon. 'But how? The male ejaculation?'

'Or the female secretion?' said Heckstall.

'Or simple lack of hygiene?' said Bacon.

They analysed their notes once again and re-affirmed clusters of infection around bawdhouses. Bacon was dismayed: the Virgin Mary and a few martyrs aside, the Church was quick to blame women for all of man's downfalls. Who originally infected whom, gender-wise was impossible to determine. Clusters also emerged in London's more deprived areas: St Giles, Houndsditch, and Smithfield.

'We can't discount miasmata,' said Lowther. 'The air around these places is noxious.'

'They buried plague victims in mass graves at Houndsditch,' said Heckstall. 'Could that create a miasma? A hundred years later?'

'I had a patient saying the jews are poisoning the wells,' said Lowther.

'That's nonsense,' said Bacon.

'There is a cluster at Clerkenwell. Maybe it is the well,' Lowther persisted.

'We can't fully discount fouled water,' said Bacon, 'but the jews are not poisoning the wells.'

The disease's virulence varied enormously. Some victims were bed-ridden within days, their balance and ambulation badly damaged. Others displayed no ill-effects beyond the ulcers and rash.

'Is the disease selective?' Heckstall wondered.

'Or are some patients more immune to the worst of it?' said Bacon.

They analysed the notes detailing their treatments. The mercury rub achieved some good results but the side-effects were devastating and often fatal. Theriac alleviated the symptoms but its cure rate was not high. In the absence of a guaranteed cure, theriac was the safest treatment.

There were so many unknowns and fear was growing on the streets.

'Why aren't we seeing any of the upper classes?' Lowther asked.

'Because the upper classes wouldn't deign to see us,' said Heckstall.

'No, they would consult their physicians,' said Bacon.

Bacon paid a visit to Sir Thomas Metcalfe who was leaving his residence near The Strand.

'Sir Thomas, we have over 200 cases. Has the pockes infected members of the Palace?'

'As if I would divulge that to you, Bacon.'

'Are there any more victims along The Strand.'

The physician brushed past the surgeon, refusing to answer,

Sir Thomas had indeed been consulted by panicked members of the Westminster court.

'Nothing to be concerned about,' he assured his patients with the bluff and jovial confidence which inspired calm in his patients. He handed out theriac from his stockpile to those who exhibited symptoms and always added an opium and henbane concoction; if the theriac didn't cure the patients at least they would feel better. At a guinea a pop, Sir Thomas's coffers swelled like his patients' genital pustules. In every event in the affairs of man, Sir Thomas reflected, someone did all right.

THE GREAT POCKES

T
he face looked familiar but patients were entering and leaving the surgery in a continual stream, almost a torrent really, and the faces melded.

'Have I treated you before?'

'Daniel,' the fellow said. 'The Black Swan.'

The brute who punched and kicked him while the others held him. Bacon was tempted to send him back to the docks. Briefly, before the surgeon's vows asserted themselves.

'It's a long way to come from Rotherhithe. You have symptoms, Daniel? Let me see.'

He hesitated.

'C'mon, you drop 'em quick enough down the Swan.'

The man dropped his breeches. Pockes. Sores. Rashes.

'How long have you had them?'

'Two months, mebbe.'

That would include him in the very first wave.

'Have you taken anything?'

'Frogs.'

It was an old "cure" from the days of the plague; cut open a frog and smear the still-living animal across the affected areas.

'Any other sores or ulcers?'

He opened his mouth. There was a line of sores along his gums. The man was shaking. It could be last night's alcohol; more likely he was terrified.

'How do you think you got those?'

'You're the surgeon.'

It was called "the French way" in polite society. Eating tack, or hardtack down on the docks.

'You've got something you can give me?'

It would be impossible to keep the mouth dry, thought Bacon. He would add elder, an astringent, to the theriac and hope it might work.

'Were you always this slim? Or are you not eating?' said Bacon.

'Not eating much. Will I die?'

'Somewhere between possibly and probably.' There was little point hiding the truth. The man was fit, his body hardened by years on the docks but the disease was indiscriminate. Geffrey Farrer was healthy and well-nourished but his body had succumbed with little resistance. 'Do you have a wife?'

'Not any more.'

At least the man wouldn't leave a widow.

'Have you been having sex since these symptoms appeared?'

He nodded.

Bacon groaned inwardly; he'd bet there was a cluster of infections in Rotherhithe.

'Other men have them too?'

'Yes.'

'How many?'

'I don't know. We don't talk about it, you know?'

Men didn't.

'But you've seen it?'

'Yes.'

'You must abstain from sex. That is how the infection spreads. You must tell everyone at the Swan to abstain or the infection will spread. Tell them to come and see me. Return when this salve is finished or if your symptoms change.'

'Will it work?'

Bacon sighed.

'It might. At the least it will help.'

The man rose to leave.

'I'm still looking for the lascar.'

'He's out to sea.'

'Where?'

'Somewhere between here and Naples. Or Genoa, maybe.'

The number of infections and deaths was rising rapidly but in the face of the crisis, Londoners responded with forbearance and unity. They exercised good, old English common sense and by and large abstained from sex beyond marriage. Priests and mayoral and parish offices preached the king's message: "this thing will pass". Those who could work continued to work. Henry's worst fears were not realised: the economy dipped but did not plunge.

Sir Thomas Metcalfe was a man of limited intelligence but he was no fool. He had consulted with apothecaries, physicians and barber-surgeons. Amidst all the crackpot theories Bacon's theory of sexual transmission was the only one that made sense. So Sir Thomas claimed it for his own. As Court Physician and thus the senior medical officer of the realm, he was lauded as a medical genius, an encomium he did little to dispel. A relieved Henry bumped him up to a Knight of the Garter, the highest honour in the land. Barabbas was moved to write:

> Make the upcoming hour overflow with joy, and let pleasure drown the brim./With mirth and laughter let old wrinkles come.

Henry was relieved. The economy hadn't collapsed, his faith in his experts was justified. Hurrah for good old English common sense!

There was little mirth and laughter for Bacon. Recovery rates remained low and maddeningly random. He was working sixteen hours a day in the surgery and on his rounds. A hammering on his door didn't waken him. Neither did the bells of St Mary's.

'What is it, Lowther?' he said finally roused by the lad's shaking him.

'It's Jane Darley. Her husband's in the waiting room, frantic, like.'

'Has she come to term?' said Bacon, fully dressed and fully aware.

'Yes,' said Darley. 'But it's the baby. Please come.'

Bacon gathered his instrument and drugs and hurried with Darley to Aldgate. It was an appalling sight. The poor woman's bedclothes were covered in blood. She was barely conscious. The umbilical cord had not been severed. Jane held the dead child to her breast where it had briefly suckled. It was hideously deformed; its tiny body covered in ulcers, its penis swollen gargantuanly. It had been born with a hare lip and a pair of nostrils where a nose had failed to form.

Bacon stanched the bleeding and gave her opium.

'I'll order you a salve of comfrey and lady's mantle.'

'Thank you,' she whispered.

'What happened to the midwife?'

'She ran.'

She would. Not her fault, thought Bacon. Midwifery was the most traditional of all practices and remained rife with superstition. She would have put it down to witchcraft and soon the word would be out. Jane would be ostracised, in all probability branded a witch and forced to flee.

'My baby.'

'Best I take him, Mrs Darley,' said Bacon, wrapping the infant in swaddling. 'I will see a priest and make sure he receives a Christian burial.'

Bacon wasn't sure he could guarantee this. There would be the baptism and then the burial and a superstitious priest might view the deformities as the mark of satan. It would be expensive. Simony, by any other name. He met with the priest at St Botwulf's and paid – bribed – him to baptise and bury the infant. Then he went to see the midwife.

'It was witchcraft, sir.'

'It was the pockes, Mrs Stokes.'

'Satan leaves his sign, sir. Covered head to toe he were. An abomination, sir.'

'It was the pockes, Mrs Stokes. Please, you must keep this to yourself.'

The English are a stoic race and had faced down the fears of the unknown but when news that the disease had infected an unborn child, resolve gave way. This was to prove the turning point, the day when good old English common sense gave way to blind English panic.

So much of human experience is perceived as cause and effect and whenever a disaster occurs it is only human nature to find the cause and apportion the blame. A great many Londoners were religiously observant and the pockes swelled congregations to capacity levels. Despite the Church's stance that diseases were the wages of sin, no one could actually blame God for the pockes and so a human agency was sought.

The first to wear the blame, predictably, were the jews. Yet again they were accused of poisoning the water supplies. Jewish businesses, synagogues and residences were attacked and looted. Several jews were murdered, their bodies dumped in an open field at Houndsditch.

Blame then turned on someone, anyone – as long as they were foreign. With the opening of trade, there had been an influx of foreigners in London. Lascars, moors and Europeans of any nationality were beaten or murdered and thrown in the Fleet or Thames.

The next to feel Londoners' wrath were, also predictably, women.

Bacon's rounds took him to a follow-up call in St Giles. He turned down the squalid lane on which his patient lived and saw an angry mob, shouting and kicking at her door.

'The lips of the adulterous woman drip honey,' cried a street-preacher, his bloodshot eyes widened with hate, 'and her seductive words are smoother than olive oil, but in the end she is bitter as wormwood, sharp as a two-edged sword. Her feet go down to death; her steps lead straight to the grave.'

'To the grave!' cried the mob.

'She who defiles herself as a prostitute must be burned.'

'Burned! Burned!'

'She has visited the plague upon us,' shouted the preacher.

'Get out of my way,' said Bacon, pushing his way through the mob.

'Who are you, sir? One who would corrupt himself with a fallen woman? One who would contaminate others with his sin?'

'I am a surgeon, sir, and she is my patient.'

'You would cross the path of the righteous, sir?'

The mob pressed forward, clutching at Bacon. Lord, even the women looked tough enough. The preacher's face was in Bacon's. Bacon saw the beginnings of an ulcer on his lip.

'That is not honey that falls from your lip, sir. You carry the pockes,' he snarled.

'How dare you?'

'I will expose you, sir, if you do not disperse this mob and let me through.'

The preacher hesitated.

'Mercy,' he said. 'The man cries for mercy.'

'No mercy!' cried a crone.

Oh, shit.

'Mercy!' said the preacher. 'Our heavenly father shows mercy, and so shall we.'

The crowd wanted blood. A man threw a punch, knocking Bacon to the ground.

'I'm warning you,' Bacon hissed at the preacher. 'I will expose you.'

'We be away,' said the preacher. 'This harlot will be gone by nightfall. She will spread her poison no more. To Chitty St, we go!'

He shepherded his mob toward another defenceless woman's hovel.

Bacon knocked on the door.

'It's Mr Bacon, Jenny.'

She opened the door.

'Are you all right, Jenny?'

'They've been forcing the girls out of their homes. That's the first I've heard of burnin'. Unclean, we are, though that never stopped the blokes when they wanted a fuck, did it?'

'These are clearing, Jenny,' he said, after examining her. She may be one of the lucky ones, he thought. A few pockes, a few scars in her pubis and abdomen were all to show. He gave her more theriac.

'I'd best leave,' she said. 'I'd stay if it was just me. But there's me kids. And that mob'll be back.'

'It's criminal forcing you from your home.'

Jenny gathered her few belongings and Bacon helped her to the parish almshouse. It was filled to overflowing with women and their children. Many had been beaten by angry mobs. They were frightened and their children were bawling with fear.

'I'm so sorry, Jenny.'

'Not your fault, Bacon. It is what it is.'

Bacon moved amongst the women asking if any needed treatment. His supply of theriac soon ran out. He promised he would fetch more and deliver it the next day. He headed for Cheapside. Street preachers were declaiming on all corners. Mobs were prowling the streets, looking for victims to calm their fears, appease their god. He returned to the surgery, deeply worried. The violence was unsettling and supplies of theriac were running dangerously low.

Supplies of frogs and pigeons – ('At least they're not shitting everywhere,' said Henry when he was informed) – were likewise running low and were commanding astonishing prices. Leeches were fetching two shillings a gross. There were those who prospered from the epidemic. The charlatans and soothsayers who peddled fake cures and predictions; Sir Thomas Metcalfe whose leechings and emeralds did no better. Since adopting Bacon's alleviations – theriac and mercury frictions – his recovery rate had improved but was still far from efficacious. As always, in time of disaster man turned to god. Sir John Morton saw his churches fill to overflow, their coffers bulge.

Conspiracy theories abounded. It was a Yorkist plot, a Lancastrian plot; the French had managed to bottle miasmata and had unleashed it on Londoners prior to invasion. Believing that sexual intercourse with a virgin cured the disease, wealthy men – and the occasional woman – bought virgin adolescents, for which a lucrative market had sprung up. Likewise, the reprobate physicians who certified the girls *virgo intacta* cashed in. Palmists discovered the hitherto unknown "pockes line" – which supposedly ran adjacent to the Line of Mars. Trade in fake theriac, mercury and emeralds flourished. One sharpie was murdered for substituting toad for frog.

Distrust spread like miasmata across the city, adding to an already oppressive air of disquiet. Citizens regarded each other with suspicion, fearing that their friends, neighbours, drinking companions may be carrying the infection, and if so, what odious or perverse behaviour had caused the infection for which God was punishing them? An accidental bump in the street might lead to fisticuffs – or worse. At a more intimate level, husbands and wives became distrustful. Adulteries were exposed and marriages and families broken.

The poor were the hardest hit. The wealthy retired to their country estates or holed up in their city mansions. Unemployment rose with infections. Construction slowed, shops and market stalls lay silent and empty as their owners succumbed to the disease. All who could afford to leave London, fled. Those who couldn't, drank. Theft and burglary, and crime, both petty and violent, spiralled; domestic violence soared.

'We were thinking about closing shop till this pockes dies down, Bray.'

The Master of Eton College had been up at Oxford with Sir Reginald. They were meeting at an Old Boys dinner put on by the Master in the college dining hall.

'Why would you want to do that, master?'

'As you know, we house our boys in a very confined area.'

'Propinquity has not been identified as a problem.'

'Yes, but, well, boys will be boys. We can't abandon games, can we? Stoolball, football.'

'Wouldn't be the same old college without games, would it?'

'And then there's the wrestling.'

'I didn't know wrestling was on the curriculum.'

'It's not an organised sport. Not in a conventional sense at any rate.'

'No tournaments?'

'No. Very informal. Often played after lights out.'

'Oh,' said Sir Reginald, suddenly reminded of his own, painful initiation into "wrestling" in the dorms after lights out.

'No wrestling, master.'

162

'Boys will be boys, Bray. So we should stay open?'

'Absolutely. We cannot deprive young men of their education. It would send the wrong sort of message.'

'Of course. If that's the government's official line.'

'It is, master.'

The curious, unexplained nature of Sir Rowland de Montfort's death shook Henry. Had a kind of madness taken him and compelled him to take his life? It didn't make *sense*. And now this wretched pockes which had somehow breached the Palace walls. Despite the grandeur of his banquets and his tourney, despite the mystique which cloaked him, Henry's majesty had not protected his inner circle. Many were openly questioning the whole Doctrine of the Divine Right of Rule. He took refuge, night and day in his ledgers and his beloved Domesday, but as revenues ebbed so did his spirits. Barabas no longer came up with new gags; he lay about in a drunken stupor, his marotte lay unshaken, its bells silent, symbolic of the malaise which enveloped the realm. His soliloquies did little to cheer his king's gloomy spirits:

> *This goodly frame, the earth, seems to me a sterile promontory look you, this brave o'erhanging firmament, this majestical roof, why, it appears no other thing to me than a foul and pestilent congregation of vapours.*

As the numbers of sick and dead rose so did Henry's anxiety. He heard the rumour that disease spread via toilet seats and assigned a 24-hour guard on the Royal Privy.

He trusted his wife. But she did have a lot of spare time. She couldn't be trying on dresses all the time, surely? He joined her in the marital bed.

'Henry, what are you doing down there?'

'Oh, nothing, dear, you know ...'

'No, I don't know.'

'Just, you know, having a look.'

163

'A look? Get out, Henry.'

'Yes, dear.'

The wisdom which passed down the line from Alfred the Great through the Black Prince to Henry himself decreed that ejaculation depleted the warrior spirit. A randy warrior is a deadly warrior. Henry had fought at Bosworth Field with a length of bow-string tied (painfully) around the royal member. By battle's end it contained a sacful of warrior spirit. Henry had long abandoned the practice but this was a fearful new enemy and Henry believed that the familiar painful constriction of his trusty old cockring provided an added defence against the predations of the pockes. His weekly consultations with Sir Thomas Metcalfe were bumped up to daily.

'Urine is clear?' said Sir Thomas.

'Yes.'

'Stools.'

'Splendid.'

'What's this, sire?'

'What does it look like, Metcalfe?'

'Yes, but what's it for, Your Majesty?'

Henry explained the theory.

'Well, can't do any harm I suppose,' said Sir Thomas. 'Best if you loosen it a notch, sire, wouldn't want it to fall off, would we?'

In fact, many infected commoners had been prescribed a cockring and, after weeks of constricted blood flow, their penises did indeed fall off.

'They're surgeons, Sir Edmund, they seem to be specialising in treatment of the pockes.'

'You say his name is Bacon?'

'Yes, sir. You asked me to keep an eye on him, sir,' said Fleck, one of Dudley's army of taxmen.

Aaah, yes, Bacon. Hardwick's mysterious associate, the recipient of 100 sovereigns of Bray's "office expenses".

'I've followed him, sir, as per your instructions. The surgery's full from bells to bells so I'm sure they're not paying their full taxes.'

'Attend to that. Anything else?'

'He seems to be spending an awful lot of time with bawds, sir.'

'Not a hanging offence, Fleck.'

'Not like not paying your taxes, sir.'

'Indeed. Is that all you've got?'

'He was observed having heated words with Sir Edward Norris.'

Edward Norris. Former Worshipful Master of the Merchant Taylors. Interesting.

'And he's taken two serious beatings in taverns off Brick Lane and down in Rotherhithe.'

Years of running Henry's tax system had honed Dudley's instincts razor-sharp – something was amiss here. Dudley took an early lunch and headed for The Strand.

'Robert Bacon? Can't say I know him.'

'I think you do, Sir Edward.'

Perspiration trickled into one eye. Sir Edward's other eye tic-ed furiously.

'One meets so many people, Sir Edmund.'

Dudley smiled sympathetically.

'I take it your taxes are in order?'

These words filled every Londoner, rich and poor alike, with the fear of God; the words made worse by an unannounced visit from HRH's top taxman. Norris well knew that Dudley could find disorder in the most meticulous of taxation records and that said disorder would result in a long stretch – either in The Tower or at the end of a rope.

He told him all he knew about Robert Bacon.

'Hardwick drew one hundred sovereigns from the treasury, Sir John. He handed the money to a surgeon called Robert Bacon.'

'The Cheapside surgeon? The Humanist?' said the Archbishop, recalling his conversation with Sir Thomas Metcalfe.

'He has used treasury money to frequent taverns and bawdhouses. Bawdhouses, I might add which cater to unnatural practices.'

"Unnatural practices" were expressly forbidden by holy scripture but not prohibited by law. Morton determined to fix that anomaly as soon as possible.

'This Hardwick was authorised to draw the money?'

'The chit was signed by Sir Reginald Bray.'

Sir John Morton was shocked. Sir Reginald was a liberal and was notoriously lax regarding church dogma. But using treasury funds on bawds? Morton couldn't decide which was the more heinous crime: Humanism or misappropriation of the king's own monies. It really depended on which hat he was wearing. He put aside his chancellor's cap for the moment; he would deal with Bray later. He had a more immediate problem to deal with. He had been made aware that Alexander had pressured Henry to appoint Giovanni de Carbonariis to the See of Bath and Wells. Morton quite rightly took it as a rebuke for his failure to enforce hardline church dogma regarding Humanism and other modernist movements. Morton had sworn loyalty to Henry, but was Henry's hold on the crown secure? Or would he be yet another battle-field monarch, destined to live and die by the sword? Morton decided his allegiance to the pope was the stronger. In the short term at any rate. He would denounce Bacon and his Humanism and toe the hard Roman line. Disease was a punishment from god. Bray and his unnatural practices would have to wait.

The Black Swan was filled to overflow but silent. All eyes, mainly hostile, were on Bacon. Daniel afforded him some protection, but there were plenty of unsavoury types, many carrying blades.

'I have patients suffering unspeakable pain. Patients who cannot speak or see or hear. Patients who are paralysed and in almshouses. Still others lie in chains in Bethlem or grow cold in their graves. You are all at risk. You must refrain from any form of sex until we have found a cure for this terrible disease. No doubt there are men in this very room who carry the pockes. I will treat them and anyone who wishes to see me free of charge.'

Daniel proved invaluable. He was a Rotherhithe man born and bred. The following morning he took Bacon on a tour of the local bawdhouses. Most were worked by women; the Swan catered to a minority taste.

Bacon sent a messenger to Heckstall; he would be in Rotherhithe for a few days. He dispatched a second message to the Stratford Langthorne Cistercians requesting theriac and mercury paste. Twenty-four patients reported to the rooms he had taken on Silver Walk. Few knew from whom they caught the disease but several confirmed that the lascar was the first they knew who carried it. No one knew the lascar's whereabouts. He came and he went according to the work.

Bacon and Daniel went to HM's Custom's House and obtained a list of the latest arrivals. Six ships had arrived overnight.

'*Il Dio Falco,*' said Daniel. 'The lascar works that one regular.'

It was a lateen-rigged, three-mast caravelle and ran a route between Rotherhithe and Antwerp for the Merchant Traders. Their representative was supervising the loading of cloth.

'He didn't show up for work this morning,' said the trader.

'When did he dock?' said Bacon.

'Two days ago. If you see him tell him to haul his backside down here lick and spittle if he wants to keep his job.'

Daniel took him on a tour of local lodgings. Dormitory types, they rented beds per night, ten or twelve to a room.

'He stayed the night afore,' said a landlady. 'Han't seen him since. He left his kit wi' me. I'll only hold it another day. Then I sells it.'

'If he was still on the docks,' said Daniel, 'he would have stayed here. Or one of the other places.'

'Would he have stayed the night with someone from the Swan?'

'They don't stay the night, Mr Bacon. Most of 'em don't see a bed when a privy or an alley'll do.'

Bacon thanked the navvie and started the long walk back to Cheapside. He crossed London Bridge and turned north-east toward Aldgate. Tracing the disease back to origin had always been at long odds, he thought, all he could do now was treat his patients as best he could, alleviate their suffering and hope he found a cure. He was about to enter the city gate when he paused and decided to turn north.

The Mitre was closed. It did not cater to the lunch time crowd. Its clientele were nightstalkers. Revels often continued till dawn. Bacon hammered at the door. And again. An upstairs window opened and a dishevelled Wilf appeared.

'Fie, Wilf.'

'A fuck to you, Mr Bacon. We're not open. What do you want?'

'The lascar.'

'He's not here.'

'That may be true, Wilf, but I think he's been here.'

Wilf nodded.

'Wait.'

The bolts were drawn and the door opened. The air inside was musty with last night's drink and piss.

'You needn't concern yourself with the lascar anymore, Mr Bacon.'

'He did show up here?'

'Best not ask questions, Mr Bacon.'

'The lascar was my only hope of finding the origin of the disease, Wilf.'

'Cup of wine?'

Bacon nodded. Will poured him a cup of Burgundy.

'He told us an interesting story before we, er, bade him final farewell.'

'C

an't you just excommunicate him?' said Henry.

'We must make an example of him, sir, as a lesson to all those who would be Humanists. And sodomites.' Morton thought he might as well throw in the latter charge.

Unnatural practices were not something Henry thought about much. Lord knows he rarely practised natural ones. He knew all about Edward II and his litany of unnatural practices, of course, but that was ancient history.

'There will be no inquisition during my reign, Sir John.

In this never-ending battle between mitre and crown, Henry was not going to cede the right to torture or execute his subjects to some English Torquemada.

'Barbaric, this burning at the stake. Not like a decent English hanging.'

'We burn witches, Your Majesty.'

'Yes, well, that's different. They're wome ... witches.'

'This man Bacon has also been spending monies obtained from your very own treasury, sir.'

'What?!'

Burning was too good for the bastard.

Morton handed Henry the incriminating chit. The authorising signature leapt out at him. Sir Reginald Bray. His oldest advisor. His oldest friend. And he'd been diddling his expenses.

'Commander!'

'Your Majesty.'

Henry had not quite taken to Sir Walter Sentjohn, the unfortunate Sir Rowland de Montfort's replacement. He peered at him apprehensively. It couldn't be ...

'What's that on your lip?'

'Hoskyns, Your Majesty. He cut me shaving, sir.'

Plausible, but ...

'Bring me Sir Reginald Bray.'

Sir Reginald realised that if this ended badly his next address would be c/- The Tower of London. He fell back on the tried and true. He obfuscated.

'Sir, I confess that the strains of office exacerbated by the current malaise which is afflicting out great city may have clouded my usual meticulous supervision of treasury funds, creating an unfortunate situation in which funds may have been channelled – '

'Enough, Bray, before I call for the hangman.'

'What I mean to say – '

'What Sir Reginald means to say, Your Majesty,' said Hardwick, leaping to his mentor's assistance, 'is that the money has been invested in medical research.'

'Medical research? In bawdhouses? In unnatural practices?'

'Absolutely, sir. Mr Robert Bacon is a prominent surgeon, sir. It was he who discovered how the pockes is carried.'

'A Humanist,' spat Sir John Morton. 'A heretic.'

'I thought Sir Thomas discovered that,' said Henry. 'Didn't we give him a gong?'

'Sir Thomas has done sterling work,' said Hardwick. 'But Bacon first alerted us to the disease. He discovered clusters of the disease around taverns and bawdhouses.'

'Did he now?' said Henry.

'All on file, sir,' said Sir Reginald, at last joining the fray. 'I am not one to argue with the Archbishop, but some might say the Church, indeed, Sir John, should be confronting this disease. While we remain inactive, the disease grows more powerful.'

'This is heresy – '

'Be quiet, Morton. Sir Reginald is prepared to wage battle with this fearsome enemy. He, at least, is doing *something*. I'd like to meet this Bacon. Guard, bring me Bacon!'

'L owther, go to Rotherhithe, said Bacon, scribbling an address on a scrap of paper. 'You will find a sailor's kit at these lodgings. Pay the landlady whatever she asks.'

It was early evening when Lowther returned with the kit. It held a sailor's essentials but little else, save for an earthenware pot which contained a smudge of dun paste. Bacon sniffed it.

'What do you make of this, Heckstall?'

Heckstall sniffed.

'No idea.'

Bacon took it first, to a friendly apothecary and then to the nearest friary.

Neither had come across the paste. Neither could identify it. Bacon returned to find a deploy of King's Guards waiting for him.

'I have committed no crime.'

'Tell that to the hangman,' said the guard commander as Bacon was marched to Westminster.

'I wish to see Sir Reginald Bray.'

'You will. He'll be joining you at Tyburn.'

'Tell Sir Reginald, I have found the origin of the disease. Tell him I may have found a cure.'

As it was, the soldiers were merely indulging in typically boisterous King's Guards humour. They brought him before Henry.

'You have found the origin of the disease?'

'How will finding the disease's origin help?' said Sir Thomas Metcalfe. 'We have this disease under control. The English physician is the finest in the world.'

'Aristotle – one of the Ancients you so assiduously study, Sir Thomas, says we cannot understand a phenomenon unless we trace it to its origin.'

'The disease is god's punishment for sin,' Morton insisted.

'Be quiet, Morton. Mr Bacon?'

'I traced the disease to a lascar, sire. A matelot working the European trade routes.'

'And you have found a cure?'

'The lascar spoke of a cure on his deathbed, sire.'

'Can you get hold of it?'

Thousands, tens of thousands of gold sovereigns danced before Henry's eyes.

'The Europeans have access to it, sir. At the moment, we do not.'

Damn, thought Henry. The cure was worth a fortune. If the Europeans have found it they will decimate our trade surplus.

'With Your Majesty's permission, I will undertake a journey to the disease's origin. And, hopefully, I will return with the cure.'

Henry was not slow to grant permission. His hold on the Crown, he realised, may well depend on the success of Bacon's mission.

3. That which hath been is now ...

B

acon found it easy to imagine the siren Parthenope calling to Odysseus across these quicksilver waters and, having failed to woo her beloved, casting herself into the sea, her body washing up at Castel dell Ove, the oldest fort in Naples which stood guard on the western side of the harbour. It was a beautiful city, Naples. The crescent-shaped harbour was ringed by hills, from Vomero in the west to the mighty snow-capped Vesuvio, at once beautiful and minatory, in the east. Palazzi and castelli, and forts and temples dating back to the ancient Greeks were visible from the deck of their caravelle as they docked.

It had been a rough crossing, especially London to Calais and thence to Antwerp. Their caravelle was laden with Merchant Adventurers' wool but flew Florentine banners and ensigns, belonging as it did to the Medici bank. The Merchant Adventurers were forced to lease the boat at eye-watering expense, hence their and Henry's determination to build an English navy, both merchant and military.

Naples had for centuries been held up as a paragon of the Hellenistic ideals of architectural purity. The villas and palazzi were classic in line and structure, achieving an architectural harmony, occasionally equalled but never bettered. A porter loaded their belongings onto a hand cart and led them to the residence of the Merchant Adventurers' representative.

'Hardwick? Bacon? Everson. Hugh Everson.'

Everson was in his mid-twenties and recently accepted into the Merchant Adventurers. He was starting at the bottom – Naples was certainly that – but he was sharp enough. They took him into their confidence.

'Are you accusing the Neapolitans of starting this disease? Be careful. The Neapolitans won't take too kindly to this. They're quick to temper and even quicker with their blades. The loss of prestige, the opprobrium from the international community will be humiliating. And as for the French. The old enemy. If they suspect you're a spy they'll hang you.'

'How long have you known about the disease?' said Bacon.

'Only recently. My trading partners warned me off the bordellos and I stay out of the tavernas which is where you hear most of the gossip. They're full of French soldiers who are riddled with it apparently and Charles's army is topped up with mercenaries – Swiss, German, Spanish.'

'They will take it back to their homelands. All Europe will be infected,' said Bacon.

'How are the Neapolitans coping with occupation?' said Hardwick. 'We've heard they're on a sort of lockdown.'

'There are restrictions but they've never been properly explained so no one takes much notice. There is a curfew but the French don't bother enforcing it. They flout it themselves. Barbarians! They have no interest in trade. They drink, they loot, they fight and rape. The bordellos and the tavernas are about the only boom business at the moment.'

As if to underscore the assertion Bacon heard shouting, then a scream. Somewhere nearby, a bottle smashed.

'So, you hope to find the origin of this disease?'

'I know of no other way of learning about it. Our cures are not very effective.'

Bacon produced the lascar's earthenware pot.

'Have you ever come across this?'

Everson opened the jar, sniffed it. He shook his head.

'No. What is it?'

'That I don't know. Have you heard of a woman called Mencia?'

'No. Who is she?'

'Some sort of herbalist possibly. Before he, er, disappeared, a lascar told some contacts of mine about a woman called Mencia. He got the pot from her.'

'A nun, perhaps? I'll get together a list of priories for you. They supply most of the medicinal herbs around here. One other thing – they're a superstitious lot, the Neapolitans. The place is full of folk remedies, amulets to ward off demons, that sort of thing.'

'I'll start with the priories.'

Given that their mission was fraught with potentially Vesuvian repercussions the pair had concocted a cover story in which they were touring vineyards and cheesemakers for possible trade with London.

'Neapolitan goods are a little cheaper than the Florentine,' said Everson. 'We're definitely the poor relations as far as London's concerned. The Florentines export out of Genoa, it's much closer. There's this wild rumour circulating that Leonardo da Vinci – have you heard of da Vinci? Clever chap. Anyway, he and this Florentine official called Machiavelli have dreamed up this idea to *divert* the River Arno *around* Pisa. It will give Florence access to the sea and deprive Pisa of water. The Pisans are up in arms, of course. Diverting a river! Can you believe it?'

'His enemies say da Vinci likes playing god,' said Hardwick.

'Yes, as you say, man playing God and the pontiff's not too happy about it. He's branded da Vinci a Humanist. Claims he is usurping the Church. He might consider you a Humanist, Bacon. So be careful. There are priests everywhere and they'll report you to Rome in a heartbeat.'

Everson called for a servant to bring more wine and cheese.

'Tell me, how bad are things in London? The disease – what do you call it? The pockes? I've also heard rumours of dissidents and a possible rebellion. Is there anything in this Perkin Warbeck claim?'

It took Bacon and Hardwick several hours to relay the London news. They turned in for the night, agreeing that Hardwick would maintain his cover story by visiting wine merchants while Bacon would begin the search for Mencia.

Although an ecclesiastical hardliner, Archbishop Sir John Morton could be a pragmatist when necessary. He had to be, serving as he did, his God who ruled heaven, and his king, who by God's divine right ruled that little corner of God's flat earth called England. There were times he was torn and his judgements favoured Westminster over Rome but Morton was fearful of the threat that Humanism posed to the power and position of the Church. Even more than the monarchy, whose reigns this last 500 years could best be described as turbulent, the Church was responsible for maintaining the status quo, which largely meant keeping the peasants in their place. This meritocracy, this social mobility which surged during Henry's reign, disturbed the realm's precarious balance; and disturbed Morton with it.

Morton felt that Bray's liberal influence on Henry was waxing while his own was waning, but he felt he had no choice but to toe Rome's official, hard line concerning disease and punishment. There was unrest on the streets of London; due to a combination of the disease, the high taxes and the rise of anti-European feeling. He was in no doubt that Warbeck was an impostor, but if there were a rebellion and if it were to succeed, stability must be restored. Cumbria, Suffolk *et al* would wage war with France. Possibly, the Dutch and the Spanish. But not Rome. Morton's position, therefore, was secure; the loyalist Bray's position was not. In such a scenario, Sir Reginald was for the scaffold. Morton asked Zorima to cast Henry's horoscope. It was not favourable. And so, Morton the pragmatist threw aside his chancellor's cap and affixed the Archbishop's mitre.

Morton had learned of Bacon and Hardwick's departure for Naples the minute their caravelle set sail. He wrote an urgent, sealed message to Pope Alexander. It was dispatched on a Merchant Adventurers' six-sail carrack which departed two days later. It was a direct sail and driven by favourable winds reached Rome a full three days before Bacon and Hardwick docked in Naples.

It was rare that events weighed heavily on Alexander – Rodrigo Borgia, as was. He was the most powerful man on earth and his principal goal was maintaining the Church's, and therefore his own privileged position, the order of which remained fluid. He had inherited wealth and privilege. His forebears were raised to the nobility and Uncle Alfonso became Pope Calixtus III. Young Rodrigo took a law degree from the prestigious University of Bologna and rapidly navigated his way through the Church bureaucracy. From an early age, his eye was fixed firmly on the prize he felt was his destiny. They could say what they liked about Alexander, and they said plenty – three very public mistresses and several not so public; four known, and an indeterminate number of unacknowledged, children were common knowledge. He tried to pass the four off as a niece and nephews but few were fooled.

Alexander set about reforming the curia by appointing his most pious cardinals in all church-related matters, leaving him to devote his energies to cementing the power of the Papal States. He initially allied himself with France in order to expand the States, seizing duchies from the King of Naples. When Naples refused to cede more land he took revenge by granting Charles VIII and his army free passage through Rome en route to Naples. Alexander regretted the move almost immediately for, having taken Naples, Charles made it clear he wanted to claim all Italy. Alexander pirouetted adroitly and formed the Holy League, whose members included Milan, Florence and Venice, Spain, and the Holy Roman Empire which at that time comprised Germany, Austria and Burgundy.

Rome and Spain were on especially good terms. Alexander's predecessor Innocent (who was anything but) was strangely obsessed with witchcraft. He appointed the Dominican friar, Tomas de Torquemada, who shared

Innocent's obsession with witchcraft, and also jews, moors and muslims, heretics and sodomites, as Grand Inquisitor of Spain. Torquemada was also confessor to King Ferdinand and Queen Isabella of Spain. Alexander, Ferdinand and Isabella enjoyed a warm relationship forged by Spain's obeisance to Rome; if nothing else the Spanish church was in safe hands with Ferdinand, Isabella and Torquemada in charge. In 1493, following Christopher Colombo's triumphant return to Spain, Alexander rewarded their endeavours by issuing a papal bull confirming Spain's sovereignty over the New World.

Heresy was a many-headed monster which Alexander confronted but could never quite slay. He charged the curia with keeping heresy in check and with people like Torquemada in tow was largely successful. However, one after the other, the Albigensians and Waldensians, the Lollards, and Hussites challenged papal authority. The Florentines were a constant source of irritation with their mania for Art and Humanism. On his last visit to Florence, Alexander had been shocked by the wall-to-wall and piazza-to-piazza painted and sculpted nudes. All right, he was titillated too, but these were temptations too much for the lower classes. And as for that madman da Vinci? He wore *woman's* clothes and *make-up*.

Alexander read Morton's missive with growing concern. Disease as god's punishment for sin was a key tenet of the Church. The twin precepts of heavenly reward and earthly punishment (and vice versa) were essential for maintaining the Church's position. Alexander didn't see the Englishmen's appearance in Naples as an existential threat, but God (or whoever or whatever) had done the Church an almighty favour by visiting the Great Plague upon Europe a century ago. Alexander's spies in Naples had already reported that this new disease could wreak the same apocalyptic havoc. Unless these English Humanists could find the origins of the disease, and worse, play god by finding a cure.

Alexander sent for Giovanni di Medici, 19 years of age, the son of Lorenzo the Magnificent and the rising star of the curia. Young Giovanni was destined for the highest office, being tonsured at seven years of age and reaching the rank of cardinal at 13. He had once confided to Alexander that he had chosen his papal name, Leo at eight years of age! The Magnificent Lorenzo had given his son but one piece of advice: Rise early in the morning. The eight-year-old Gio had taken this to heart and was known for his almost non-Catholic work ethic.

'I want you to go to Naples,' said Alexander, 'and see what these two Englishmen are up to.'

'Si, papa.'

There was no shortage of priories in Naples. London may have boasted the highest number of churches in Europe, but Naples outranked her with her houses of the holy. Bacon spent four days traipsing the steep, rutted lanes and streets of Naples and the surrounding hills, visiting the men and women of Holy Orders. He met with friars Conventual and Minor, Capuchins and Bernardine – and these were just the Franciscan sub-orders.

'Theriac?' he asked a Capuchin friar.

'Si.'

'Can you give me the recipe? La ricetta?'

The friar chuckled.

'It's very expensive,' said Bacon, when given the theriac.

The friar spoke no English but Bacon learnt that classically concocted theriac took forty days to brew and twelve years to mature. Recipes contained as many as 100 ingredients and it wasn't the ingredients, but the interaction between the ingredients that gave the drug its potency. The friary's recipe was taken from a recipe over 500 years old.

'Do you prescribe – prescrivi mercurio?'

'Troppo pericoloso.'

Yes, as Bacon knew, it was very dangerous.

'Do you know what this is?' said Bacon, offering him the earthenware pot. 'Or where I might get some?'

The friar sniffed it and shook his head.

'Do you know a woman called Mencia?'

'No, signore.'

Bacon tried the farmacie next.

Each had his own supplier of theriac: Franciscan or Augustinian or their sub-orders in the main. Not one had come across the unguent, nor knew what it was. No one knew of the mysterious Mencia. Like London, there were sharpies – ciarlatani – working the streets and from small shopfronts in dark alleys, selling home-made or home-brewed cures, amulets and charms.

Bacon returned, weary and footsore, to Everson's villa.

'No luck? That's a pity,' said Everson, handing him a missive. It bore Sir Reginald's seal. The number of infections and deaths continued to rise. A mass grave had been dug at Houndsditch to cope with the numbers. His Majesty was wondering if there was any news ...

'What next?' said Everson.

Bacon sighed.

'The bordellos.'

There was no difficulty finding bordellos. Like St Giles, there was one on every street corner. The women were puzzled or suspicious that Bacon wanted only to look. Some refused even when payment was offered. Word of the strange Englishman preceded him and he was met at each bordello with omerta. More than once a smiling madam showed him her collection of canes, switches and racks. Flagellation and penitence were conjoined with sex for many clients. If love of God replaced love of man or woman, perhaps it was not that surprising. He finally found a bordello in Vomero where a young woman acquiesced to his request. The poor woman was infected, but she was one of the fortunate ones; a few pockes and a mild rash were all that remained. There was no doubt it was the pockes.

'Do you know where you got it?' he asked.

'I soldati Francesi.'

'French soldiers?'

'Si.'

The following day a second and third woman confirmed the story.

'I soldati Francesi.'

All the cases had been contracted before it had appeared in London, so Bacon's hunch was right – the disease had not originated in England. But he was still faced with the quandary he faced in the early days of his investigation: who infected whom? And where did it all start?

None of the women had heard of Mencia, let alone knew her whereabouts. Bacon reported his findings to Hardwick.

'Cripes. The French? Does this mean we have to go to Paris?'

'I don't know, Hardwick. Perhaps.'

'We have to tread carefully here,' said Hardwick. 'If London finds out about this there'll be hell to pay. Cumbria and his chums will blame it all on the French. They'll be up in arms – literally – and he'll have popular support. It'll mean another war.'

Like many Englishmen, Bacon and Hardwick had grown weary of the constant wars which killed thousands and which resulted in little more than a change of king and a massive debt to pay.

'We still don't know which way Alexander will jump,' said Everson. 'If he honours the Holy League's alliance with France it could drag all of Europe into it. It will be an absolute disaster for trade.'

'I'll see if I can talk to some French soldiers.'

'Be very, very careful, Bacon,' said Everson. 'The French hate us, and don't forget it.'

It was not difficult finding French soldiers. The taverns were full of them, very drunk and very rowdy. Bacon's French was excellent but he couldn't pass himself off as a Frenchman.

'Taking in the sights,' he said in answer to their questions.

He quickly learnt to target the younger soldiers. The older men had fought in wars with the English and preferred to speak with their fists. Or knives. Or guns. The French had brought no law or order with their occupation of Naples; the death of an inquisitive Englishman would not be questioned. Bacon finally found a relatively friendly group of young Frenchmen who, fuelled by a local wine called Lacryma

Christi del Vesuvio – Christ's Tears at Vesuvio – were eager to vent their anger on the local prostitutes.

'La maladie italienne,' they cried.

'You mean you caught it from the Italian women?'

'Oui.'

For one young Frenchman, the wine was well-named as his bonhomie turned to tears.

'Vais-je encore baiser?' he wept. 'Ma bite tombera-t-elle?'

'Your cock won't fall off,' Bacon assured him before excusing himself and returning to their lodgings. He reported his findings to Hardwick.

'The Italians are blaming the French?'

'And the French are blaming the Italians.'

Europeans.

As the number of deaths continued to surge, Sir Reginald implored Henry to display leadership. In the absence of any actual wars, he argued that a martial tone might demonstrate Henry's combative spirit.

'We face an implacable enemy, a powerful enemy but we are English,' Henry declaimed. 'We shall fight it in the cornfields of Kent and the green pastures of Wessex, on the stoolball pitches and in the taverns. We will fight as long as English blood flows in our veins and one day soon we will reach the sunlit uplands and be free of the tyranny of our foe.'

Sir Reginald sighed and called in the scriveners who were responsible for composing the court proclamations.

'Something short and sharp,' he said, 'after all, the majority of the population is illiterate.'

'Just say no!' offered a scrivener.

'Be alert!'

'Keep it buttoned!'

'No thanks – we're English!'

Sir Reginald was pleased; it was a most productive session. Proclamations warning against physical contact were issued and displayed on parish churches and halls throughout the realm. Town criers were briefed – 'Spread the word, not the pockes!' – and exhorted Londoners to use their "good old-fashioned English common sense".

The death toll continued to surge. Perhaps, they should have locked the gates, Sir Reginald reflected.

"What will happen to my economy? Henry moaned, as shops were forced to close, construction sites and dock yards lay idle and most importantly, untaxed.

'I fear this febrile atmosphere is proving an ideal breeding ground for dissidence, Your Majesty,' said Sir Reginald.

God had anointed Henry King of England, yet this pockes threatened his Divine Right to Rule. Was God punishing him?

'And news from Naples?' he said hopefully.

'Alas, no, Your Majesty.'

'What am I to do, man?'

'Perhaps we ought call a meeting of the King's Council.'

'Another one?' Henry snapped. 'Is that the best you can come up with?' His shoulders sagged. He sighed. 'Very well then.'

The full Council was hastily convened. Henry pulled himself together. He tightened his cock ring a notch and marched into the Painted Hall, his blood hot and his humours at a high pitch.

'I've got advisors coming out my arse,' Henry thundered, 'and people are dying in droves.'

No one was game to speak. Even the Archbishop, with god at his side, remained silent.

'Well?'

'Best leave this in the hands of experts,' said Sir Thomas smoothly. 'Put your faith in the medical profession, sire.'

'Given the number of dead, Sir Thomas, surely our faith is better placed with god,' said Sir John Morton.

'You have been promising us a cure for months, Metcalfe,' said Henry.

'Yes, sir. The cures have not been as effective as we had hoped, sir. But English physicians, English treatments remain the world's best.'

'I can't ask my subjects to stop fuc – '

'Fornicating, Your Majesty,' said Sir John.

'Fornicating.'

'Perhaps if they fuc – fornicated at a social distance,' said Sir Reginald.

Advisors.

'Our treatments *are* working, Your Majesty,' said Sir Thomas. 'But they take time.'

'Hundreds are dead, Metcalfe. Thousands are infected. And the numbers are growing daily.'

'We could all be doomsayers, sire, gloomsters,' said Sir Thomas, 'but look at how many are *not* infected. All down to English medicine.'

It was a glimmer of hope, Henry thought, something to hang his cap on.

'It is written in the stars,' said Zorima, not to be outdone. 'that when a man and a woman wish to consummate the act of Mars and Venus they must ensure that Saturn, that most mischievous companion is not present. However, Saturn has entered the sign of the water carrier while Jupiter rises in the sign of the archer.'

'What does that actually mean, Zorima?'

'It is as it is, sire,' said Zorima. 'And is as it should be. The godhead of the pure is the way of the true.'

'Oh, for Christ's sake.'

Like the Court Physician and the Court Astrologer, the Court Apothecary and the Court Herbalist were firmly of the mead-mug half-full school of thought.

'English apothecaries are the finest in all Europe,' declared the Court Apothecary.

'Our herbal cultivation and decoction manufacture are second to none,' said the Prior Warden.

'Sir John?'

'"You have walked the way of the kings of Israel and into whoredom,"' said Sir John.

'What was that?'

'Not you specifically, sire, your subjects. "Behold, the Lord will bring a great plague on your people and all your possessions, and you yourself" – again not being specific here – "will have a severe sickness with a disease of your bowels, until your bowels come out day by day".'

'A great plague?' said Henry, panicking.

'Disease is god's punishment for sin, sir.' Sir John Morton was not a man to change his mind. 'It is god's will. The scripture is quite clear on it.'

'The people are looking to blame someone,' said Henry, 'and I don't want it to be me. Can we blame god?'

'No, Your Majesty, that would never do. But, given you rule by god's divine grace it is understandable that many of your people question your divine right.'

'But I have the pope's support. The bull, man.'

'Bulls come, bulls go. What one pope giveth, the other taketh away.'

'If I may trespass on Sir John's domain,' said Bray. '"There is a season for every activity under the sun. A time to be born, a time to die. A time to embrace, a time to refrain, a time to scatter stones, a time to – "'

'It's not stones my subjects are scattering, Sir Reginald.'

Henry was paralysed by indecision. Lord Cumbria sat quietly, the ghost of a smile on his lips. He seized the moment.

'The people are restless.'

Four words which chilled Henry's heart. Might this pockes incite Henry's greatest fear, open rebellion?

'The people know that their health and safety are His Majesty's chief concern,' said Sir Reginald.

'The people know that the economy and their financial security are His Majesty's chief concern,' added Sir John.

'We must not live in fear, Your Majesty,' said Sir Thomas. 'We must learn to live with the disease.'

'Is that it?' said Henry. 'We do want to stop the disease spreading, correct?'

In truth many of the Councillors were torn. Sir John Morton had never seen his churches – and the collection plates – so full. Sir Thomas was also conflicted. It wasn't often he had queues of patients happy to fork out their guineas. Zorima could barely keep up with panicked clients seeking his soothsaying skills. Even Sir Reginald was conflicted. The dissident nobles, Margaret of Burgundy and James of Scotland was a formidable, if not formal, alliance.

They had the numbers to defeat Henry in open combat. Could this be the time to scatter his stones and jump ship?

Lord Cumbria left the meeting, buoyant of spirit, and met with his fellow dissidents.

'He shows no mettle,' he reported. 'He seeks to blame god.'

'The people question his very right to rule,' said Suffolk.

'Margaret and James are abreast of the situation,' said Devon.

'The time is ripe,' said Cumbria 'This pockes is a godsend. The king is dead!.'

'Long live the king!'

Bacon wasted another four days in the bordellos and tavernas. They had been in Naples more than a week and were no closer to solving the mystery. It was approaching nightfall and was a long walk back to Everson's villa. Tired and thirsty, Bacon saw welcoming lights and the sound of laughter. As soon as he entered he realised he shouldn't have. There were no women. Beautiful young men with a few older, clearly wealthy males. But the padrone's smile was welcoming and Bacon sat at the bar.

Just the one.

'Blanco, grazie.'

The padrone poured him a goblet of white wine. It was refreshingly sharp, cool, grassy in flavour. It slipped down easily. The padrone poured him another.

A young man sat down beside him. He was wide at the shoulder and slim at the hip. Olive skin and almond eyes; perfect lips and teeth revealed in a beautiful smile. A young Apollo. Or St Sebastian, perhaps.

'Ulisse.'

Or Ulysses.

Time to go.

'I'm Robert.'

Just the one more.

They ordered a carafe of wine and shared a classically Neapolitan dinner of pasta with a meat ragu followed by seafood and rice. The taverna provided upstairs rooms.

They undressed. Bacon hardly dared to look.

There were no ulcers, no sores nor rashes. No pockes.

'You have to stop working here, Ulisse. There is a plague in Naples.'

He kissed Bacon's hand and then his lips. Bacon fought his devils, but unlike his patron saint, St Robert of Molesme, the notoriously abstinent founder of the Cistercians, he quickly yielded.

'Are you all right, Sir Walter?' said Henry. 'You look a little peaky.'

'I enjoy splendid health, Your Majesty. All thanks to God's grace and of course your own bountiful favour.'

'Are you sure you don't want to sit down?'

'Quite sure, Your Majesty.'

Henry had still not warmed to Sir Rowland's replacement. It wasn't just his looks – no one in the realm could match Sir Rowland's fair countenance – Sir Walter also lacked his predecessor's boyish charm. The gloomy countenance wasn't entirely the poor knight's fault. His breastbone had been smashed in the Championship and a rib had pierced a lung. When he spoke he wheezed like a pipe organ with a punctured bellow. Sir Walter had also sustained a broken hip which the coffin cullies had been unable to mend and he hobbled about, reminding Henry of his predecessor Richard III.

'Call them in, sir knight.'

A cadre of nobles, emboldened by the divided and fearful state of the nation had petitioned the king to discuss "the Scottish problem" and the perennial and even graver worry, "bloody Europe", as the more polite dissidents called it. They were the usual lot: Cumbria, Suffolk and their chums. John Blanke's final alarum had barely died out when Lord Cumbria was on his feet. What had happened to the old Which Way, Henry wondered?

'Is it true,' Cumbria thundered, 'that Your Majesty still favours *peace* with France. That the lands his noble predecessors rightfully took, on which brave Englishmen shed their blood, will remain in foreign hands?'

'The time is not ripe for attacking France,' said Henry.

'And when will the time be ripe, Your Majesty?'

'That is for me to decide,' said Henry.

'Is Your Majesty aware that as we *talk*, as we *discuss* the *situation*, the French forces are planning to attack Genoa?'

'Aye, aye,' muttered the nobles.

'I am aware.'

'And if France should take Genoa, she will grow stronger and more wealthy, while we *cower* a mere seven leagues across the channel?'

'His Majesty has spoken. The time is not ripe for attacking France,' said Sir Reginald.

The mutters grew louder.

'And what about the Scottish, Your Majesty? More skirmishes on the border. And does not King James insult us, baring his hairy, red arse at us by protecting the pretender Warbeck?'

Henry knew Cumbria supported Warbeck, knew Cumbria would support him in a rebellion against Henry. And Cumbria knew Henry knew.

'The time is not ripe for attacking Scotland.'

Henry felt the hostility sweep across the table in waves.

'Would it be fair to say that Your Majesty is an *appeaser?*'

Henry the Appeaser. Nasty. The barb stung.

'Now that the Stannaries Exemption has been repealed,' said Sir Reginald, 'I am delighted to inform you that construction of a new fleet of warships will shortly begin. This will ensure that England remains one of, nay, *the* greatest nation in Europe.'

'Well, when are we going to use these bloody warships,' said Cumbria. 'When are we going to invade France?'

'If and when I judge it,' said Henry. 'You are dismissed.'

The nobles refused to rise.

'You would have me call my guards?'

Sir Walter snapped to arms, wheezing like a capsized bagpipe.

It was a stand-off. For a few moments, there was silence, neither side prepared to yield.

'Let it be known, Your Majesty,' said Cumbria finally, 'that your loyal servants will not allow mighty Albion to cringe before France any longer.'

He and his fellows rose, bowed and departed.

Cumbria's leadership shook Henry as much as his outburst. He took to his bed before supper, complaining of chest pains. Sir Thomas Metcalfe prescribed a mixture of mandrake, opium and red wine. Henry drank a jugful and ordered another but sleep would not come. According to Foxe, it was from this day that the ill-health which dogged Henry for the rest of his days took root.

'Where did you get to last night?'

'A few drinks. A meal. It was quite the walk from Veromo.'

Hardwick was puzzled. There was a spark in Bacon's eyes, a flush to his cheeks that he hadn't seen before. But he was lying and Hardwick was apprehensive. Hardwick's career didn't depend wholly on their mission's success but he believed that a rapid rise through the Westminster ranks was within his grasp. A knighthood. A country estate. A seat on the King's Council and ultimately his mentor's job – Privy Councillor. Lord Chamberlain. For the early attainment of these goals, he was dependent on his childhood friend.

Bacon and Hardwick were breakfasting on traditional Neapolitan "lobster tails" which had nothing to do with marine crustaceans but were pastry shells stuffed with savoury meats or sweetened cream.

'You look excited. What have you discovered?'

'Nothing new. The Italians are still blaming the French. The French are still blaming the Italians.'

Bacon returned to his room. He tried to plan the day's investigation but thoughts of Ulisse intruded. There was a tap on the door.

'Un visitatore,' said his elderly proprietaria.

A visitor? It was Ulisse. Bacon hauled him into his room, terrified that Hardwick might spot him.

Ulisse was just as beautiful in the daylight. There was an intelligence in his eyes and a personality that was free of artifice. Despite his fear of discovery, Bacon was delighted to see him.

'I want you to stop working at the bordello.'

Ulisse shook his head and began undressing.

'I cannot see you if you keep working there.'

Ulisse hauled him into bed.

Bacon's Italian was improving; his schoolboy Latin helped. Conversation was difficult but the eyes have it and their looks conveyed a multitude of meaning. There was no misunderstanding with the sex. There was an emotional depth which communicated more intensely, more truthfully than words and gestures.

'You don't understand the dangers – '

'Bacon?' Hardwick knocked on the door.

Bacon cupped Ulisse's mouth.

'Are you in there?'

Bacon waited for the receding footsteps. They dressed. Bacon offered him money but he refused. Bacon heard the proprietaria pottering around in the kitchen. They scurried along the hallway and into the street.

'Are you off, Bacon?'

The silence spoke louder than any words. Or actions. It seemed to go on forever.

'Are you going to introduce me to your friend?'

'Hardwick. Ulisse.'

'Delighted, Ulisse. Are you two planning some sort of odyssey for the day?'

'I'll continue my search.'

'Ulisse is helping with your enquiries?'

'Local knowledge.'

'Do not forget your duty to your king and country, Bacon. Business before pleasure. I look forward to your report this evening.'

Hardwick nodded politely to Ulisse and left.

Ulisse took Bacon by the arm and led him to a *piazza*. He sat Bacon at an eating-house and ordered a jug of water, honey and local spices.

'No, Ulisse. I really must get on.'

'Importante.'

He gestured for Bacon to wait.

'Very importante.'

He disappeared into a side-alley. Bacon saw French soldiers swagger into the square. They stopped and stared at him. Did he look that English? Bacon realised how vulnerable he was, a lone stranger in an occupied land. He was beginning to get nervous when a troupe of mummers appeared, masked and costumed. A crowd gathered. One performer portrayed a lecherous old miser; another a bullying but cowardly soldier and Bacon saw that Ulisse played a poor, young man, one of a pair of star-crossed lovers. Ulisse had poise and grace. He was talented, Bacon realised with something approaching pride. The troupe provoked laughter and applause and a hat was passed around. Bacon contributed, noting that there were plenty of coins in the hat. Business had not suffered under the French occupation. The French soldiers stared suspiciously at Bacon a final time then, bored, moved on.

Ulisse joined him.

'Come. Molto importante.'

Cumbria's star had never risen so high nor shone so brightly. His denunciation of Henry the Appeaser had brought him respect. His fellows had previously dismissed him as a loud but empty vessel; now they looked on him as their leader. The dissidents met secretly in a hunting lodge near St Albans.

'James stands by in Scotland and Margaret in Burgundy,' said Suffolk.

'Cornwall is on the verge of open rebellion because of the Stannaries Tax,' said Sir Richard Treloy, a Cornish noble, new to the cause, who was able to muster 3,000 of Cornwall's finest.

'And London is a hotbed of resentment because of the pockes,' said Devon.

'One of my agents tells me that the disease is spreading through Europe,' said Suffolk. 'That it may have originated in Naples.'

'And Henry wants to trade with them?' Cumbria spat. 'It's because of Henry that we are struck with this disease.'

'Probably not,' said Suffolk, 'but the people will believe us.'

'The time to strike is now,' said Devon. While this pockes sows fear.'

'We have 15,000 men at the ready,' said Suffolk. 'Plus Scotland and Burgundy.'

The die was cast. No Which Way for Cumbria now, no turning back. If the rebellion were successful, Perkin Warbeck would be king and Cumbria would hold lands and riches beyond his most extravagant dreams. Cumbria the Kingmaker! Then again, failure would mean death – on the battlefield or swinging from a rope, his entrails trailing in the wind. Would he live to see the birth of his son?

'Cumbria?'

'I say aye,' said Cumbria.

His fellows cheered.

Live or die, Cumbria thought, his son would be proud.

Business concluded the conspirators turned their attention to pleasure. They opened jugs of wine, ordered in food from an eating-house and a flourish of St Albans's choicest strumpets.

Cumbria's thoughts turned to his beautiful young wife. He wavered.

'Are you sure that's wise,' he said. 'The pockes and all that?'

'Why do you think we chose St Albans?' said Suffolk. 'The pockes has barely reached here.'

'My father died in the mud and blood at Agincourt that his son had the right to fuck who and when he pleases,' said Devon.

Try as he might, he could not dismiss thoughts of his Lady Cumbria, lying abed, her belly gently swelling with his young son.

'What is wrong with you, Cumbria?'

'Show us what you're made of.'

'Be a man.'

'Who is it from?' said Henry.

'Hardwick, sir.'

'Who's he again?'

Sir Reginald reminded him.

'It's in the balance, sir,' said Bray, précising Hardwick's report. 'Charles is listening to the pope but French troops in Naples are openly bragging of an attack on Genoa.'

'What then? Pisa? Siena?'

'Hardwick believes he has bigger fish to fry.'

'Florence?'

'The wealthiest city in all Europe, sir.'

'Do the dissidents know of this? I suppose they're meeting. Planning. Plotting.'

'My agent reports that they've met in Hertfordshire, sir. Somewhere near St Albans.'

Henry groaned.

'Regrettably, it gets worse, sir. Charles has made overtures to da Vinci, inviting him to Paris.'

'Da Vinci? The painter?'

'Charles does fancy himself as an art lover. But no, da Vinci calls himself a *scientium*. He has designed a range of sophisticated weapons and it is in this capacity that Charles wishes to consult him.'

'Weapons? What sort of weapons?'

'Details are sketchy, sire, but weapons capable of massive destruction.'

'Any chance of inviting da Vinci to London?'

'I doubt it, sir. Cesare Borgia has his eye on these weapons too, we believe.'

'Cesare Borgia's a madman.'

There was a brief silence as both men contemplated the consequences of weapons of massive destruction in the hands of a madman.

'If Charles teams up with Borgia and they're mad enough to go to war with the Holy League, all Europe will be at war.'

'Unless Charles backs down,' said Bray.

'Is there any good news?' said Henry despairingly. 'What of the plague?'

'The pockes, sir. And no, sir, numbers continue to rise. No good news there.'

Henry dismissed his Lord Chamberlain and wandered downstairs to Court Accounts, known around the Palace as the Counting House.

'Hello, Dunne. Mind if I spend some time with you?'

'A pleasure and an honour, Your Majesty,' said Dunne. 'Care to look at a few ledgers, sir?'

'I would enjoy that, Dunne. Thank you.'

Dunne retrieved the latest accounts from their file and handed them to Henry.

'Look at that, will you, Dunne? Symmetry and balance. These figures speak to me. They have metre. Ten/pounds four/shill/ings and six/pence. Bugger Chaucer. This is poetry!'

Henry whiled an uplifting couple of hours in the counting-house before retiring to his chambers. The fears resurfaced. He had difficulty breathing and was struck with a crippling stomach ache. He called for Sir Thomas Metcalfe.

The physician shook his head.

'We'll have to bleed you, sire.'

Henry's heart sank. He hated leeches.

'Fine little bleeders, these, sire. Thoroughbreds. Two shillings and two pence a gross!'

'Is it absolutely necessary?'

'Your humours, sir. Completely unbalanced. Surplus of phlegm, yellow and black bile.'

'Which leaves blood.'

'Correct, sir.'

'So why the fuck are you bleeding me?'

'It's bad blood, sir.'

'Is there anything good left in me?'
'I'm sure we'll find something, sir.'

'Vieni con me.'
Ulisse took him by the hand and led him to a humble cottage. Try as he might Bacon felt uncomfortable with the hand-holding and cheek-kissing between Italian males. Thankfully, it would never catch on in England.

'This is Baptista.'

He had been one of the mummers. No more. It was a severe case. Paralysis had set in and he was confined to bed. Sores and pockes covered his body. Less than two months since he first noticed the ulcer, he said.

'Have you and Baptista – ?'

'No. He prefers women.'

Bacon suppressed a sigh of relief.

'Can you help him, Roberto?'

Bacon had collected a number of samples from the priories and apothecaries. It was little more than educated guesswork but he thought he could decide on the most effective. He rubbed the theriac on Baptiste's body and wasting limbs and dispatched Ulisse to the Capuchins for a fresh supply.

'Do you know how you became infected?'

Baptista's speech was laborious. No, he did not. He was a travelling mummer and had had a hectic social life; a girl in every village. How many had he infected, Bacon wondered. And how many had they infected?

'Prostituta?'

'No!' he said with what remained of his pride. 'How long before I am cured?'

'There is no cure, Baptista. Theriac and mercury – '

'Prayer, Roberto. I pray to Santa Nichola.'

He held up the scapula he wore. It was enscribed with a brief prayer to the saint.

'I doubt that prayer – '

'Si, si. A viaggiatore gave it to me.'

'A traveller? A camp follower for the French army?'
'Si. She had the disease but she cured herself.'
'A charlatan, Baptista.'
'She had pockes. Tiny pockes. But nothing else.'
'Was she Italian? French?'
'Spanish.'
Bacon's heart sank. Where was this disease leading him? It seemed to have an intelligence, it seemed to be playing with him. Would he have to journey to Spain? Hope did not spring eternal in Bacon's sinking heart; he was down to his last drops.
'Who is this viaggiatore? What's her name?'
'Mencia.'

Henry sat morosely in the Painted Chamber. Not even John Blanke's catchy alarum lifted his gloom.
'Fr Giovanni di Carb ... Carbonara,' Sir Walter wheezed.
Bloody marvellous. No good news ever came from Rome.
'What does he want?' said Henry.
'He is anxious to gain the See of Bath and Wells.'
'Any progress?'
'It's a lengthy process, sir.'
'Good.'
'And Captain John Cabot,' said Sir Walter.
'Who's he?'
'I've no idea, sir,' said Bray.
'He looks like a bloody Italian.'
Cabot was an Italian. It was an unusual practice peculiar to the times, whereby individuals were known by different names in different countries. He was born Guiseppe Caboto in Genoa but was known as Zhuan Chabotto in Venice and John Henry Cabot in Bristol.
'The Holy Father sends his warmest regards and a special blessing, Your Majesty,' said Fr de Carbonariis.
'Tell, Alexander, thank you very much and our very best in return.'
'I shall, Your Majesty.'

Bray saw that Henry was already losing concentration.

'How can we help you, father?'

'How can we help each other, Sir Reginald?'

'Indeed. How can we?'

'May I introduce Captain Cabot. He is preparing an expedition to the New World.'

This caught Henry's wavering attention.

'And he requires sponsorship.'

'For an expedition?' said Henry. 'To the New World?'

'But the Holy Father has granted Spain sovereignty over the New World,' said Sir Reginald.

Cabot spoke in Italian which de Carbonariis translated.

'Spanish sovereignty extends only to lands already discovered and claimed,' said the priest. 'Captain Cabot is convinced there are more lands, vast lands to the north and the south. He also believes there is an alternative route to the east in the north-west of the New World, a north-west passage if you will.'

This had Henry and Bray listening. New lands and a quick route to India. And China. It would be far easier – and cheaper – claiming land than taking it through war.

'An intriguing proposition,' said Bray. 'What do you need?'

'A fleet of five fully-outfitted ships with as many men as required. Should Your Majesty invest, the fleet will sail under the English flag. The expedition will be charged with sailing, finding, discovering and investigating whatsoever islands, countries, regions or provinces of heathens and infidels, in whatsoever part of the world they be placed, which before this time were unknown to all Christians.'

Bray was impressed; Cabot had some pretty nimble lawyers working for him.

'All commerce resulting from your discoveries must be conducted with England alone,' said Sir Reginald who fancied himself as agile as any Roman avvocato.

'Of course.'

'And all goods will have to be brought to England.'

'Certainly.'

'Who else have you approached regarding sponsorship?'

'His Royal Highness, King Joao has expressed interest.'

Portugal. Henry clenched his jaw. Joao the bloody Perfect.

'And Doge Barbarino is likewise keen to invest.'

Duke Augustino Barbarino. The Lion of Venice.

'I have secured initial investment from the Florentine banks,' said Carbonariis.

That would be the Medicis, thought Henry. With their poncey bloody art and sculpture and music.

'But you need a Royal Patent,' said Bray.

'As you say, Sir Reginald.'

The Royal Letters Patent authorised the bearer to claim land in the name of a royal signatory – who, of course, ruled by Divine Right. The Royal Letters patent was as good as a hand-written note from god himself.

'We will need time to consider your proposal,' said Bray.

'Of course. Have you had time to consider our, er, other little matter?'

'Well in hand, Giovanni. All going according to plan.'

'Which plan is?'

'I have issued invitations to sit on the standing committee, the members of which will, of course, be making recommendations on the composition of the select committee. I anticipate the invitations will, in the fullness of time, be accepted.'

'So we are on the first step, Sir Reginald?'

'The first step. But a very large step, Giovanni.'

'And how long before we reach the final step?'

'Aaah, that would be god's will, Giovanni.'

Always useful to invoke God, thought Sir Reginald. If nothing else God had a very safe pair of hands.

'I see.'

The obsequies observed, Cabot and de Carbonariis departed.

'Well?' said Henry.

'I advise caution, Your Majesty,' said Bray. 'The Holy Father may not be pleased and Spain certainly won't. On the other hand, we are violating no treaties. The undiscovered regions of the New World may be greater, may be more bountiful than those discovered. And a quick route to India to boot!'

'And China,' said Henry. Visions of coffers overflowing with gold flashed before his eyes. Forget the Westminster redesign, the counting-house would need a total renovation!

'Free trade with the New World. India. China. The world!' Henry enthused. 'We could stay out of Europe. Let them fight amongst themselves.'

'No,' Bray insisted. 'Caution, sire. Europe remains our major trading partner – for the present.'

It made sense. With a bulging Exchequer and a decent chunk of the New World, Olde England would soon be back on top of the table again. Wheels spun furiously in Henry's mind. Cyrus the Mighty. Suleiman the Magnificent. Alexander the Great ... An English Empire which stretched east and west, from one side of god's flat earth to the other. An empire on which the sun would never set. That would put the French and Italians and Germans and Swiss in the shade. Henry the ...? Henry the Greatest? That'd show Joao Perfect and Il Doge the bloody Lion. And of course, Charles.

'We'll do it.'

'First things first, sir. The dissidents.'

'Brief me again.'

'Cumbria has assumed the mantle of leadership. He has 4000 men standing by.'

'Arrest him. Execute him. tell the executioner to disembowel the bastard first.'

'The 4000 men might be soldiers manqué but they are gainfully employed on Lord Cumbia's estates. It would send the wrong message to the other nobles, sir. They'll be, literally, up in arms.'

'So, we sit around while Cumbria and Suffolk and the others raise armies against me?'

'I think this latest news may stop them in their tracks, sire.'

Cumbria returned to his vast estates to ready his men. He had refused to pay the 5000 sovereigns. It was illegal to maintain an army as Cumbria well knew but he had circumvented the law in the time-honoured way by arming his labourers, estate workers and anyone vaguely associated with his lands; even his valet and footmen were skilled with halberd and mace. His militia numbered nearly 4000 men and he had sent word to James IV and Margaret of Burgundy that he and his allies were standing by, ready for war.

The Lady Cumbria's pregnancy was progressing well. The morning sickness had passed. Cumbria was not cast from Sir Rowland's blond and peachy mould. His hair was thinning, and sandy in colour, his complexion the rufous side of ruddy. A *real* Englishman. He had sired four daughters by his first wife but daughters didn't count. They cost a fortune in dowries unless they married upwards or at least sideways. But they were cast in their father's sandy, ruddy image and he had duly paid up on the dowries. Two remained unmarried and they were sure to cost him another small fortune.

Lady Cumbria was carrying low; her hair was lustrous, and she was craving pickles and relishes – all sure signs the child was a male. A son was different. A son represented a future. Cumbria again wondered if he should cast his lot with Henry. It would mean stability and security for his boy. If it came to open rebellion and the dissidents lost, Henry would attaind his lands and his son would be left with nothing. Yet again Which Way Cumbria wavered – and the battle lines had yet to be drawn.

When the messenger arrived, summoning him to yet another meeting of the King's Council, he was not warmly welcomed. Presumably, Henry wanted his 5000 sovereigns. He briefly thought about refusing to go. He couldn't use his wife's pregnancy as an excuse; what would the men on the Council say to that? He kissed his wife tenderly goodbye. By God she was looking beautiful, Madonna-like, despite the less than immaculate conception. He wished he could remember it; he must have been very drunk.

L ondoners are a resilient lot. Once they understood the cause of the pockes, once the fear of the unknown had gone, those that had left the city drifted back and those that had left their jobs returned to work. Many Londoners had become sick from the pockes, but many more had grown sick of it. Barrie Vagg no longer featured reports in his cries. Warnings on parish notice boards went unread, and, torn and tattered, they added to the detritus littering London streets.

The St Stephen's tower bells tolled five o'clock. Heckstall had never been to Westminster Palace but he soon found his way to the Court Physician's chambers. Sir Thomas was inclined to refuse the surgeon's request for an audience but curiosity got the better of him.

'What do you want, man? Get on with it.'

'I come offering an olive branch, Sir Thomas. I am sorry for my colleague's forthrightness. I am aware his manner can be abrupt. However, it has never been the surgeons' intentions to threaten or usurp the physicians' pre-eminent position. Physicians diagnose, surgeons treat. That is how it should be. Surgeons and physicians must work together. For the benefit of our patients.'

'Yes, yes, of course, our patients. Their welfare must come, er, first.'

Metcalfe was mollified by Heckstall's charm as much as his words. More than this he didn't like to get his hands dirty – literally in the case of the pockes with its ulcers and pustules.

The men shook hands and peace was restored to the medical profession.

Heckstall found his way to the Chief Minister's chambers. Sir Reginald was in a contemplative mood. Henry's health was declining; his spirits failing. Likewise, Sir Reginald's influence was declining. Henry was increasingly turning toward the Church for spiritual nourishment which meant Sir John Morton's influence was rising. Sir Reginald was depending on Bacon and Hardwick to find a cure, to sound a rescuing bugle call from across the sea but he hadn't heard from Hardwick in weeks and had no idea where they were or what they may have discovered. Heckstall's arrival was timely.

'The Buckinghamshire Heckstalls?'

'Yes, sir.'

'Wrong side of the bed. Buckingham supported Richard at Bosworth. Still, young Buckingham is proving loyal to Henry. But I'm sure you know all that. You are one of the surgeons at Bacon's clinicum, correct?'

'I am.'

'Have you heard from your colleague?'

'No, Sir Reginald.'

'Oh,' said Sir Reginald, his hopes dashed. 'Well, what have you got to report, man? Get on with it.'

For a man who had developed a whole new and lengthy form of official-speak and whose reports at Council and speeches in the Lords had broken all records Sir Reginald Bray demanded concision from others.

'The numbers continue to rise, sir. I fear our message is not getting through.'

Given that the message was largely composed by Bray and his scriveners this effectively meant it was his message.

'Are we looking at another plague, Heckstall?'

'Unless a cure is found, we must face that possibility.'

Which would be manna for the dissidents. Not bad for Morton and the Church, as the people increasingly turned to God. A disaster for Bray, the Chief Minister and advisor.

'Funny thing numbers,' said Sir Reginald. 'They can be interpreted in so many ways.'

'That is true, Sir Reginald.'

'At first sight, these numbers are appalling, but one can be optimistic ... can't one?'

'Yes, well... the number of infections is rising rapidly. Relatively speaking, however, the number of deaths is low.'

'Aaah! Relative to what?'

'The plague, Sir Reginald. Death occurred very quickly from the plague. Death from the pockes is sometimes very slow – '

'Aaah!'

' – and sometimes not at all.'

'So, you can, er, adjust these figures to reflect this uncertainty?'

'I can, Sir Reginald.'

'And this brilliant medical strategy is all down to England's wonderful medical practitioner and his advisors?'

'Indeed, Sir Reginald. His Majesty's Chief Minister has been most supportive.'

'Splendid!'

'One small matter, Sir Reginald. It has come to my attention that there is no position of Court Surgeon.'

'An oversight, my dear Heckstall.'

'The position would come with a knighthood, would it not?'

'Indeed it would.'

Bray duly reported to Henry.

'It would appear, sir, that my strategies, going forward have delivered the desired, indeed optimum result. Case figures have plateaued, sir, and deaths have begun to decline. Whilst we must err on the side of caution we may, without being unduly precipitate declare victory over a formidable foe and ask Mr Blanke to sound a celebratory alarum.'

Henry's spirits lifted; finally, it seemed, luck was running his way.

'That's one for good old English common sense, eh?'

'It played its part, sir.'

'Call in the nobles, Sir Walter. Sound an alarum, Mr Blanke. Can you lend it "a fuck to you" note?'

The nobles were duly announced.

'Play it again, Mr Blanke?'

Henry's ears were as solidly tin as any Cornish stannary, but he listened appreciatively.

Cumbria didn't like Henry's cheerful look nor the sound of John Blanke's aggressive alarum.

'I have brought you in today, gentlemen, to include you all in plans for our – what did Barabbas call it?'

'This sceptr'd isle, this other Eden, this fortress built for herself against the hand of war, this silver stone set – '

'Thank you, Sir Reginald. Can you inform the nobles of our progress?'

'Construction has begun on seven warships with a further twenty-four planned. Thirty-one warships within twenty years. That is our promise. The finest navy in the world, my lords.'

All eyes turned toward Cumbria.

'While you are shipbuilding our oldest enemies grow stronger and wealthier by the day,' said Cumbria.

'I have broader horizons than our northern borders, my lords,' said Henry. 'An expansionist view that sees further than Brittany and the Clyde. What say you to an English empire where the sun never sets? An empire stretching west to the New World and east through India, yea, unbroken to China?'

That shut the bastards up.

'I am in the process of issuing letters patent to Captain John Cabot to sail west, to explore and claim land in the New World and to find the north-west passage to India. What say you, my Lord Cumbria? My Lord Suffolk?'

The nobles were speechless.

'Oh, and we've beaten the pockes. Listen, my lords, can you hear that?'

There was nothing to be heard, save for Sir Walter's wheezings.

'That is not Mr Blanke's trumpet. It is our buglers sounding the charge! The great pockes is in retreat!'

Henry waved the report documenting Heckstall's revised figures as evidence. It was a subdued, indeed craven banner of knights that trooped from the Painted Chamber, farewelled by an eructative arpeggio from Blanke's trumpet. The celebrations in a local eating house were almost requiem. As night fell, Cumbria excused himself, having to prepare for the long ride north. He retired to his room with a cleaving headache.

'**L**aissez moi partir! Unhand me.'

THE GREAT POCKES

Both soldiers wore falchions on one hip and daggers on the other. Bacon could smell the wine on their breath, but both were battle-hardened soldiers and needed nothing more than brute force and a pole-axing blow to the solar plexus to subdue him. Bacon saw the ulcers ringing one of the soldier's mouth. They half-carried, half-dragged him to the French garrison which was housed in the Castel Saint Elmo, and brought him before the garrison commander, Capitaine Leconte.

'What is your business in Naples, monsieur – '

'Bacon.'

'Monsieur Jambon?' guffawed Leconte. The soldiers chuckled at their commander's sally.

'I am visiting Naples with my friend, an envoy on an official trade mission for the English government.'

'An "envoy", eh? On an "official trade mission"?' The soldiers chuckled again. 'I thought your "friend" was a street performer.'

They'd been following him.

'I am an English citizen and I have papers to prove it.'

'You are an English spy and I will have you executed.'

'I am not a spy.'

'You have entered a war zone, M. Jambon, and your execution will have no repercussions.'

'I repeat – I am not a spy. I am a surgeon.'

'Why does a surgeon visit Naples?'

'I studied at Bologna. I am revisiting the country for pleasure.'

'And I am detaining you at my pleasure, sir. Take him down.'

Lady Cumbria lay abed. She had endured seven months with child. She had considered telling her husband the truth but her courage failed her every time. Blanke was the first black man she had ever seen let alone Sir Rogered, and she had no idea what to expect. One of the estate's golden mastiff bitches had been served by a black male and the offspring had emerged either fully black or fully golden. Cumbria's calves, on the other hand, came out a mixture of spots and splotches. Would she be lucky and bear a white child? Or a black child? Could her child – god forbid – emerge in some combination of white and black? Spots? Splotches? Lady Cumbria had seen no precedent and simply had no idea.

Cumbria entered her chamber, bearing a mug of spiced and watered wine.

'You have never looked lovelier, my dear,' he said, kissing her fair hand. Not for the first time of late Lady Cumbria noticed the gentler, more considerate side of his nature which had remained dormant through the loveless years of their marriage. He was so chuffed, so boyishly excited by the impending birth. Again she thought of confessing and this time her courage didn't fail her; her heart did. Cumbria cleared his throat self-consciously and looked embarrassed. He took a sheet of parchment from his pocket.

'What is this?' she said.

'Doubt thou the stars are afire?'

he began hesitantly.

'Doubt that the sun doth move?

Doubt truth to be a liar

But never doubt that I love thee.'

'Oh, Cumbria.'

'A bit soft?'

'Never. Did you write it yourself?'

Cumbria thought about claiming the credit, but there comes a time when a man – even Cumbria – must peer into his soul, and hope to find truth.

'Well, no. I slipped Barabbas a shilling and he knocked it off for me.'

Cumbria had already commissioned scaled-to-size bows and arrows, a halberd and a mace for his unborn son. There was much to look forward to. He would get this fatherhood right second time around. He kissed his wife once more and retired to his library. The walls were lined with books. He'd glanced at the few that had pictures but had never read a word. He took a volume from the shelf. No wonder he hadn't read it; it was written in some foreign language. French? Latin? He removed the letter he had received from Suffolk which he had hidden in its pages.

Liverpool, Manchester and Hull, the cinque ports had been devastated by the pockes. Likewise Bristol. Given Henry's crown was won on the battlefield, the notion of "divine right to rule" had become openly challenged, especially in the badly-hit north.

'If yon Tudor fook is so fookin' divine why can't he cure fookin' pockes?' became a constant refrain in northern alehouses.

But it was the taxes that fanned the flames of rebellion. Henry couldn't help himself. He was building the finest navy in the world and he was mounting an expedition to the New World. Yet again, the thought of depleting his counting-house coffers had unnerved him and he instigated tax rises to pay for his plans. As always, the poorer north had borne the greater burden. The west country had also been badly hit by the hikes, and Cornish resentment against the Stannaries Tax had festered into outright hostility. "Always bloody London to get off lightly" had been the common complaint. Up in Scotland, James was aware of these developments and had sent word south that he was prepared for war.

Cumbria scratched at the rash that had developed on his torso. When he first discovered the ulcers, he dispatched his valet to that clinicum on Cheapside. The man had returned with theriac and a mercury friction. Cumbria knew the dangers of mercury but he was determined to live to see his son. He rubbed the friction on his body. He gazed out his window. Sheep, fat with offspring grazed on his green pastures. Lovely creatures, sheep. He wondered why he'd never noticed before.

T he gaoler unlocked the prison door.

'Venez,' he grunted.
'Where are you taking me?'

'La potence,' the gaoler chuckled.

The gallows.

The guards dragged him to a room which was bare save for a crucifix which hung from the wall. Commander Leconte sat at a table, a carafe of wine and glasses before him.

'Care for a mug?' said Leconte.

'No last meal?'

'We haven't got to that. Yet. You are a spy. We both know it. My soldiers report that you are taking a great interest in la maladie italienne – '

'Or la malattia francese.'

Perhaps he shouldn't have said that.

'I have received word that you have an outbreak in England,' said Leconte, forcing a smile. 'Perhaps the disease originated in England. Perhaps you English have deliberately infected French soldiers as an act of war.'

'The disease was introduced to England by a lascar who caught the disease here in Naples. From a French soldier, perhaps. And now you are preparing to march on Genoa and you and your Swiss and Spanish mercenaries are going to take the disease and spread it throughout Europe. You will probably kill more innocent people fucking than you do with your weapons.'

He definitely shouldn't have said that.

'We have spoken to your "special friend",' said Leconte.

Ulisse.

'Aaah, l'amour. L'amour improper, you might say.'

'He has nothing to do with – '

'Your "trade mission"? Oh, we know you are here to investigate French soldiers. That you believe the disease originated in France. That you blame us. That you are a spy.'

'No!'

'Your friend showed resistance. Perhaps he truly loved you. But there is only so much pain a man can endure.'

'No.' Bacon's pain was as intense as any torture.

'Preparez la potence.'

B

acon regretted his outburst almost immediately. Of course the French would not want it known that they had brought the disease to Naples. Of course they would not want it known they were about to spread it throughout Europe. Of course they were going to execute him. His eye fell on the crucifix. He crossed himself and offered a prayer to the god he wasn't sure he believed in. The door opened.

'Hardwick?'

'We have to leave. Immediately.'

'How did you find me?'

'Everson tried the diplomatic approach which failed.'

'How much?'

'A silver ducato. Come.'

'Nice to know my life's worth, what? A shilling sixpence?'

'It'll be worth the length of a rope if we don't hurry.'

They scurried along a corridor and through a dry stores room. Another corridor and then through the armoury.

'Do you think we should – ' said Bacon, eyeing the weaponry.

'Do you really think we can fight off an entire garrison? This way.'

They came to an oak door. The key was in the lock.

'That's lucky.'

'It's expensive, luck. Your whereabouts cost a silver ducato. The luck cost a hundred gold florins.'

'Worth it, I trust?'

'The florins did not buy your life. They bought but five minutes of it. We must hurry.'

Hardwick unlocked the door and they clambered down the stairs beyond. They hurried through the powder magazine and across a cellar which led to an unlocked gate and thence into an alleyway.

'Our things?'

'They've been collected. They await us at the docks.'

They paused in the alley as a pair of French soldiers passed. They emerged onto the street.

'No. We're going the wrong way.'

'The docks are this way, Bacon.'

'I've found Mencia.'

'A fuck to Mencia. We have to leave. Now.'

'She may have the cure, Hardwick. I have to go.'

'And a fuck to you, Bacon.' Hardwick saw his seat on the Privy Council and the Chancellor's black velvet cap drift disappear before his eyes. 'Oh, all right. Where are we going?'

'Soccavo.'

'Which is where?'

They made their way by back lanes and alleys toward Camaldoli mountain beyond and to the west of the city.

The viaggiatori had set up a camp comprising thirty or so tents pitched in a field at the foot of the mountain. Women sat alone or in small groups outside their tents. Pots of soup or stew simmered on open fires. Several of the women bore rashes on their arms. One or two had sores ringing their mouths. A French soldier emerged from a tent, buckling his belt, drunk, and aggressively arguing with one of the women, who was naked from the waist down.

A viaggiatore pointed them to a woman who was hanging bedclothes on lines strung between a pair of poles.

'Mencia?' said Bacon.

'Si.'

'We have come from London. A sailor, a lascar, brought a disease to England. I believe you knew him.'

She led them into her tent and offered them wine. A baby slept in a crib. Conversation was difficult. Mencia was Andalucian and knew little English but they managed to make themselves understood.

'Your child is healthy?' said Bacon.

'Si. Praise to god.'

She sat on a paillasse which served as a bed. The Englishmen sat on cushions on the floor. After contracting the disease, she had taken it as a warning from God and abandoned her life as a prostitute. She returned to her religion and eked out a living laundering sheets and clothes and running errands for the other prostitutes and the French soldiers.

'When did you become ill, Mencia?'

'Six months ago.'

The earliest case.

'May I examine you?'

Mencia's symptoms had indeed cleared; a few pockes were all that remained.

'You've recovered well, Mencia.'

'Si.'

'Tell me about the lascar.'

'He was a client and then my lover.'

Gender was of little importance to the lascar.

'Did he recover?'

Bacon shook his head.

'He had an ointment. An ungüento.'

'Si. Gaiac. There was very little left. Only a smear. But he stole it from me, God forgive him.'

'Gaiac? Do you have any more?'

'No.'

'Do you know who infected you, Mencia?'

'Yes, sir. I know exactly who gave it to me.'

Bacon and Hardwick evaded the French patrols, returning by the same circuitous route, and thence to the docks.

'That's ours,' said Hardwick, indicating a Portuguese carrack. 'It's leased to the Merchant Adventurers and bound for London. Our things are stowed.'

'We have to see the captain,' said Bacon. 'We must go to Spain.'

'No, Bacon. We've found the origin of the disease. We've found a possible cure. Our mission is accomplished.'

'We need proof, Hardwick. I will go alone if I must.'

Navvies were loading the cargo. Hardwick scanned the docks for French soldiers.

'Can we disembark in Spain?' Bacon asked the captain.

'No stops,' said the captain. 'We sail direct for London.'

'We are on a mission from the king himself.'

'Yes, yes, of course you are.'

'Hardwick? The papers, if you please.'

Hardwick handed the captain Sir Reginald's letter of introduction. The captain cursed under his breath.

'Whereabouts in Spain?'

'Palos de la Frontera.'

'I'll drop you at Cadiz. Thirty sovereigns.'

'That's outrageous,' said Hardwick.

'Each.'

'You'd better be right about this, Bacon.'

Hardwick didn't have sixty sovereigns. He would have to write a promissory note and good luck getting your sixty sovs out of Dunne, he thought maliciously.

'Away!' the captain shouted.

'Away!' called the mate.

'Un momento!'

Bacon saw a young priest hurry up the gangplanks and converse with the captain.

'I'll see what's going on.' Hardwick joined the priest and the captain then returned to Bacon.

'He's an emissary from the pope.'

'Look,' said Bacon, pointing to a French patrol led by Leconte and heading their way.

'Will you please cast off?' Hardwick shouted. The captain ignored him. Bacon saw the priest pass him coins.

'Would you hand over your countrymen to the French?' Hardwick screamed at the captain who saw the Frenchmen a hundred yards from his ship and coming fast.

'Away!' cried the captain.

'Away!' called the mate.

The moorings were hauled, the boarding planks heaved in and the ship, aroused from its slumber like some ancient Kraken, lumbered from the dock.

The Englishmen watched Naples slowly recede.

'No change?'

'No change, Sir Reginald.'

No change was, in itself a change.

'The number of infections and deaths continue to rise but I can say with confidence that the *rate* of both infection and deaths are decreasing,' said Heckstall. 'That's what my figures suggest.'

'You're very good with figures, Heckstall. Marvellous news.'

'Complacency remains our biggest enemy. Should the people relax, should complacency replace good old English common sense physical contact may resume and there could be a second wave of infections.'

'We shall bear that in mind. Anything else?'

Heckstall hesitated briefly. He had argued the matter with himself but neither Hippocrates nor Galen had mentioned it. His surgery was not the confessional, after all.

'One more thing. We received a visit from Lord Cumbria.'

'Seeking what?'

'Theriac and mercury friction.'

'Aaaahh.'

'Indeed.'

'Bad case?'

'Very bad.'

Sir Reginald was thrilled at the good news and just as – almost as – important, he had beaten Sir John to the punch. He requested an audience with Henry before the good news inevitably leaked. The king had taken to his bed with a racing heart and congestion to his lungs. (Bad blood and excess of phlegm, according to Metcalfe who added corn silk and crushed cranberry to the tray of concoctions on Henry's bedside drawers.)

'The numbers of afflicted are tumbling, sir. The economy is back on track. Our foe is vanquished. '

'Beat the drums? Sound the victory bugle?'

'Indeed, sir.'

Henry felt the congestion in his chest ease slightly.

'Oh, and Cumbria has fallen to the pockes.'

'Dead?'

'Not yet. But I suspect the rebellion will fall apart without their leader.'

Henry should have been happy at the downfall of his foe, but he was sick at heart and sick of body and wearied by the pockes and a monarch's duty. And even though it took a good while for Which Way to make up his mind, he had, after all, been with him at Bosworth.

'Check with Cheffie to see if we have any grapes, Bray. The purple ones, preferably.'

'I shall, sir. According to Zorima, good tidings arrive in threes.'

'Let's hope it's not long.'

It wasn't. A missive arrived from Naples before nightfall.

'You've got to hand it to Zorima, sir,' said Sir Reginald. 'Not so great on the weather. Nor romance, come to think of it. But we have news from Naples.'

'Yes?'

'Hardwick says he has traced the origin of the disease.'

'Naples?'

'Presumably so. It took four weeks for this to arrive.'

'So the *Euros* have infected *us*?'

'Amusingly, sir, the French are blaming the Italians. And the Italians are blaming the French.'

'Excellent. There'll be a knighthood for that young man.'

'Hardwick also believes he has found a promising treatment which he is trying to source.'

'Grant the man an estate! Shroppy's up for grabs, isn't it?'

Things *were* looking up. For the first time in weeks, Henry chuckled. He felt the phlegm dissipate from his lungs. He felt the bile leech from his blood as it coursed through his veins.

'How will this affect our trade agreements?'

'Favourably, sir. If the Europeans are responsible for this disease I'm sure we can renegotiate our existing agreements on more suitable terms.'

The most accurate intelligence network in Naples comprised the local parish priests. Within hours of arriving in Naples, Fr Giovanni Medici's agents had informed him of Bacon's tour of the local bordellos and his visit to the viaggiatori.

He sat in the rude tent which had been vacated by Bacon and Hardwick only minutes earlier.

'Will you bless my child, father?'

Medici's love fell short of the Franciscan ideal when it came to children; babies in particular. The infant bawled through the entire, if abbreviated, ceremony.

'And will you hear my confession?'

Medici was no pastoralist but his holy vows prevented refusal. It was a lengthy confession and Medici pronounced an even lengthier penance.

'The Englishmen? What did they want?'

'They seek the origin of the disease.'

'And they thought you might tell them,' said Medici with barely concealed sarcasm.

'I did, father.'

At first, Medici thought she was joking. Then he realised she wasn't.

'The disease is god's punishment for sin.'

'I know, father. But there is a cure and the Englishmen seek it.'

'Have they found it?'

'They know where to look.'

'Which is where, my child?'

His interview completed, Medici spurred the donkey he had borrowed from one of his informants and headed for the docks.

A cabin boy served jamon and manchego cheese with soft Spanish bread and olives and a red wine from Jerez called tintilla.

'The finest Iberian jamon,' said the captain, 'comes from the Dehesa plains. Pata negra pigs fattened on the acorns from the encina trees.'

It was very good.

Hardwick and Bacon had been invited to dine with the captain and the priest.

'What brings a pair of Englishmen to Cadiz?' Fr Medici enquired.

'I'm a trade envoy looking for new goods to market in London,' said Hardwick.

'And you, Mr Bacon?'

'I'm riding along on my old friend's coattails, taking in the sights.'

'But surely that is a medical bag you carry with you.'

Bacon had earlier treated a sailor who had fractured his arm, after falling from the rigging.

'I am a surgeon.'

'Did you find anything interesting, medically speaking, in Naples?'

Bacon knew it was pointless, suspicious even, lying.

'La maladie italienne. Or la malattia francese. Whichever you prefer.'

'And has this terrible disease reached England?'

Bacon sensed the priest knew the answer despite his show of unworldliness.

'It has.'

'Perhaps you will find a cure.'

'Perhaps you can tell me where to look, father.'

'That is beyond my knowledge.'

'Do you believe that the disease is a punishment from God, father?' said Hardwick.

'With all my heart.'

'The disease may be heaven-sent, father, but its origins lay somewhere on earth,' said Bacon.

'Again, that is beyond my humble learning.'

'Captain, we have been twenty-four hours at anchor,' said Hardwick. 'I can see Cadiz from the quarterdeck. When will we be landing?'

'As soon as I am given permission, Mr Hardwick.'

A four-oar vessel heaved portside of the caravelle the next morning. Hardwick saw a Spanish customs official arguing heatedly with the captain and, to his surprise, the priest.

'What is that priest's game? For a man of God he takes an inordinate interest in worldly matters.'

Hardwick approached the captain as the four-oar cast off.

'Are we docking?' said Hardwick.

'Immediately,' said the captain.

With no breeze to speak of, "immediately" turned into half a day. Bacon and Hardwick waited impatiently on deck.

'Hold steady, sir,' the customs officer said before the boarding bridge could be deployed.

'What is it?' demanded the captain.

'This is a Neapolitan ship, and no one from Naples may disembark.'

'Why's that?' the captain demanded. 'I have documents.'

'You bring disease, sir. La enfermadad italiana.'

'It's not the Italian disease. It's the French disease. La enfermadad francese. You stupid Spanish fuck,' he added *sotto voce.*

The customs official would not be swayed.

'It's a ruse,' the captain told the Englishmen. 'Soborno. A bribe. They'll make us wait until we pay up.'

'We are not Neapolitan,' Hardwick called from the deck. 'We are English. *Inglés.*'

'You may have the disease.'

'We do not have the disease.'

Hardwick discreetly dangled his purse.

'Where are you going?' said the official, sensing a few easy *escudos.*

'Palos de la Frontera.'

The official considered the matter.

'Wait here.'

He moved along the dock. Hardwick and Bacon waited anxiously.

'What are they up to?' said Hardwick, watching the captain and the priest conferring.

'Hola, Ingléses,' said the official. 'There is a ship departing for Frontera in an hour.'

'They're not going anywhere,' said the captain. He gestured to his sailors who surrounded the Englishmen.

'Oh?' said the official. 'In that case, neither are you. You are denied permission to disembark. You are denied permission to unload. And your ship is denied permission to leave Cadiz harbour.'

A carrack of gnarled old English salts is no match for a Spanish customs official. The captain conceded and stalked off. Hardwick and Bacon tossed their bags onto the quay and jumped.

Bacon saw the priest watching them with ill-concealed fury.

'Fifty *escudos,*' said the official. 'Each. In advance.'

'I'm not letting my horses out at this time of night.'

'I've been held on the docks all day and forced to pay a bribe,' said Fr Medici, producing a document.

'I can't read, can I?' said the ostler.

'You can see, can't you? This is the Seal of the Ring of the Fisherman,' Medici snapped.

'The Holy Father?'

'It is addressed to Fr Tomas de Torquemada.'

'*Santa mierda.*'

'Exactly.'

'How many horses, was it?'

It was a twenty-league ride to Sevilla and Medici rode all night. He asked directions from the first priest he met and made his way toward the Dominican monastery where Torquemada headquartered. The Dominicans were keen on mortification of the flesh, practising self- or mutual flagellation. They were known to kneel for days on end whilst shouldering heavy weights. They were rumoured to emulate some of the more grisly tortures endured by the martyrs.

Medici heard a piercing, almost unearthly scream. He smelt the odour of burning wood and flesh. This augured well. An enthralled crowd watched the flames of an auto-da-fe; a heretic was burning alive. It must be serious; the auto de fe was reserved for the most egregious of heresies. She – it was hard to discern the gender, but almost certainly a female – was probably a witch.

Torquemada was chairing an inquisition and Medici had to wait. He was finally admitted to a modest chamber where he met the great man. He was unremarkable-looking. He was in his mid-seventies by now, a little fleshy, not in the best of health, but his spirit remained fired by the zealot's passion. Medici introduced himself and gave Torquemada his letter from Alexander.

'A very great honour to meet you, Fr Tomas.'

'All honour to god, my son.'

The Grand Inquisitor was a Dominican friar who had displayed unusual levels of piety since infancy. He was confessor to Princess Isabella before she married Ferdinand and became Queen. The royal couple elevated him to the role of Inquisitor and then Grand Inquisitor. He successfully engineered the expulsion of all jews and muslims from Spain in 1492. Ironically, he was of jewish heritage himself. He had one simple aim: to rid Spain of all heresy and he had made a mighty job of it. He finished reading Alexander's letter.

'We must stop these Englishmen,' he said.

Palos de la Frontera was a port town of some 1500 souls. It was from here that Christopho Colombo sailed for the New World on the evening of August 5, 1492. It was the only fame attached to the town; Palos remained a minor trading hub with fishing its principal industry.

Hardwick and Bacon found lodgings and wasted no time looking for their man; one Ximeno Abascal, a local fisherman. According to Mencia, this was the man who passed her the pockes. They called at a church near the small docks.

'We are looking for Ximeno Abascal,' said Bacon.

'Aaahh ... '

'Can you tell us where we might find him?'

The priest shook his head sadly.

'No,' said Bacon.

'Dead?' said Hardwick.

The priest led them to a humble grave.

'The disease?' said Bacon.

The priest refused to answer.

'You know something about the origins of the disease, father?' said Hardwick.

'Only what Ximeno told me in the confessional.'

'Would you care to share it?'

'You know I cannot violate the sanctity of the confessional.'

'Ximeno is beyond caring about the sanctity of the confessional.'

'I have sworn a holy vow.'

'People are dying, father,' said Bacon. 'Quickly. Or slowly like Ximeno. Man must have dignity, father.'

The priest shook his head.

'I am trying to save lives, father.'

'It is god's will, gentlemen. You have come a long way but if that is all you learn your journey has not been wasted.'

The priest pointed to the gateway out of the graveyard. The Englishmen returned to the docks.

'Abascal can't be the only infection,' said Bacon.

'Someone must have known him,' Hardwick suggested.

Their enquiry at a dockside taberna met with open hostility.

'Soborno,' Bacon whispered.

Hardwick took a coin from his purse and placed it on the counter. The tabernero pointed toward the docks where the fishing fleet was returning.

'Which one?'

'*Ysabel.*'

They made their way to the *Ysabel* where a fisherman and a boy, perhaps 12 years of age were unloading their catch.

'I'm told you knew Ximeno Abascal.'

'Who are you?' said the fisherman. 'And what do you want?'

'There is a terrible disease ravaging Europe and we are told Señor Abascal knew something about it.'

'Ximeno is dead.'

'Be quiet, boy,' said the fisherman.

'Yes, we know,' said Bacon impatiently.

'We're so terribly sorry,' said Hardwick. 'And you are?'

'His brother,' said the boy.

'He died of the disease?'

'We cannot help you,' said the fisherman. He took a gutting knife from its sheath and slit a fish's belly.

'You must help us,' said Bacon. 'People are dying.'

The fisherman paused. He said nothing. His bloodied knife looked wickedly sharp.

'Come, Bacon.' Hardwick hauled him away. They returned and enquired about lodgings.

'No point tarrying here in Palos,' said Hardwick. 'I'll book us a passage to London.'

'Señor?'

It was Ximeno's brother.

'Si.'

'My brother. My other brother. He is very ill. Can you help him?'

'I can try,' said Bacon.

They followed the lad to a humble, whitewashed cottage near the docks.

The lad spoke to his mother. She shook her head furiously.

'I am a surgeon. A medico. My name is Bacon. Perhaps we can help.'

The woman relented and led them to a bedroom. A man huddled in a corner of the room which was devoid of any furniture beyond a bed and dresser. A crucifix hung on the wall.

The man's eyes were open but he was clearly blind.

'Señor?' said Bacon.

'He cannot hear you. Or see you.'

He was whispering some incantation, barely pausing for breath.

'How long has he been like this?'

'Two years.'

'Two years!'

There was nothing to be learned. Bacon examined the man. There were no ulcers or rash; he was past that stage. Bacon refused to offer false hope.

'All you can do is pray.'

The woman began arguing with the boy.

'It is time for you to go. My mother is very upset.'

'Can she tell us where he got this disease?'

'A prostitute called Mencia.'

The old woman spat on the floor.

'Gaiac,' said Bacon. 'Do you know anything about a cure? Something called gaiac?'

'All gone. Please go.'

Bacon and Hardwick returned to their lodgings to gather their belongings. There was little else they could do.

'I'm sorry, Hardwick. I feel like I've led you on a fool's errand.'

'It was worth the shot.'

'Is this where it all started?'

'Mencia said it started here.'

'Why do I think they know something, Hardwick? Why aren't they telling us?'

'Because it started here, Bacon. Shame. Humiliation. The fear of God.'

'I was sure if I found the disease's origin we would learn something.'

'As I say, Bacon, it was worth the shot.'

Their dueña served them a final luncheon of jamon and manchego, tomatoes and olive oil.

'You know, I'm starting to get a taste for this olive oil,' said Hardwick.

'Hardwick?' said Bacon. 'The olive oil.'

'What about it?'

'The jug.'

Hardwick looked at the jug quizzically. Bacon rummaged in his travel bag and held up Mencia's empty gaiac pot.

'The jug and the pot – '

'I'd wager they were thrown by the same hand.'

'Señora? Where did you get this olive oil?'

Don Pedro Montoya's ancestral estate stretched as far as the eye could see. The serried groves of olive and orange trees, and vineyards, from which Don Pedro produced tempranillo and syrah wines, had made him a fabulously wealthy man. The olives were crushed on the hacienda and the oil was sold in jars and amphora thrown in the Montoya pottery. It was situated two or three leagues from Frontera. The Englishmen arrived by wagon.

'Don Pedro sees no one,' said the estate's capitaz.

'Tell Don Pedro we have travelled from England. We are on a trade mission from King Henry to source fine wine and would be honoured to sample your wares.'

The capitaz nodded doubtfully but disappeared into the sprawling casa. They waited patiently until he returned.

'Don Pedro is not well. He has lost the use of his legs. But he has agreed to see you.'

They followed him along a corridor, colourfully tiled and cool beneath the searing sun, and across a courtyard where a fountain splashed a host of cavorting nymphs. The parlour opened off the courtyard.

Don Pedro was formally dressed to receive the king's emissaries. He was in his forties but his frame was emaciated, his cheeks hollowed, his eyes sightless. He sat in an armchair, his useless legs splayed, his wasted arms folded before him.

Hardwick produced his papers.

'My eyesight failed me two years ago.'

Two years. Bacon glanced at his companion.

'It has partially returned but I'm afraid I can no longer read.'

'Perhaps you can make out the seal of our Lord Chamberlain?'

Montoya's ran his fingers over the embossed wax.

'You are trade envoys?'

'I am.'

'And I am a surgeon also on a mission from our government. I am investigating the disease which afflicts you.'

'You are too late to help me.'

'I fear I am.'

'So you are not interested in my wine?'

'I must ask you both to leave,' said the capitaz.

'Please, Don Pedro. The disease has ravaged Italy, Spain, France and England. It will continue to spread.' Bacon produced the empty pot of gaiac. 'I believe this is a cure.'

'My sense of smell has not left me,' said Don Pedro.

'Where can I obtain it?'

'Fetch Palta, Juan.'

The capitaz departed. Bacon questioned Montoya about his illness. It was a copybook case. He had survived two years but he would be lucky to last another month.

The capitaz returned with a young woman. She was perhaps 20 years of age, quite short but slim and toned. Her eyes were dark, almost matching her black hair, her skin was smooth and tawny.

'Is she not the most beautiful woman you have ever seen?'

Bacon believed she was. He was put in mind of a pagan goddess or at least a princess. Perhaps she was.

'Her name is Palta which means pear in her native tongue. Ironically, the pear is their symbol of good health.'

'Palta is not from Palos, Don Pedro,' asked Bacon.

'No, she is from the New World. Colombo returned from his journeys with fifteen natives. I purchased Palta.'

'And the disease?'

'Palta had the disease some years ago. Most of the natives get it but it passes without the ravages we Europeans experience. You must understand, Palta did not bring the disease with her. None of the natives did.'

'It was Colombo's sailors,' said Bacon.

Don Pedro nodded.

'And the gaiac?'

'The natives use it. It is very effective for the natives.'

'But not so effective for Europeans?'

'No.'

'But it remains our best hope, Don Pedro? What is this gaiac? Do you have any?'

Fr Medici had endured forty-eight hours in the saddle without sleep when he arrived in Palos de La Frontera and saw his quarry sailing serenely from the harbour. Forty-eight hours is insufficient time to develop a *fistula in ano* but sufficient to develop a severe case of saddle sores. Medici spoke with the local priest and then the Alvaros. Faced with the prospect of another sleepless, bumpy night on horseback, the indefatigable Medici suddenly looked defatigable. He had once knelt naked for twenty-four hours on cold bare flagstones, a hundredweight of lead suspended from each shoulder, but he would make chorizo of those horses before he got on them again.

Medici was not a nautical man but when he saw the calm sea he knew a smaller lighter vessel might catch the Englishmen before Cadiz. He approached the *Ysabel*.

'Will you take me?'

'I have fish to catch,' said the fisherman.

'And I have fish to fry and I travel under the authority of he who wears the fisherman's ring.'

There is a superstition among sailors that priests are bad luck on boats, that their presence offends Palaemon and his Oceanids.

'I go to mass. I try not to sin but – '

'I am special Inquisitor assisting Cardinal de Torquemada.'

Oh.

'When did you want to go?'

'**G**od's will, god's wrath, god's punishment,' said Bacon, staring down at the calm blue waters of the Gulf of Cadiz. They were a long way from the New World and the gaiac which might or might not save European lives.

'Maybe it is god's will that it is god's will.'

At least, one mystery was solved. Ximeno and Colombo's other sailors had brought the disease back from the New World. Ximeno had infected Mencia and perhaps others who had infected ... well, who knows how many thousands of others.

'Bacon? Isn't that the *Ysabel*?'

'That man, the one throwing up. Isn't that the priest?'

'I believe it is.'

'It can't be a coincidence.'

They were barely a league from the docks but it took several hours to negotiate the calm waters and the bustling harbour to their berth.

'Is it normally this busy?' said Hardwick.

'No,' said the captain of the small carrack which they had boarded in Frontera. 'Colombo has arrived.'

'Here in Cadiz?'

'He is stocking provisions for another journey to the New World.'

The docks were festooned with flags and banners. Crowds of Cadiz locals, gaditanos as they were known, crowded the quay.

'He's quite the hero, your man,' said Hardwick.

'We will be the greatest nation on earth,' said the skipper proudly. 'And much of it is due to the great Christopho Colombo.'

Bacon counted the ships.

'Seventeen.'

'They say there are more than a thousand men,' said the skipper.

Their vessel finally docked.

'Can you see the priest?' said Hardwick.

'There!'

Medici stood on the fringe of the vast crowd.

'Let's go the other way,' said Bacon.

'We'll never get through this lot,' said Hardwick as they disembarked.

He had no sooner said the words than the crowd loosed a mighty roar and surged away from the dock.

The Englishmen paused by the fleet's flagship, the largest of Colombo's ships, a Portuguese-designed, triple-masted nau.

'*Marigalante.*'

'The Gallant Mary.'

The crowd cheered again and swept toward them, blocking their way.

'It's Colombo,' said Bacon. The crowd surrounded the great man and surged toward the dock. Bacon and Hardwick clutched the *Marigalante's* gangway for fear of being driven into the water and crushed between the ship and the dock.

Colombo passed within a few feet of them.

'Señor Colombo,' Bacon cried.

Bacon forced his way through the mass of cheering admirers. He clutched Colombo's arm and shouted above the din.

'Señor Colombo.'

The soldados ushered Colombo toward his ship.

'The gaiac,' Bacon screamed in the great man's ear. 'Where can I find gaiac?'

The crowd swept Bacon aside. Colombo paused and waved to the crown then moved serenely up the gangway. Bacon tried to follow him but a pair of marineros, guarding the *Marigalante* shoved him back into the crowd. He stumbled and fell. Feet trampled him, kicked him. Hardwick grasped his arm and hauled him to his feet.

'He's deaf. Colombo has the pockes, Hardwick.'

Again, Bacon tried to force his way toward the gangplank.

'I must speak with him.'

'Bacon? I think they're looking at us ... '

A company of armed soldados marched toward them, clubbing gaditanos out of their way.

Sevilla was one of the original centres of the Grand Inquisition and so Torquemada's return was something of a homecoming. The courtroom with its seal of the cross, the olive branch and the sword remained unchanged. The cells and the subterranean chamber where he supervised the tormento sessions were still operable.

A pair of Inquisition guardias led Bacon into the courtroom. Torquemada sat at a high bench flanked by a pair of Inquisitors, two of the six appointed by Alexander to assist the Grand Old Man of the Inquisition. His hair was precisely tonsured but the fringe of greying hair was unruly, untouched by vanity's brush or comb. There was no fire in his eyes; no cruel twist to the thin lips. The eyes seemed calm, all-seeing, yet fixed on things beyond the temporal. He radiated piety, it came off him in waves. Perhaps that is what happened the closer you got to God, Bacon mused. An Inquisitor began the formalities which blurred in Bacon's ears.

' ... a special inquisition ... by grace of God ... authority of our Holy Father Alexander, Successor of the Prince of Apostles, Supreme Pontiff of the Universal Church, Servant of the Servants of God ... and of Ferdinand of Aragon and Isabella of Castile under whose divine right we exercise our duties ...'

Despite his fear, Bacon felt comforted by Torquemada's serenity. Lord, the old man *smiled* at him.

'What are the charges, Inquisitor?' said Torquemada.

'Blasphemy and sodomy.'

'What?' said Bacon. 'No!'

Bacon had never blasphemed in his life. He was prone to cursing but that was merely foul language. And he was not a sodomite. He had lain with men, many men, in mutual pleasuring. But sodomy, no, because, well, nothing hurt like buggery. These charges had to be made up. Then he saw Medici sitting quietly amongst the spectators, thin, ascetic, and to Bacon's ever-professional eye, still looking a little peaky.

'Please be quiet, sir,' said Torquemada's assistant reasonably.

Bacon saw an Inquisition official move to a row of garments suspended from the wall. One featured a cross, another, burning flames. The official fetched a short black robe embossed with burning flames.

'Sanbenito,' he said, indicating the robe. Bacon struggled but the guardias pinioned him and the official slipped on the garment.

Burning flames? What did that mean? A symbol of hell? Not a bonfire, Bacon prayed, anything but a bonfire.

'Pride is their necklace/'They clothe themselves with violence,'

the Inquisitors sang in unison, if not quite perfect three-part harmony.

'From their callous hearts comes iniquity;

Their evil imaginations have no limits.
They scoff, and speak with malice,
With arrogance they threaten oppression.
Their mouths lay claim to heaven, and their tongues take possession of the earth.'

That's not me, Bacon wanted to scream.

'Do you admit to your sins ... ?'

'No. I do not.'

'You will be returned to your cell,' Torquemada began. The court waited for him to finish the pronouncement. And waited. An Inquisitor whispered in Torquemada's ear.

' ... where you will reflect on your sins. Confess, repent, and you shall be penanced.'

The guardias led Bacon back to his cell. It was empty.

'Where is my companion?'

'He has been set free.'

'Why am I being charged?'

'Because you are a maricon. Worse, you are a blaspheming maricon.'

'I am not a sodomite.'

Bacon was left to reflect on his sins. A few minutes of hellish imaginings passed when the door opened and a guardia showed Hardwick in.

'Hardwick. At last. Please, get me out of here,' he begged.

'Not quite that simple.'

'It was obviously simple for you.'

'I had my letter from Sir Reginald.'

'What about me?'

'I don't know what's going on, Bacon, but that priest is behind it and he's an envoy from Alexander himself.'

'The pope ... ?'

'It's because of our mission, I'm sure of it. We've challenged the official line, Bacon."

'Do you know the punishment if they find me guilty?'

Hardwick's eyes fell on the sanbenito's flames.

'They're going to burn me alive?' said Bacon.

'Officially speaking, it's called an auto-da-fe.'

'But they can't burn a man alive without evidence.'

'It seems they do have evidence. From your friend in Naples.'

Ullise.

He was fucked and he hadn't fucked anyone.

'How long do I have?'

'It is at the court's discretion. I'll see what I can do, Bacon.'

The guardias returned. They hadn't given him much time to reflect on his sins. He was led back to the courtroom which was packed with expectant spectators. The black robe and red flames always attracted a crowd. Outside a pair of friars swept the ashes from the auto da fe.

'Do you confess your sins?' said Torquemada.

'I do not confess.'

Torquemada looked genuinely sorry.

'Derribalo.'

Take him down.

Bacon was led to the basement chamber where the infamous instruments of torture were at the ready. A fire burned in a brazier, in which branding irons were glowing white-hot. Bacon saw thumbscrews and a giant device like a nutcracker, big enough to crack limbs, and a spiked device like a carpenter's horse. Presumably, you sat on it and the spike went up ... 'No, don't think about it,' he muttered under his breath.

Torquemada and his Inquisitors prayed while the guardias roped his hands behind his back. They looped the rope through a chain which was attached to a pulley.

'You would torture me?'

'No tortura. Tormento.'

'Oh, you'll torment me. That makes a difference?'

'It is forbidden that your blood be spilled,' an Inquisitor explained.

'You must remember,' said the second Inquisitor, 'it is not a punishment.'

'No?'

'It is – ' Torquemada fell silent again. An Inquisitor nudged him.

'An aid to reflection,' whispered the Inquisitor.

' – an aid to reflection,' said Torquemada.

Bacon was not a follower of the ancients but Hippocrates had diagnosed a singular form of madness amongst the aged which he called *paranoia*. Galen also identified the madness, calling it *morosis*.

'You're mad. You are suffering from *morosis paranoia*. You are in no fit state to try me.'

Bacon screamed as the atormentador hauled on the rope, suspending him, merely inches above the floor. The nearness to firm ground only increased the pain which was terrific.

'There is a strict time limit,' said the Inquisitor.

'How long is the strict time limit?'

'Fifteen minutes.'

Struggling made it worse. Much worse. All the while the Inquisitors, the guardias and the atormentador knelt and prayed.

After exactly fifteen minutes, Bacon was let down. He collapsed to the floor.

'Do you confess your sins?'

Bacon shook his head.

The guardias carried him back to his cell.

H ardwick sipped his wine and chewed on his supper of suckling pig. He now knew the origin of the pockes and had identified a possible cure for it. But Colombo was headed for the New World, so that ship had literally set sail and the cure would only be found half a world away. Still, no one could deny that his mission was a success. He would return to England and be amply rewarded, his career assured, a knighthood in the bag. Sir Reginald would be secretly delighted that the Spanish were responsible for the disease; it would give him leverage in any future trade agreements.

There was little he could do to help Bacon. He could send a message to Sir Reginald asking for help but Bacon would not survive that long. There was no envoy, not even a Merchant Adventurer in Sevilla that might intercede. Hardwick would be magnanimous on his return to London and acknowledge Bacon's contribution to their mission's success.

No.

Hardwick pushed aside his suckling pig. He was an ambitious man but he was also a man of honour. He could not let an old friend, a fellow Englishman die at the hands of a madman like Torquemada. The only people who could talk sense into Torquemada were Ferdinand and Isabella. It was his only hope.

'How long will it take to ride to Madrid and back?'

'Ha ha. Inglés humour, right?' said the ostler.

'I need to see King Ferdinand and Queen Isabella.'

'Aaah, you Inglés' the ostler chuckled.

'I'm serious.'

'Three weeks. Maybe four to Madrid and back.'

Bacon would be ashes long before.

'But the king and queen are in Cordoba. They farewelled Colombo yesterday.'

'Your finest pair, sir. A man's life is at stake.'

'The maricon Inglés? He'll confess. They always do. You don't want to miss the burning.'

'Those are your only two?' Hardwick pointed to a pair of grey-muzzled, bow-legged roans. 'Your sign says Finest Horses in Andalusia.'

'I'm a bit short, right now,' the ostler grumbled. 'My other two are knackered. A bloody priest, a man of God, eh? Flogged 'em like they were bloody penitents. Five escudos. Each.'

It almost drained Hardwick of cash.

The ride to Cordoba on the ageing swaybacks took almost twenty long, slow and very painful hours to complete. Ferdinand and Isabella were staying at the Alcazar de los Reyes.

'My name is Nicholas Hardwick. I wish to see the King and Queen.'

'Cabrear, Inglés.'

'I will not piss off. I am an emissary of King Henry, by Grace of God, King of England.'

Hardwick presented his papers. The soldado looked at the papers blankly and shrugged.

'You don't read English. I might have guessed. El rey, si? De Inglaterra?'

The soldado scowled and showed the letter to his colleague. They conferred and finally handed it to a passing officer. The officer looked suspiciously at Hardwick. He crooked his finger and Hardwick followed him across a garden of palms and orange trees, through the marvel of Islamic tiles that was a cloister and along a corridor which ended, finally, at an ante-room. The officer handed the papers to an official. He looked at them quizzically. Blasted Spanish. Didn't anyone read English?

'The seal of Henry VII. El Rey de Inglaterra.'

The official disappeared into an adjoining office. The ante-room was painted in golden rays which ascended into the blue dome of the ceiling. It was an Islamic representation of heaven and Hardwick found himself sinking into a serenity he had rarely known before. Hours must have passed because it was dusk when the official nudged his shoulder. He led him into the royal throne room.

Ferdinand and Isabella sat on a pair of adjoining thrones. They were the first undisputed rulers of a united Spain; no one questioned their divine right to rule. They were both about forty and had ruled since their teens. Like Torquemada, they radiated piety and virtue.

Hardwick had heard that they did everything together, were joined at the hip. They passed the papers between them, casting serene, untroubled glances at Hardwick.

'We don't read English,' said Ferdinand, finally.

Was that the royal we or the grammatical we, Hardwick wondered.

'I am an emissary of His Majesty King Henry by Grace of God King of England.'

'Please convey our warmest regards to Henry,' said Ferdinand.

'Our good friend Henry is in our prayers,' said Isabella.

'And your gracious Queen Elizabeth,' said Ferdinand.

'She too is in our prayers.'

'I'll tell them that.'

'What is your mission, Signor Hardwood?' said Ferdinand.

'My colleague is a cirujano, a surgeon. Our country has been blighted by a plague, a pockes.'

'La enfermeda francesa,' said Ferdinand.

'Or la enfermeda italiana,' said Isabella.

'Some call it that, yes. And my colleague is searching for a cure.'

'Disease is the wrath of god.'

'His punishment.'

'Yes, yes. Absolutely. But by god's will, by his divine grace can we not seek a cure?'

Ferdinand and Isabella exchanged glances. They gestured for Hardwick to continue.

'God, in his divine grace has ordained that my colleague save the innocent ones, the wives, the children of the sinners. This disease is devastating our country. It is devastating Europe. Henry has entrusted Mr Bacon with this mission. Your right to rule is divine. Henry's right to rule is divine. This mission he has entrusted to Mr Bacon is god's will. Henry will be most upset if you allow the execution of an Englishman who may save thousands of English and Spanish lives.'

'Execution?'

'My colleague has been arrested in Sevilla.'

'By whom?'

'Fr de Torquemada.'

'On what charges.'

'Blasphemy.'

'Oh,' said Ferdinand.

'And, er, sodomy.'

'Oh,' said Isabella.

'Fr de Torquemada is the Grand Inquisitor.'

'He has our full authority.'

'And blessing.'

'He is wrong.'

'Fr Torquemada is never wrong.'

'Not wrong,' said Hardwick. 'A misunderstanding.'

'Fr Torquemada understands everything.'

'It is god's punishment.'

'And Fr Torquemada is god's instrument of punishment.'

Hardwick had one last card to play.

'Henry will be most displeased because Mr Bacon has discovered the origin of the disease.'

Ferdinand and Isabella were listening now.

'The disease is not la enfermeda francesa or italiana. It is la enfermeda española. Christopho Colombo and his sailors defied their church. They lay with heathen women, pagans, worshippers of false idols and they brought the disease back to Europe. Your national hero, the man you have built statues to, Christopho Colombo has the pockes, Your Majesties and he and his men have unleashed a disease that is devastating Europe. Does Torquemada try Colombo and his sailors? No? Does the Church condone it? How is that the will of God?'

'Guardia!'

The soldiers snapped to attention.

'You are a spy, sir,' said Ferdinand, 'and you will be executed.'

'Without trial,' Isabella added.

The soldiers pinioned Hardwick by his arms.

'Be that as it may, Your Majesties, my report is on its way to London as we speak. Our great nations are allies, trading partners. You would jeopardise that for the life of a single Englishman?'

His friend's life, Hardwick knew, lay in the balance. Ferdinand motioned the soldiers to release him.

'It was the heathens who carried the disease,' said Isabella.

'Heathen *women*,' Ferdinand amended.

'Of course it was,' said Hardwick. 'No need to mention Colombo or his sins. Let history record that the slaves Colombo brought back with him spread the disease. Would that suit?'

'I

n the future, every penitent will have his fifteen minutes of pain,' Torquemada had proclaimed when he was first appointed Grand Inquisitor.

In Bacon's second fifteen minutes of pain his ankles were tied and an adjustable length of timber was placed between his knees. The timber was ratcheted, forcing the knees agonizingly outwards.

'This is not a punishment,' Torquemada reminded him,

'Thank you.'

Somehow Bacon survived the tormento and was carried, his legs bowed into a near-perfect ellipse, back to his cell.

Hardwick had also suffered the agonies of the damned as he returned from Cordoba on the spavined and sway-backed roans.

'I have come from King Ferdinand and Queen Isabella,' he said, presenting his papers to an Inquisitor who read them and considered the contents gravely.

'Fr Torquemada answers to a greater authority,' he said quietly. Torquemada smiled vacantly from the Inquisitor's bench.

The Inquisitor held the letter to a candle.

'With the greatest respect, sir, you are mad,' said Hardwick.

The ink and Ferdinand's wax seal exploded, showering them in sparks.

'They saw tongues of fire that came to rest on each of them,' said Torquemada, 'and all were filled with the mercy of the Holy Spirit.'

4. ... and that which is to be, hath already been

F r Medici would choose one of Torquemada's choicest tormentos over a horseback return to Rome any day. He caught a caravelle from Cadiz to Civitavecchia, a journey of about 400 leagues. The winds tailed them and it was a relatively quick voyage. He walked the last few miles to Rome where he was granted an immediate audience with the pontiff.

'The Englishmen have learned that the disease came from the New World?'

'They have, Holy Father.'

'Have some cake, Gio,' said Alexander. 'My baker calls it tira mi su.'

'Pick me up? It's very good, Holy Father.'

Alexander was god's representative on earth. His every Bull, his every utterance, was deemed the word of god himself. Many doubted that Alexander's inspiration was divine; few doubted that he was a man of vision.

'France has decided it wants all Italy,' said Alexander.

'But surely the Holy League has scared him off?' said Medici.

'Charles the Affabile has turned Charles the Folle. But I am not too worried about France. Maximilian's son – '

237

'Philip the Handsome.'

' – is to marry Ferdinand and Isabella's daughter – '

'Joanna the Mad.'

'Best not to say that too loudly, Gio, but yes. Their son, assuming they have one, will rule Germany, Austria, Burgundy and the Lowlands.'

'And so France will be surrounded ...'

'Exactly. France is no longer a threat.'

'You engineered this, Holy Father?'

'It would be fair to say we had a hand in it, Gio.'

The pair ate their tira mi su and sipped their chianti.

'But what of the Englishmen, Holy Father?'

Alexander's vision extended far beyond Europe. He wished to establish the Church as *the* global power. Alexander used the term "global"; the Church had long known that the earth was not flat even though it contradicted several passages in the scriptures. That secret would soon be out, he reflected, with da Vinci and all these renaissance Humanists and thinkers studying the human body and the stars and whatnot. Spain, led by the arch-conservatives Philip and Isabella and inspired by Torquemada's fanaticism was the perfect ally to conquer the New World and establish the Church as the most powerful institution on earth.

Until a pair of Englishmen came along and upset the apple cart.

Alexander was on excellent terms with Henry – he had upheld Innocent's bull recognizing the legitimacy of his rule, after all – and wondered if Henry might be open to marrying off one of his daughters to his one, unmarried son. Trouble is, Alexander reflected, Cesare had a reputation for unpredictability; some thought him downright unhinged and those rumours of him and his sister wouldn't go away. Alexander had gained a foothold in Scotland by funding the university in Aberdeen. But James had no daughters. Pity, Cesare and the Scots were quite a match.

But deep down the one ally Alexander didn't trust was the English. If anybody was going to challenge papal authority, perhaps even break from the Church, it would be England. Alexander's efforts to install his man di Carbonariis in the

Archdiocese of Bath and Wells had met with early resistance. Fortunately, Alexander's plan to offer John Cabot to Henry in return for di Carbonariis's appointment to Bath and Wells looked like bearing fruit. With Anglo-Roman ties thus strengthened, it confirmed the Church's position as the pre-eminent global force.

'Colombo's secret will be revealed sooner or later. The idea that disease is spread by pagan harlots suits our narrative,' said Alexander. 'Disease is a punishment from god. His wrath is heaped upon the pagans and those who are tempted to lie with them. That is our official line – our hard line. I won't have to issue a Bull, a proclamation should do the trick.'

'Congratulations, Holy Father.'

'Have another slice of tira mi su, Gio.'

The port of Hull was one of the major trading hubs in England. Wool and cloth from the northern and eastern counties: Northumberland, Cumbria, Yorkshire and Lincolnshire were traded out. Wine was traded in from Italy, Portugal and Spain.

They were a day's sail from Hull. The bells rang. Six bells or seven o'clock. Night was falling when Bacon was driven to his bunk with a cleaving headache.

'No, god, please. I have much work to do.'

He reached for a looking glass and lowered his hose. An ulcer, the size of a shilling had risen in his groin. He had no opium and had to bear the excruciating pain. There was little sleep that night. At dawn's seven bells the pain eased. He examined himself in his looking-glass. Eight ulcers. There was no doubt. Emotions roiled his stomach. The wrath of God? For what? He had fallen in love and had expressed it physically. What was the sin?

Their ship berthed and Hardwick set out to find a connecting passage to London. Bacon had to decide whether to treat himself with theriac, mercury or a combination of the two. Gaiac offered the best chance of a cure but he would have to wait for Christopho Colombo's return. For a brief moment he fantasised about joining Cabot's expedition; they would need a surgeon after all. He obtained directions to a Carthusian friary with a small, attached hospital.

'Can you mix me a theriac decoction, brother,' he said to the priory's herbalist.

'The disease has taken hold in our city. Our theriac is spoken for, my son.' The friar directed him to another friary beyond the walls. 'It is a closed order – The Reformed Cistercians of Our Lady of La Trappe.'

Trappists. The strictest, most secretive order of them all.

'They have a herbalist. He may be able to help you.'

It was a three-mile walk. Bacon followed a track to the end of a narrow, steep-sided combe. The friary lay in shadows, shrouded by glades of oak and elder. Moisture seeped from its walls which were cloaked in dark green moss. Bacon struggled to breathe; the air, moist, fungal, seemed thicker, heavier here. He knocked on the oak portal. It echoed off the rocky walls of the combe and faintly within the walls. A bolt was shot and the portal opened.

'I was directed here by a Carthusian friar, brother. Can you mix me a theriac decoction?'

'You carry the disease.'

It was a statement, not a question.

'I do.'

The friar opened the gate. Heavy as it was and clasped to its jambs by iron hinges, it moved silently.

The friar led him into a courtyard.

'Please do not leave the cloister. The buildings are forbidden to outsiders.'

'I understand, brother. Thank you.'

The friar disappeared into the priory. The cloister was dark. There were no windows in the walls, nowhere for light to enter. Bacon felt the weight of centuries of silence bearing down on him. His shoulders sagged, his head bowed. He heard chanting; caught the odour of sulphur and base metals burning. He thought he sensed something else. It was indefinable, something beyond his consciousness; the presence of Trimegistus himself, of transmutation, of the great hermetic mysteries about to reveal themselves. He panicked and fled. He passed through a door and almost collided with a cowled friar and child. The child was also cowled and tonsured. The pair stared at Bacon.

They shared a flame of red hair and an albinoid complexion. They were clearly father and son. They turned to leave.

'Wait.'

Bacon snatched at the friar's arm and stared into the face which was cratered with pockes scars. The child stared sightlessly at Bacon. His lips were twisted with a cleft palate and he too bore the marks. Bacon recalled Jane Darley's child.

The friar pulled himself free and dragged the boy away.

A dazed Bacon tried to collect his thoughts. The child was eight perhaps ten years of age. Assuming he was born with the affliction he had been infected several years before Colombo's voyage to the New World. What did that mean? That the pockes had originated in England?

Bacon took a wrong turn at the cloister and found himself in a graveyard. The grander tombs lay closer to the altar of the chapel and thereby closer to god. They were the most expensive. It was simony in all but name and the practice was rife in priories and monasteries. Presumably, an order like the Trappists, who were holiest of the holy commanded higher prices.

Further away were the more humble graves of friars and laypersons. And then another area which was sectioned off behind a firethorn hedge. The tombstones bore simple inscriptions: a name and a date. Sinners. Infants. Infants should not be buried here. Several female names. Nuns? Buried in an all-male Trappist graveyard? It was not permitted, surely. What tales could these bones tell?

Bacon found his way back to the cloister where the herbalist, white with fury waited for him.

'Outside contact is expressly forbidden.'

'You have the pockes within your walls. I'm guessing it's been here for generations.'

'Do not speak against the Holy Order of Our Lady and all who serve here.'

'I know how the infection spreads. How long has it been here?'

'There is no pockes here, sir. Take your medicine and go.'

'I will return with king's men, father.'

'They will find nothing.'

'You are concealing the truth.'

'There is a greater truth. Who will be believed? A fornicator such as you? Or the word of men who have devoted their lives to poverty and prayer?'

T he quickest route to London was by sea; 135 nautical miles, 40 or so leagues. They sailed on the morning tide and moored at the India dock 48 hours later.

'You'll send a message when Sir Reginald wants his report?' said Bacon.

Hardwick nodded.

Bacon returned to the clinic. The waiting room was packed. There had been no abatement in the disease's spread.

'Common sense prevailed and the infections dropped,' said Heckstall. 'But then complacency set in.'

'I need to gather my thoughts and write my report,' said Bacon.

'It's grand to have you back, sir.'

'Thank you, Lowther.'

Bacon left his colleagues to deal with the patients and withdrew to his rooms. He re-read his case notes. He scoured his texts, both ancient and modern It was past midnight when he finished his report. He washed and lanced the ulcers. He disinfected with honey, lavender and Persian aloe then applied the theriac. He had retained the lascar's tiny smudge of gaiac, but wished to leave it for the king and the Council and further examination by London's leading herbalists and apothecaries.

When he awoke the next morning he saw the ulcers had spread to his chest. It looked a severe case. He dressed and joined Heckstall and Lowther for breakfast.

'Good morning – '

THE GREAT POCKES

The words choked in Heckstall's throat. Bacon saw the shock in his face.

'What is it, Heckstall?'

'Your lip, Bacon. Best you take a look.'

Bacon went to his room and steeled himself to look in his looking-glass. Two reddish sores at the corner of his lower lip. They had come on very quickly. He applied the antiseptic and the theriac and returned to his colleagues. Lowther looked sick with apprehension; Heckstall, merely sickened.

'Do you know how you got it?' said Heckstall.

'The usual way. In Naples. I didn't know he, I mean she – I didn't know this person was infected.'

The disgust remained on Heckstall's face. Lowther tried to digest the information.

'Will you be all right, Mr Bacon?'

'God's will, Lowther.'

'There are implications, Bacon,' said Heckstall brusquely. 'For our practice, I mean. Our patients.'

'Yes, you're right.'

'We will discuss it later. Lowther, we have patients.'

The pair left for the examination rooms. A messenger arrived with a missive from Hardwick requesting his presence at Westminster at 11 am. Bacon did his best to conceal the sores, gathered his papers and notes and left for the Palace.

'Sorry it was such short notice,' said Hardwick, leading him toward the Painted Chamber, 'but the King's Council is meeting and it seemed an opportune time to present our report. What's that on your lip?'

'Nothing.'

Hardwick stopped.

'Bacon, they're ulcers.'

Bacon was too distressed to lie.

'I carry the pockes, Hardwick.'

'Naples?'

Bacon nodded.

'I'm so sorry. I – '

They waited in the ante-room until called.

It was a full convention of the King's Council. All were present, including, to Bacon's surprise, Heckstall.

Sir Reginald introduced Hardwick to outline their mission.

'Your Majesty, my lords, gentlemen, I, along with my colleague, the eminent surgeon Mr Robert Bacon, was entrusted with a mission to discover the origins of what is now known as The Great Pockes. Our mission took us to Naples, Cadiz and Palos de la Frontera. The journey began with research here in London where Mr Bacon examined a number of sailors who informed us that they had contracted the disease either from a sexual liaison in Naples or with someone who had recently been in Naples. We journeyed to Naples where the Neapolitans claimed that the disease arrived with the invading French forces. Working back, we discovered that the French had caught it from Spanish mercenaries who had caught it from Spanish viaggiatori. We learnt that the disease first appeared in Europe in Palos de la Frontera. The disease was brought back from the New World by Christopho Colombo and his sailors who had caught the disease from native women with whom they had had sexual congress.'

The Council collectively inhaled.

'I shall hand over to Mr Bacon who will report on his findings.'

Bacon saw Metcalfe and Morton watching him with open hostility. Why did he think he was surrounded by enemies? Oh, yes, because he was surrounded by enemies. Or would be when he delivered his report.

'Thank you, Mr Hardwick. If it pleases Your Majesty, my lords, gentlemen. Colombo and his men did indeed bring the disease back from the New World. The disease is highly contagious and acts without fear or favour. For the natives of the New World, however, it is little more than a discomfort. Somehow they have become resistant to it, perhaps over the generations. For Europeans it is far more virulent and as we know, often fatal.'

'You are saying that these pagans are superior to christian Europeans?' Sir John Morton demanded.

'In terms of the disease, your Grace? Yes. Why the disease is less virulent with the New World indigines than with Europeans is open to conjecture. Is it the same disease? I believe it is, despite the differing outcomes. We know the infection is passed via sexual intercourse and other sexual practices.'

'Embracing?' asked Lord Suffolk.

'Touching?' asked Sir Edmund Dudley.

'Toilet seats?' asked Zorima.

'I doubt that it is passed through secondary means.'

Bacon held up the gaiac pot.

'Our second goal was to discover a cure. In this too we were successful. Sort of. This is gaiac. We were informed by a native from the New World that it is a decoction extracted from the bark of the gaiaca tree and that the natives use it with great success. It is less successful when treating Europeans, but is almost certainly our most efficacious cure.'

'You have said nothing, sir, to convince me that this is not God's punishment for sin,' said Morton. He produced a document. 'I have received a missive from the Holy Father himself, proclaiming the disease as God's punishment for sin.'

'The pope is wrong.'

'The pope is infallible! You, sir, are a heretic!'

'The pockes is not God's punishment for sin, Sir John.'

'Heresy! Heresy!' cried the Archbishop.

'I believe that tiny organisms invisible to the naked eye pass the disease.'

'Where did you get this idea of tiny creatures?' Metcalfe demanded.

'The idea was first proposed by Marcus Terrentius Varco in the first century BC.'

'Long discredited,' Metcalfe shouted.

'And developed by Avicenna Ibn Senna in 1070.'

'A muslim!' Morton thundered. 'You would believe the word of a Saracen before your own religion! Heresy, sir.'

'It is not the sexual act that transmits the disease. It is something *associated* with the sexual act. Furthermore, there is something within individuals' bodies – indigines for example – that promotes resistance to infection.'

Bacon's radical theories produced uproar. He demanded silence.

'Where is this cure? This gaiac?' he said hopefully.

'Alas. It is temporarily beyond our reach, Your Majesty, but Mr Cabot may return with supplies.'

Sir John seized on the setback as evidence of God's intervention.

"A-hah. God's will!'

'You are saying that pagan indigines are more proficient at medical practice than Oxford-trained, English physicians?' thundered Sir Thomas Metcalfe.

'That these savages manufacture superior medicines to our own?' cried the Court Apothecary.

'I refuse to believe that these pagans' knowledge of the stars can compare to our own,' said Zorima.

Bacon ignored them.

'Let me conclude, gentlemen, by saying that the origins of the disease remain shrouded in mystery. I have found reports of the disease from Pompei and Metaponto in Roman times. Furthermore, the disease existed in this country *before* Colombo returned,' said Bacon, 'before he sailed to the New World. The disease has been in Hull Port for years. Perhaps a century or more.'

'This is a serious accusation, Bacon,' said Sir Reginald, fearing humiliation, international opprobrium and an unfavourable renegotiation of trade agreements. 'What proof do you have?'

'My own eyes, Sir Reginald. A Trappist monk and his son. The monks' own cemetery with its gravestones dating back a hundred years.'

'How dare you, sir!' cried Morton. 'Are you suggesting that Trappists, that ordained men of God indulged in sexual intercourse?'

'For a hundred years or more, your Grace.'

'Torquemada should have torched you, sir,' said the Archbishop.

'You asked for proof.'

'You would exhume bodies from consecrated soil?' demanded the Archbishop.

Bacon turned to Heckstall for support.

'What you have found in Hull is some other affliction, Bacon,' said Heckstall. 'The disease originated in the New World. God punished the pagans for their sins and this punishment was passed on to sinful Europeans. That is the Barber-Surgeon's official line.'

'Hear, hear,' cried the Councillors in unison.

Bacon was too shocked by Heckstall's betrayal to argue.

The Councillors were outraged to a man. Bacon had managed what neither the House of York nor the House of Lancashire, what neither the Normans, Plantagenets, or Bolingbrokes had achieved in battles which had raged over hundreds of years and taken thousands of lives. For the first time in centuries, the King's Councillors were united.

Lord Cumbria requested an audience with his king. He congratulated him on his grand plans for the navy and his vision of an empire unrivalled in history. Like all his fellow Councillors, Cumbria had realised that the social system worked in his favour. Why break it? And there was his son to think of. Why risk his losing his lands – and his head – for Perkin Warbeck and a little more power?

'You have made England great again,' he said.

'Do you swear fealty, Cumbria?' said Henry.

'I do, sire. And I vouch for Lords Devon and Suffolk. Can't speak for Cornwall. You know the Cornish.'

'Thank you. Are you all right, my Lord? You look a little peaky.'

'A touch of the ague, I fancy, sir. Thank you for asking.'

'What is that on your lip?'

'I was cut while shaving, sire?'

Probably time to retire Hoskyns, thought Henry, before he does someone a real damage.

Cumbria bowed and exited.

'I have the minute-by-minutes of the King's Council meeting, sir,' said Sir Reginald.

'Best destroy it, Bray, don't you think?'

'Oh, no, sir. I couldn't possibly do that, sir,' said Sir Reginald. 'It is safely filed, far from prying eyes.'

'Very well, Bray.'

'I have booked the private dining room for lunch, sir,' said Sir Reginald.

'Not today, thank you, Bray,' said Henry.

Sir Reginald met Hardwick in the private dining room where they dined on Cheffie's finest. Cheffie himself was on hand to carve the haunch of venison.

'But first, gentlemen,' said Cheffie. 'A little French brandy.' He poured a liquid from a glass decanter into a silver ladle.

'You're not going to set fire to it, Cheffie?' said Hardwick.

'Is that wise, Cheffie ... ?' said Sir Reginald.

The brandy gently ignited and Cheffie poured the flaming liquid over the meat.

'Bravo, Cheffie!'

The art of flambé cooking was in its infancy and Cheffie had yet to learn that you *never* pour brandy on flaming dishes. The room itself seemed to inhale as the flames sucked oxygen. The decanter exploded, firing flames and shards of razor-sharp glass in all directions. A Flemish tapestry – gifted by the Burgundian King Philip (the Good) of Valois caught fire and was incinerated. Hardwick and Bray escaped with flesh wounds. Cheffie was not so lucky. A shard of glass severed his femoral artery. It was his final entremet.

Henry made his way downstairs to the counting house where he and Dunne, in what would become a long-standing ritual, totted a few figures and balanced a ledger or two.

'Can you smell smoke, Dunne?'

'I can, sire.'

'And venison?' Henry shuddered. Cheffie's rich cuisine played hell with his indigestion. He was convinced it was taking years off his life. The pair lunched modestly on Mrs Dunne's cold roast fowl which had become a firm favourite of Henry's. He never learnt that a dagger-shaped shard had embedded itself in the chair he was to sit in; that Cheffie's cooking might indeed have taken years off his life.

Cumbria made his way across the Palace to the Royal Physician's chamber.

'Is there anything you can do, Sir Thomas?'

'It is God's will that you have this disease,' said Sir Thomas Metcalfe, toeing the official line. 'Theriac and mercury are our best hope. Do you agree, Mr Heckstall?'

'I do agree, Sir Thomas.'

'I also find that crushed emeralds in concert with freshly-cut snake assists absorption of the concoctions.'

Heckstall may have dragged a reluctant Metcalfe toward the sixteenth century but the physician was unable to abandon his old ways completely.

'As you say, Sir Thomas.'

Heckstall supplied Cumbria with opium for the headache that inevitably forced him to his bed come nightfall. Like many military men, Cumbria was terrified of disease. He prayed. He went to confession. It was a lengthy one. So was the penance. The birth of his son was imminent and he was desperate to return to his estate. Of course, he didn't want to witness the actual birth. He just wanted to be there, to hold his new-born boy. Once the midwife had cleaned him up, of course. He slept peacefully but awoke the following morning, struck blind. The journey from London to Carlisle is a perilous one, even for an armed man with perfect vision. He was driven, however, by his squire and his newly-found, if literal, blind faith. He returned home safely as his wife went into labour.

It was a boy. Bonnie, bouncing and with a pair of lungs that sounded musical to Cumbria.

Where did he get that from? he chuckled, cradling the son he couldn't see. There was no musical talent, no artistry of any sort in the Cumbria genes. He dispatched a footman to the garden with trowel and tray. His son's feet would first touch this world on rich Cumbrian soil.

He clasped his wife's hand and kissed it. If god granted him safe passage through this disease he would serve his king dutifully. Without him and his 4000 men, the rebellion must surely collapse – like one of Cheffie's entremets.

Never again would Which Way Cumbria change direction.

B acon waited for Hardwick in his office.

'Sorry. There was a lot to catch up on.'

'What happened, Hardwick?'

'I'm not exactly sure. Henry and Alexander have done some sort of secret deal. Nothing written down, nothing signed.'

'And?'

'As I understand it, Alexander fears that Henry wants to break free of Rome which is why, despite Spain's claims on it, he hasn't opposed Henry and Caboto's expedition to the New World. In return, the pope's agent – a Fr de Carbonariis, will be the next Archbishop of Bath and Wells. Plus we agree to convert all the new world heathens to the one true faith.'

'And the pockes?'

'All this business about la maladie italienne or la enfermeda francesa – let the Europeans fight over that one. Henry won't allow our English reputation be sullied by your claims.'

'I don't have to remain silent, Hardwick.'

'You think Barrie Vagg would risk his job? Or Foxe the Chronicler for that matter? If you were to breathe a word of this, Bacon, the Church will try you for heresy, the Crown will charge you with treason. I won't be able to protect you.'

'And what of my report?'

'It is on file.'

'Never to be seen?'

'In the lap of the gods, Hardwick. Or rather, Sir Reginald's, which in this case is one and the same.'

The pair parted, unable to embrace for fear of infection. Bacon returned to the surgery.

'What were you doing at the Palace, Heckstall?'

'Sir Reginald liked the cut of my sail.'

'The Berkshire Heckstalls?' Bacon sneered. 'Eton and Oxford?'

Heckstall ignored the jibe.

'Why were you sitting with the King's Council?'

'I was invited, in my unofficial position as Court Surgeon."

'Court Surgeon? Metcalfe would never agree.'

'Metcalfe is surprisingly compromising if he's handled respectfully. We have settled a truce. Diagnosis will remain with the physicians. Treatment will become the surgeons' responsibility – '

'Metcalfe has never touched another human being in his life. How can he diagnose?'

' – and in time and with Sir Thomas's support we surgeons will have our own Company.'

It was not something Bacon could argue with.

'As for our practice? I will not have an infected surgeon treating our patients, Bacon. Look at you. I won't ask you how you got the pockes. But I could hazard a guess. You will leave in the morning. Do not resist. Or as Court Surgeon-in-Waiting I will call the King's Guard.'

Bacon collapsed on his bed, not bothering to undress. He tried to remain optimistic. His career was not over. If he could beat the pockes he would set up a new practice. Out of London. Highbury, perhaps. Or Highgate. Green pastures. Fresh air. A fresh start. Things could not get any worse, he consoled himself.

Lowther arrived unannounced with his instruments and earthly possessions which totalled thirty pounds and four groats, courtesy of his judicious wagers on the jousts.

'It's not the same without you, Mr Bacon.'

'No, Lowther. Stick with Heckstall. Don't destroy a promising career.'

But Lowther would not be swayed. He moved in and set out the red and white pole. He saw patients but would have to cut hair if needs be; it covered their lease, food and Bacon's medicines.

Then things did get worse. It was a shocking case. Bacon self-medicated with opium for the various pains and theriac for the pockes but his sight was fading and he was losing his hearing. Bacon knew he was dying. He decided on the ultimate deterrent – a full mercury friction. Kill or be killed.

Then the deafness set in. Followed by the blindness. Deprived of his senses, Bacon's imagination took flight. He saw the tiny living organisms which caused disease. He saw how they invaded human cells, how they infected the human body and how they multiplied and spread. He saw the genesis of the disease and how its carriers mutated over the centuries, how they changed from benign parasites to lethal killers. He imagined a world where surgeons and physicians worked together, united in their sacred duty to fight disease.

He lost the use of an arm and a leg. He hovered near death. His heart stopped beating and he felt himself cross over. And then he passed through the *krisis*. His sight gradually returned, though he would remain deaf in one ear. He tried to remember the strange visions. He had been so close to seizing this knowledge, this certainty, but spectral-like, it slipped through his grasp. He regained the use of his limbs though he would walk with a limp for some years.

Lowther kept him informed by relaying news from the outside world.

'According to Barrie Vagg, James has sent Perkin Warbeck packing.'

'Henry is safe.'

'The Cornishmen aren't happy with the taxes. There's talk of rebellion.'

'London is all that Henry really cares for and Cornwall is a long way from London.'

The pockes continued to claim its victims: tens of thousands seriously afflicted, thousands dead.

'Henry has given up on the pockes,' said Bacon. 'He has declared it God's will and he'll wait for it to die out.'

'People have decided to live with it,' said Lowther. 'Rotherhithe has never been busier. Daniel sends his best. There's new buildings springing up all over Aldgate. The poor can't afford to live here.'

'What of our futures, Lowther?' said Bacon, despairing at his slow recovery and his failure to curb the disease. 'What is to become of us?'

'We're surgeons, Mr Bacon. We, er, surge?'

'We practise, Lowther.'

'What about those green fields and fresh air you've been on about?'

A south-easter whipped across the Thames. Clouds scudded across a pale, autumnal sky as Bacon took his first walk in many months. He needed a cane and the walk was short.

'Perhaps it is God's punishment after all,' Bacon thought. 'But I live. Perhaps he has deemed my punishment sufficient. Then again, perhaps it is by God's grace that we live or die.'

Thankfully his vision was sharp; he could still practise surgery. He returned to their cottage and helped Lowther pack their instruments, books and other possessions.

'Where to, Mr Bacon? The green fields of Highgate?'

'Where are we needed most, Lowther?'

'If you are asking me what is the most wretched borough in London? Smithfield? St Giles?'

'St Giles, it is.'

THE END

Reviews mean a lot to indie authors.

If you enjoyed my book please review it – in as few or as many words as you like – by following this link:

www.amazon.com/review/create-review/?&BO94TGS4G4=

If you have any questions or you'd like a chat with me please visit my website:

www.rbtaylorwriter.com

Printed in Great Britain
by Amazon

35478892R00149